THE
ASSISTANT

BOOKS BY NICOLE TROPE

NICOLE TROPE

THE
ASSISTANT

bookouture

Published by Bookouture in 2024

An imprint of Storyfire Ltd.
Carmelite House
50 Victoria Embankment
London EC4Y 0DZ

www.bookouture.com

ISBN: 978-1-83525-675-6
eBook ISBN: 978-1-83525-674-9

To all the enthusiastic readers who eagerly await each novel. Thank you for your support.

PROLOGUE

It will be declared a suicide.

There are no signs of a struggle. No signs of forced entry. The empty bottle of vodka and the crushed packet of sleeping pills point to an obvious conclusion. There's no note but there isn't always a note. Sometimes people take their lives because they have run out of ways to tell the world they're unhappy. There's nothing left to say.

The computer has one tab open: a job advert for a personal assistant.

> *Are you looking for a new challenge? Do you thrive in a fast-paced environment? Then this might be the position for you. Our CEO is seeking a forward-thinking candidate with the ability to use initiative and adapt. Ideally, we are seeking a candidate who is able to be with the company long-term.*

There will be a brief investigation.

'Yes,' her former employer will confirm. 'An unfortunate series of incidents made her position within the company untenable and we had to let her go.'

There will be loved ones left behind, people who are devastated and who will question themselves. *Why didn't we know? Why didn't she say?*

But those aren't the only questions that need to be asked.

When they find out she was fired from a cherished job, they need to ask why.

When they are told her heart was broken by a mysterious lover, they need to ask who he was.

And when all the secrets she was keeping are revealed, they need to ask who didn't want the truth to come out.

Those who loved her will struggle with confusion and guilt but they won't ask the right questions, so it will be declared a suicide...

ONE

GRACE

At the clinic, towards the end of my stay, there was a lot of discussion about coping strategies.

'What are you going to do when life becomes stressful and the urge to go back to your drug of choice strikes?'

Meditation, journaling, calling a helpline or your therapist, taking a walk, physical exercise, doing something special for yourself like taking a bath in scented water by the light of a single candle. Those are the correct answers. I know because I heard them repeated often enough.

I knew how to give the right answers by the end. The answers that would make my therapist smile and nod.

But meditation only magnifies the noise in my head – the hideous thoughts clash into each other, getting louder and louder until I want to scream.

I dislike taking a walk without needing to get anywhere and I have little interest in exercise.

Journaling irritates me when I read it back. The whiny person who wrote about her suffering has no relation to me. I loathe her more with each nauseating sentence.

I don't want to talk to a helpline or a therapist ever again. I have nothing left to say to anyone. I have talked myself in circles and it always comes back to the same thing: my life as I knew it is over and I can never get it back.

So how on earth will I stay away from my drug of choice when the stress of everyday life smacks me in the face?

I know exactly how – not that I told this to my therapist.

Quite simply, I will remember who I used to be.

I have a photo of myself that I carry with me everywhere, tucked into a pocket or a bag. My hair is in shining waves, my make-up perfect, my clothes soft and expensive. It is a picture of the me before my life went so terribly off the rails, the me I wanted to be forever, the me I thought I would be forever. I am seated behind a desk with a bottle of champagne in front of me, the very expensive kind with a shiny gold label. The photo was taken to celebrate my success. I am smiling at the camera, at the person taking the photo, and I can remember exactly what I was thinking at the time: *I've done it. I've actually done it.*

I felt the way mountain climbers must feel when they reach the peak, the way runners feel when they cross the finish line first, the way an actor feels as she takes a bow in front of an audience on their feet.

The photo was snapped on a cold winter's day with rain streaming down the windows of my office, the city outside obscured. But inside I was warmed by the air conditioner and the glow of my success. It was one of the greatest days of my life.

And when it all gets too much, and I know it will, I will take out the photo and stare at it. I will admire the smile on my face and the light in my eyes and remind myself that I was once that woman. And I can be her again.

It was difficult to look at the photo in the first few days I spent at the clinic, difficult to look at someone who had the world at her feet. To me, her smile was not genuine but smug, her make-up not perfect but a mask, her hair not shining but badly styled. I wanted to reach into the photograph and shake her. *You have no idea*, I wanted to scream, *no idea at all*.

But I don't feel that way anymore. I like her, the woman I was. I feel a warm love for her and everything she has endured.

I will be her again.

And I don't care who has to suffer in order for that to happen.

TWO

AVA

Is there some point when all of this gets easier? she thinks as she struggles out of her car, her arms loaded with files.

It certainly couldn't get any harder.

She admonishes herself for that thought. There are people all across the world fighting bigger battles than she is. She and Finn are healthy, the kids are healthy, they have a house and food, warm beds and enough money for their necessities. She is living the life she always imagined she would, and yet every single day is a struggle.

There are millions of women who work full time and manage to run their homes and parent their children and have everything under control. Why can't she be like them? Why is she the only person she knows whose life seems to be in perpetual chaos? What is wrong with her?

Opening her eyes in the morning, her first thought is always, *Oh God, another day to get through.* And she hates herself for that thought. She has so much more than most people, so many reasons to be grateful.

Juggling the files in her arms, she locks her car, checking

again that she has everything she needs, and then she makes her way to the elevator.

It will be easier when I have a new assistant, she tells herself. And then because it helps to repeat some positive thoughts, she keeps going as she rides the elevator up to the sixth floor, where her office is.

It will be easier when the girls are a little older.

It will be easier when Finn finally manages to sell a painting.

It will be easier when I know that Collin will not be promoted above me.

It will be easier when I've sorted out the supply issues.

It will be easier when it's not so hot.

It will be easier when...

The elevator doors open and Ava abandons her positive thoughts.

At reception, Collin is leaning over the front desk, whispering something into Melody's ear as she giggles.

It's not right. He shouldn't be doing that. Melody is so much younger than he is and he's her boss and it's simply not right to be behaving like that in the workplace.

Ava would like to say something but she wouldn't say anything in front of Melody anyway. As the files grow heavier in her arms, Collin moves away and runs his hands through his dark brown hair, where the greys are beginning to take over. Combined with his stubble, it only serves to make Collin more attractive. He was good-looking ten years ago when Ava started working for Barkley Education and Training and he has only gotten better-looking, which hardly seems fair. Ten years ago, Ava was ten kilos lighter with perfectly dewy skin and the ability to go clubbing all night and turn up to work the next day looking and feeling as fresh as a daisy. Ten years ago, she was Melody, holding exactly the same position.

'Morning, Ava.' Melody smiles sweetly and Ava returns the smile.

'Look at you, taking work home. Aren't you good,' says Collin, with a smile of his own. It's more of a sneer than a smile.

'I had a lot to catch up on. Emily leaving has made things difficult. Would today be a good day for me to have some time with James, or tomorrow, any day – just until I get a new assistant?' says Ava. She asked Collin to lend her his assistant, James, three times last week and he kept saying that this week would be better.

'James is very busy with my stuff, Ava. Aren't you inter-viewing people all day today? You'll find someone, I'm sure.'

'Collin, I really need some—'

'Oh, sorry, I need to take this call,' he says, pulling his phone out of his pocket as he holds up his hand to stop Ava speaking.

Ava sighs and Melody shrugs sympathetically, and then the reception phone rings and Melody answers quickly. 'Barkley Education and Training, how can I help you?'

Ava moves off to her office, where her desk is still piled high from yesterday.

She drops the files on the one empty square of desk space and slumps into her chair.

It will get easier, she reminds herself.

It will get easier.

THREE

Dear baby girl,

I am writing to tell you I'm sorry, so sorry, and to explain. I want to explain everything but I suppose in order to do that, I need to start at the beginning.

When you were born, they placed you on my chest. That's how most birth stories begin. But the words 'when you were born' don't begin to describe the pain of labour, the agony of a baby emerging from your body or the intense rush of profound love that engulfed me as I stared down at you. After the first cry, you were silent, your eyes blinking as you adjusted to the world.

I know that a lot of women confess to finally understanding their mothers when they have children of their own.

In my case, I understood my mother even less, found the way she had treated me even more perplexing.

I wondered if she'd felt the same intense and deep love when I was born, or if she'd been filled with anger and disgust for me even then.

I never wanted to be parted from you. I wanted to protect you and care for you.

My mother didn't seem to feel the same way about me. I know that, despite the fact that my memories of my first years are through the eyes of a child. I have blocked some of it out but I can tell you what I do remember, what images my mind has held on to. My mother never wore pants, favouring slimline dresses in muted colours, and her brown hair was always sprayed into submission and wound tightly into a low bun.

I remember being three years old and asking for a treat at the grocery store. I can still see the chocolate on display, the purple and red and gold wrappers tempting me with the promise of the dark sweetness inside.

'Please, Mum,' I said.

'No,' she replied.

I wasn't sitting in the shopping trolley, but rather walking next to her, and so, despite her refusal, my hand seemed to move of its own accord as I grabbed a large purple bar.

My mother said nothing. She paid for the chocolate bar at the till and let me take it home, and I thought I'd had some sort of victory.

But at home, she took the bar from the grocery bag and held it out to me. 'I said no, remember,' she said, and then she tore the wrapper off the bar. The rich smell of creamy cocoa and sugar filled the air, and my mouth was flooded with saliva.

'I said no,' she said, breaking off a block of chocolate and throwing it in the open garbage bin.

'I said no,' she repeated with another block. She did that until the whole bar of chocolate was in the bin in separate blocks, and then as I watched, she picked up a can of insecticide and sprayed it onto the chocolate in the garbage bin.

'In this house we control our urges and we listen to our parents,' she said. 'Now go to your room.'

There was no dinner that night. No bath, no bedtime story.

She completely ignored me as though I wasn't there. When my father came home, I opened my bedroom door, hoping that he would convince her to let me out, but I heard him say, 'Yes, you're right, my dear. She has to learn.'

In the morning, I took myself to the bathroom and then returned to my bedroom until she came to get me.

'What do you have to say to me?' she asked.

'Sorry.'

'What did I say?'

'You said no,' I replied.

She nodded and I was allowed out to eat.

I never took a bar of chocolate again. I never even asked for one.

FOUR

GRACE

No one enjoys the job interview process. The employer is bored after the first one and each candidate is slightly desperate to be liked and wanted. Everyone smiles and nods too much. Everyone lies.

The prospective employee lies about being a team player and about having an abiding interest in how boxes are produced or how search engine optimisation can change sales figures or how important a mailing list is – or whatever else the company does. They lie about being happy to work after hours and not spending their time dreaming about their next holiday.

The employer lies about their company being a fabulous place to work where everyone is happy all the time and feels like they are being paid the right amount. I'm generalising, of course, but it's mostly the way things work.

I can't remember how many interviews I've been to since I started looking for my first job at sixteen. Dozens, at least. I learned quickly to tailor my résumé, to say what needed to be said, to lie sometimes. Only when completely necessary, of course.

But today's interview is different. Today, while Ava Green

assumes she is interviewing me, I will, in fact, be interviewing Ava Green. I've been watching her for some time already, tracking her on the internet through her social media. But she's not to know that. A boss never likes to imagine that their employee knows more about their life than the basic information, but I know so very much more about Ava Green. More than she would believe.

I check my lipstick in the rear-view mirror one last time, a pale bronze that accentuates my lips just enough. I used to wear deep reds, dark browns, lipstick shades that drew attention. But I need to fade into the background as an assistant, to be there and not be there at the same time. It wouldn't do to outshine my boss.

I climb out of my car, feeling the heat of February in Sydney slam into me, grateful that I don't have to walk too far. The building where Ava Green works is in the city. Twenty-seven floors of offices, filled with every kind of business imaginable. Lawyers on one floor share the building with a suite of dentists on another and a modelling agency on another. The list goes on. It must be exciting to get into the elevator and never know exactly who you're going to meet.

Or perhaps it is exciting at first but just becomes annoying on a Monday morning when you would rather be somewhere else.

I check the board next to the elevator, confirm I'm going to the sixth floor.

A man comes to stand next to me, glancing briefly up from his phone and offering me a small smile. I drop my eyes to my shoes. My hair is tied back today but I can sense his appreciation of its lovely copper colour – dyed but he's not to know. I am wearing a fitted grey sheath of a dress, stretchy and comfortable, but whereas it would cling to curves on another woman, it's loose on me. Fury and stress burn a terrific number of calories. There are days when I forget to eat. At the clinic there were mandated times for meals and there I ate just to pass the time, but in the couple of weeks I have been living by myself, I have only eaten when it occurs to me to do so. I am not hungry for real nourishing food. Instead, I snack on cheese and crackers, pieces of fruit, things that require no actual preparation. Cooking for one person always feels pathetic, so I don't bother with it.

The offices of Barkley Education and Training take up the whole sixth floor and the place is filled with people, all moving around with an air of important busyness.

The receptionist is filing her long red nails as she speaks to someone on her headset. 'Yes, no, yes, I understand. I'll pass that along and I'm sure Ms Green will call you back as soon as she's out of her meeting. Yes, it will be today. No, I'm afraid I can't give you a time, but rest assured, she'll get back to you. Thank you, bye now.'

She touches a button on the headset and rolls her eyes before she sees me.

'Oh.' A blush spreads across her face when she notices me. 'Welcome to Barkley Education and Training. How can I help you?' A wide smile. She has thick black hair and blue eyes and her white top clings to her generous breasts, one button straining to keep everything hidden. I imagine her as the most popular girl in high school, as the one everyone wanted to date. A receptionist job must be a bit of a comedown for her but I'm sure she has a busy Instagram page where thousands declare her 'just gorgeous'.

I wait for just a moment, staring at her until she shifts in her seat. 'I'm here to interview with Ava Green,' I say.

'Oh.' Her shoulders relax. I'm not important. 'And your name is?' she asks in a slightly imperious tone. She has a job after all. I'm just another in a long line of people hoping to work for Ava Green. On LinkedIn, I saw that forty people had submitted their résumés for the position of personal assistant.

They shouldn't have bothered. This is my job but the young receptionist is not to know that.

'I'm Grace Enright,' I say pleasantly. *Silly little girl.*

'Great,' she says, her fingers tapping her keyboard, 'you can just take a seat and Ms Green will be out in a moment.' She points, without looking at me, at a collection of leather tub chairs in pale brown lined along one wall.

I don't want to sit down. I would rather pace, relieve myself of some of this fizzing energy, but I do as instructed.

I am carrying a slimline leather bag and I open it, checking over my printed résumé again. It's all lies but I'm banking on forming a connection with Ava Green. It was my greatest skill in my former life, the ability to instantly know what a person needs and wants to hear.

The references will check out because I'm owed some favours. That's all I really have left now – favours – and those are running out quickly.

A young man clutching a battered briefcase walks past me, chewing on his lower lip. He reaches the lift and stabs the button to go down aggressively. I assume his interview did not go well. As he gets into the lift, I stare down at my résumé again and take a deep breath before sliding it back into my bag.

A rush of air and the scent of musk alerts me to someone's presence and I look up to see Ava Green standing in front of me. I immediately make three observations.

Her hair is a blonde bob but there is a streak of grey at the neat middle part, meaning she hasn't had time to go to the hairdressers to get her roots touched up, meaning she has little time for herself. She's thirty-five and the grey hair is an indication of more stress in her life than she needs.

She is wearing a pale blue skirt, slightly too tight, and there is a small stain on the white blouse she has teamed with it. I know she has children but not their ages because she doesn't put their pictures on social media – which is the way of many young mothers these days – but now I know they're probably quite young. Young children are perpetually sticky creatures.

Even in the frigidly cold office, I can see light sweat stains under her arms, so Ava is harassed and rushed.

Perfect, I think. *I got here just in time.*

'I'm Ava Green,' she says, holding out her hand.

I stand and shake it. 'Grace Enright.'

'Follow me, Grace,' she says, turning away.

I follow her obediently to her office, where chaos rules. The desk is stacked with paper, desk drawers are open, I can see her phone is pinging with constant messages or alerts, and there are two half-drunk cups of cold coffee, milk scum on the surface.

'I'm so sorry,' she says, as she watches me take it all in. 'It's just been crazy here today. A whole lot of my trainers are out sick and I've been on the phone all morning to just try and get the slots filled. And in between that I'm conducting interviews. Please sit,' she says, indicating the one empty chair.

'That must be difficult,' I say, doing as she has asked and taking my résumé out of my bag.

'It's ridiculous,' she says, sitting behind her glass desk, 'and that's why I need an assistant. Emily, my former assistant, left three weeks ago to have her baby, and even though we started looking long before she left, I haven't been able to find anyone as yet. Although I have a lot of interviews lined up,' she adds quickly, lest I assume she really needs me.

But she's said too much. And she *does* need me.

'Do you know anything about the company?' she asks, leaning back in her black leather chair.

I am still clutching my résumé but she hasn't asked for it so I put it down on my lap. 'I know that you offer training and counselling on careers for all high school students. You have trainers who go out to schools all over Australia to take students through a two-day aptitude test on their strengths and skills. All students are given personalised results. And you back that up with resources sent out to the guidance counsellors at each school.'

'Yes, great,' says Ava, seeming relieved that I have a basic understanding of her work. 'It's not that we have invented this concept but more that we actively try and find the students work experience for a few days in an area where we believe they are suited. We have a huge group of businesses and professions that work with us but it takes a lot of coordination and maintaining of relationships—' Her phone trills, a boppy, upbeat song with children's voices in the background – perhaps a theme song from some television show. She stops speaking and picks up the phone. 'Oh God,' she mutters, 'sorry, please excuse me, Grace. Yes?' she says, swiping her hand across the screen and lifting the phone to her ear as she turns her chair around.

She listens for a moment. 'I can't go and fetch her, Finn. I'm interviewing and work is very busy,' she whispers. 'I simply can't get away.'

She ends the call and swings her chair around again, drops the phone back onto the desk and shakes her head.

'Sorry, I didn't take your résumé,' she says, leaning over the desk.

I hand it to her and watch as she reads. She apologises too much but then that is a particularly female trait. We all apologise constantly. Until we can't apologise anymore.

'Why did you leave your last job?' she asks.

'I'm going to be honest with you,' I say.

She nods, a flicker of worry crossing her face. I speak quickly, before she can cross me off her list of possible applicants.

'It was, as you can see from the name, a company, a group that owned a string of beauty salons. I was an assistant to the general manager and I noticed over the last year that there were a lot of customers complaining about our services. The CEO was cutting costs, hiring very junior beauticians and using inferior products, and customers were suffering with rashes and skin complaints.'

Ava relaxes back into her chair, her brow furrowing slightly as she listens. She is interested. Good.

'I understood that she had to cut costs but it felt like we were cheating our customers. When I work for a company, I feel responsible for how that company performs, even though I'm just an assistant. I like to know that the people I work for are operating in an ethical manner. I left on good terms with Liza, my boss, but I knew I needed to leave. Liza was not responsible for the cost-cutting and she was just as frustrated as I was, but she's a single mother and needs her job.' I watch Ava nod in agreement with this. I am saying all the right things and I feel my body relax because I know she likes what I'm saying.

'I was sorry to leave her but I didn't want to make things difficult for her at work.'

Liza will give me a very good reference. She owes me big time.

'Fair enough,' says Ava and I can tell she's impressed. She should be. It's a good story.

'And do you feel like you are still happy to work as an assistant? You have a lot of experience and you could find yourself a more senior role, one with a higher pay bracket.'

I have listed my work as an assistant at seven different companies, with a long list of achievements at each one, but I'm banking on her only calling Liza and Geoff. Geoff is a cousin of mine. I rarely see him, but when I was flying high, he came to me frequently for small loans that I knew he would never pay back. Geoff loves a get-rich-quick scheme and because he is sweet and charming, I always helped. I had the money after all. He's an adept liar and readily agreed to help me find a job. He will be answering his mobile phone with the words 'Trident Human Resources' every day until I tell him to stop.

I realise that Ava is waiting for my answer. One thing my

drug of choice does is slow down my brain nicely so I can concentrate on one thing at a time. Otherwise, my thoughts are always racing ahead of each other.

'I understand but I have always been happy to be the support in the background. You cannot work if the unimportant things in your life, like paperwork, aren't handled,' I say, moving my hand to indicate her messy desk.

'You're right about that,' she says with a smile.

'And as a personal assistant, I have no issue with helping you with everything in your life that needs to be done. No task will be too big or too small. It's my job to allow you the space to shine in your job.'

There is a look that people get, an expression that flashes across someone's face, that lets me know I have said exactly the right thing. It's a mixture of relief and joy and peace, as though the person is thinking, *You can see me, actually see me, and you know exactly what I need.* That expression crosses Ava's face and I know I have her.

'That's an incredible attitude,' she says. 'It's not often you hear that anymore. Most people are looking out for themselves.'

'Yes, but if everyone only looks out for themselves, then how do we function as a society? Not everyone can be the queen bee. I am a worker bee and I am happy to be one.'

'True,' she agrees as the phone trills madly on her desk.

'Please answer it,' I say. 'I'm happy to wait.'

Ava nods and takes the call. I hear someone crying on the other end. 'Just calm down and talk to me,' Ava snaps and then she looks up at me and blushes. I believe she must be talking to one of her trainers because it sounds like a young woman but not a child.

'Oh, that's awful,' she says as she listens. 'What school was it? Right, and the teacher was in the room? Okay, I will look into this. You did the right thing, Jamie, just leave now and I'll sort this out, I promise.'

She ends the call. 'Year twelve boys can be brutal with the younger female trainers. I had no choice but to send Jamie, and she could hear them whispering about her looks and laughing at her. Now I'm going to have to call the principal and I have no idea what to say since they've been a good source of revenue in the past. I usually send a male trainer.'

'That poor girl,' I say. I would love to jump in and tell Ava what I think should happen in this situation but I don't have the job yet. I clasp my hands together, discreetly pushing a fingernail into the palm of one hand to remind myself to be patient.

I don't want Ava to think I am stepping on her toes before she's even employed me. I am seventeen years older than she is, but right now we look closer in age. At thirty-five, Ava's skin looks dry and her eyes are puffy and shadowed. I don't imagine she is eating or sleeping well.

'I need to speak to the head about this. If we lose the school's business, that's fine. Young men cannot be allowed to get away with behaviour like that anymore,' she says, making a note on a loose piece of paper.

'I agree,' I say. 'The world is a very different place now.'

'Too true,' she says, nodding.

She eyes my résumé again.

'Look, Grace,' she says, glancing up at me, 'I have other people to interview but no one who has been doing this as long as you have. I need someone who can hit the ground running and I assume that's you. Should we give it a try for a week and then see how we go?'

'I do have...' I start to say, letting a beat of silence linger so that she fills in the information herself.

'I'm sure you must have some other interviews and offers to consider,' she says quickly.

'Yes, but... I think that you know when something feels right, so a trial week would be wonderful,' I say.

'When can you start?' she says with a wide smile, surveying her desk.

I want to tell her that I can start right now. I'm itching to get my hands on her desk but it wouldn't be a good idea to appear too desperate.

'I can be here first thing tomorrow morning,' I say.

'Fabulous,' she sighs, standing, 'I'll see you then.'

She sees me out, walking me past the young receptionist who had better up her level of professionalism if she wants to hang on to her job.

Ava thinks she's just hired me but it's the other way around. She needs me, and when that gorgeous husband of hers meets me, he will realise he needs me too. In fact, the whole family needs me and it's wonderful to be needed.

I am filled with glee as I get into my car, navigate my way out of the city and make the forty-minute drive to where I live. Tomorrow I will catch a train in.

As I park my car in front of my building, I receive a text message from Liza.

> *Got a call from a woman named Ava Green, sang your praises. I hope this means I won't have to do this again. I really dislike lying.*

A flash of irritation makes me grit my teeth. Liza owes me more than just one good reference. I fire a message back.

> **I assume you told her I was competent and very capable of doing the job. That's not a lie.**

> *I really hope you know what you're doing, Grace. You don't need this to blow up in your face.*

Thank you for your kind concern.

Liza doesn't reply to that message but she wouldn't. She's not one for confrontation. Neither was I before everything went haywire.

Once I am home in my apartment, I clean the place from top to bottom. It's sparkling already but dust and filth could be lurking anywhere. I need to make sure I find it and get rid of it.

As I move a pot plant a tiny cockroach runs out from behind it. I squeal and then I raise my hand and I smash it and smash it and smash it. 'How dare you?' I spit. 'How dare you invade my space?' I see her face as I bring my hand down again and again until there's nothing left of it.

Once I've washed my hand, I am calm and I happily continue with my cleaning.

Tomorrow is a new day and a new beginning.

I can't wait.

FIVE

AVA

After pulling her car into the garage, Ava turns off the engine and drops her head onto the steering wheel, breathing in the moment of silence. Work Ava is off duty now and mum Ava needs to take over, even though she is beyond exhausted. She closes her eyes and imagines what it would be like to walk into the house and find it sparkling clean and silent so she could pour herself a glass of wine, kick off her high heels and sink onto the leather sofa, taking time to mull over her day and begin planning for tomorrow without having to do more than order dinner home-delivered.

And then she lifts her head and gives it a shake, guilt making her sigh. She doesn't want an empty house, not at all. 'Come on, come on,' she says aloud, dragging the energy from somewhere inside herself to get out of the car and walk into the house, where she immediately trips over a pair of purple light-up sneakers that flash pink lights. She leans down, picks them up and puts them on the shoe rack. *How many times have I asked for the shoes to be put on the shoe rack? It's right here.*

In the kitchen, the dishes are piled in the sink, the dish-

washer still half full of clean dishes, which was how she left it
this morning when she realised how late she was running.

A shriek from upstairs is followed by the pounding of foot-
steps, and then Hazel and Chloe appear in the kitchen, both of
their faces covered in lipstick.

'Oh no,' she wails.

'Hi Mum,' says Hazel. 'It's okay, we was just playing dress-
up and Daddy said that we could do what we wanted as long as
we just left him to bloody work.' Hazel has dark brown eyes and
black hair like her father and she even shares his high cheekbones, but Chloe is more like Ava, with fine blonde hair, blue
eyes and a dimpled smile. Both of their faces are covered in the
maroon lipstick she favours, and Ava knows it will be the expensive one she left on her dressing table this morning as she rushed
to get ready for work.

It's after 6 p.m. and obviously neither of the girls has had
dinner or a bath.

'Don't touch anything,' says Ava as both girls approach her
for a hug. She searches in the pantry for a packet of baby wipes
and then struggles to clean the girls' faces and hands without
them touching her. Finally, she gives up and picks up five-year-
old Hazel in one arm and three-year-old Chloe in the other and
battles up the stairs to the bathroom. 'You know you're not
allowed to touch my make-up, Hazel, that's not very nice. I need
to wear it for work.' Her tone is strident, anger contained in
every word.

'It was just a little bit,' says Hazel, whose whole face is
smeared in the deep wine colour.

She sets both girls down and puts the plug in the bath,
turning on the water. 'Get in,' she commands as she makes sure
the water is the right temperature. The girls are silent and
obediently strip off and climb in. They sit down in the water as
the bath fills and trade worried glances, and Ava feels like the
worst mother in the world. She grabs the bubbles and squirts

them into the water so the girls can play. 'It's bubble time,' she sings. And then she sits on the floor of the bathroom and watches them.

After ten minutes she hears Finn calling for them. She concentrates on her breathing, trying not to let tears of exhaustion and desperation fall. Every single night she comes home to this, no matter how many times she points out how unfair it is. Every single night. Her drive home is always filled with anxiety about how much she is going to have to do when she gets home. Her day never ends, it just starts again. She will not get any time to herself until much later tonight, and then all she can hope for is a few hours of uninterrupted sleep. And that's if she's lucky. If one of the girls calls out in the night, Finn sleeps right through it. And if she confronts him about it in the morning, he says, 'I'm with them the whole day. They want you at night.'

'We're up here,' shouts Hazel, and Finn comes up the stairs and into the bathroom.

'Oh dear, what did you two little rascals do?' he laughs.

'Really?' spits Ava, standing. 'I just walked in from work to find them like this.'

'Sorry, I had to finish up a piece I was working on. I was really feeling inspired. I thought they were going to watch a movie on television. Hazel, you told me that you were going to watch a movie,' he says, his voice devoid of any discipline. He's mostly amused.

Hazel shrugs as she plays with the bubbles. 'Chloe didn't like it.'

'You told them to leave you alone to bloody work,' says Ava, her voice pitched just below hysteria. She is exhausted beyond what she thought possible.

'Yes, well, you know kids. I had to finish up, but I'm done now. Why don't you get changed? Do you know there's a stain on your blouse?'

Ava leaves the bathroom before she lashes out at her husband.

She locks herself in the en suite bathroom and turns on the shower. Under the pounding water she lists her grievances against her husband. She does this in silence because she would like to scream them at him. She does this so she can stay married instead of get divorced, and so that her children can grow up differently to the way she did. She does this because she wants to scream and cry and she has two little girls who need her to be a mother to them tonight and forever after that.

He doesn't clean up the house. He doesn't do the laundry. He leaves the girls unsupervised. He insists his work has meaning even though not one single person has bought a painting from him in a year. He doesn't care when everything is in chaos. He obviously hasn't made anything for dinner. He insists on finding every naughty thing the girls do funny...

The list goes on for five more minutes until she has calmed herself down.

She ends with, *I hate you. I hate you. I hate you and I want a divorce.* She doesn't hate him and she doesn't want a divorce. She loves Finn. She just needs him to be a real partner.

In order to balance out the terrible list, she makes another as she stands in the water watching her fingers prune. *He loves the girls and they adore him. He's funny and kind about everyone he meets. I'm still attracted to him even after seven years of marriage. He's nice to my mother even when she's rude to him. He makes the best roast lamb. He lives in the moment and sometimes I need to be reminded to live in the moment.*

She gets out of the shower, dresses in shorts and a T-shirt, and finds the girls sitting on the floor of the other bathroom, wrapped in towels, the bath empty and stained with remnants of the lipstick. Chloe is holding a tube of toothpaste, which Ava grabs and puts into the bathroom cabinet, relieved to have prevented another mess.

'Where's Daddy?' Ava asks.

'He said he needs a bloody drink to deal with all this chaos. What's chaos, Mum?'

Hazel parrots her father perfectly, takes pride in remembering exactly what he says. Finn returns to the bathroom with a beer in his hand. 'I opened a bottle of wine – you look like you could use a drink,' he says with a smile. He is so completely oblivious it amazes Ava.

'Part of my son's charm,' Ava remembers Finn's mother, Doreen, telling her when they first met, 'is his ability to keep himself above the fray. He's always calm, always happy. You're a lucky girl.' Doreen views her son through the rosy lens of an adoring mother. She is as charmed by Finn as everyone else is.

Finn clashed with his father, Sam, all through his childhood. Sam did not find his son's endless escapades that got him suspended from school even remotely amusing. But whatever discipline he tried to instil in his son was overridden by his wife, who saw her son as a free and creative spirit who needed the space and time to express himself.

And Finn is a talented artist, no one can deny that, but the world is filled with talented people, and in order to harness that talent, you have to work at it, go out into the world and sell yourself and your talent. Finn loves his work but he is less fond of taking the next step and selling it. He won't compromise and he won't cold-call. He has a few contacts, and he assures her when they discuss it that one of those contacts will be his ticket to fame and fortune. 'When the time is right, I will have my show and it will all be easier after that,' he has said. Finn will decide when the time is right, and until then, Ava is in charge of keeping a roof over their heads.

Yes, I'm a lucky girl, she reminds herself.

She leaves the bathroom and goes down to the kitchen, where she cleans up and throws together spaghetti bolognese for dinner with sauce from a jar.

The laundry is filled with clothes that need to be washed but she cannot begin to contemplate doing anything about that now.

The girls are boisterous through dinner and it takes until eight thirty to get them both down and into bed. Finn takes care of story time – because he loves story time and he's really good at doing the voices – while Ava cleans up and packs lunch for both girls for school and preschool tomorrow. She empties out their bags and finds a note from two weeks ago in Hazel's reminding parents about the end of summer fair to be held at the school. It's tomorrow. She knows that Hazel is supposed to bring something for the cake stall.

Ava digs in the pantry and finds a store-bought, ready-made cake, only a day past its use-by date. She mixes up some icing for it and then she covers the whole thing in Smarties as well. It will have to do.

'Look at you, little homemaker,' says Finn, coming into the kitchen.

Ava bites down on her lip because if she says anything, she knows that Finn will give her his wounded puppy dog look. And then he will launch into his usual spiel: *I never wanted children. We agreed that we would both just concentrate on our work. I give up time to be home with the girls so you can go to work. I have compromised my career and my creativity so that you can have your career. I'm not cut out for this and I'm really trying to make things work here. Our children are happy and loved and you come home every day filled with anger and complaints.*

I make the money, she wants to scream back at him but she's never done it. She makes the money but she also wanted children. Hazel was planned, Chloe was a wonderful surprise and Ava loves them with all her heart, but she is dangling on the edge of sanity, not just at home but at work too. At least she will have a new assistant tomorrow, so work will hopefully be under control.

'Why are you doing that at this time of night?' he asks, amused.

'It's for the cake stall tomorrow,' she says shortly.

'Hmm, well, it looks nice enough. I'm going to get some more work done. You should see this piece, it's incredible.'

Ava stops what she's doing and looks at her husband. How is it possible that he doesn't understand? And how can she make him get it? She contemplates picking up the cake and throwing it at his face but that would mean she would have to get in her car and go and get another one.

'You need any help here?' he asks.

'No, I'm good,' she says, because the cake is done and the kitchen is clean, and she knows by now that it would be pointless anyway, and so he leaves her in the kitchen.

She gets into bed before him and just before she turns out her light, she gazes at the family picture she keeps on her bedside table, reminding herself of all that she has.

They are a picture-perfect family in their double-storey house in the suburbs but Ava is drowning, and even if she screams for help, Finn won't rescue her.

Leave him, she can hear the world at large saying, but what then? She will have to pay him child support to take care of the kids because he's the primary caregiver at the moment. And she doesn't actually trust him to take care of them full time so what will happen to the girls? Ava is as trapped in her life and marriage as she would be if she was a stay-at-home mother. She could get a divorce and get a nanny, place the children in after-school care, but that's so unfair to them. The girls would miss Finn terribly if they couldn't see him every day and he would be devastated as well, even though children had not been part of his life plan. How do you break up a marriage and a family and hold down a full-time job? It would all be up to her. She would have to find the lawyer and she would have to organise to sell the house and pack it up after it sold.

'He's a man-child,' her friend Lucy said after the first time she met him eight years ago.

'He just seems like that because he's an artist. He's incredibly kind and sweet and he makes me laugh,' Ava protested.

'That's all very well for now,' said Lucy as she took her glasses off to give them a clean, peering at the lenses until they were pristine, 'but you're on your way to running a big company and you need a partner if you want to have kids with him. You don't need a kid to have children with.'

'He'll grow up as soon as kids arrive, all men do.'

'Ava,' said Lucy, putting her hand on Ava's arm, 'I'm married to a chess-playing brain surgeon and sometimes I want to thump him when he asks me where the nappy rash cream is – it's been in the same place since Charlie was born. Finn is delightful and very good-looking but just have fun with him, don't marry him.'

But Ava was already in love with Finn's smouldering looks and his slight Irish accent, which he'd held on to despite having lived in Australia for twenty-three years at that point, since he was five years old. Once Finn proposed, Lucy stopped saying anything negative about him, becoming the most supportive maid of honour she could be.

After they got married, everything was perfect for a while. Ava had pushed for one child, just one child, and Finn had given in because he loved her. Ava had imagined that they would make it work, that it would all be fine, and it was until it wasn't, and now Ava has no idea what she's going to do. Her whole life feels out of control, a spinning top that can't be stopped.

She thinks about Grace from the interview today, so beautifully put together in her grey sheath dress. The woman is at least mid-forties, maybe older, but incredibly attractive with thick, copper-coloured hair and green eyes. She made Ava feel unkempt. But perhaps she'll help to get everything at work truly under control so Ava can have more mental space to figure out what to do about things at home.

She's never hired anyone this fast before, especially before she even checked out the references, but there is something about Grace, something that made Ava feel she was the right choice. And her former employer sang her praises and confirmed that Grace left the company because she didn't want to cause trouble with the CEO.

Ava interviewed a lot of people for the position, and each time she ended an interview, she had the feeling that the candidate was using the assistant position as a stepping stone to somewhere else. It's unusual to have someone who is happy to be in the role long-term. Hiring Grace was a good decision, she's sure of it. If only sorting things out at home could be so clear-cut.

She closes her eyes and counts breaths in and out to calm her body. It's a problem for another day and now she needs to rest.

As she drifts off to sleep, she sees an image of Grace smiling at her.

Grace is going to make everything better; Ava is sure of it.

SIX

Dear baby girl,

I grew up in a middle-class suburb, filled with people living the Australian dream of a house and a plot of land. My father was an electrician by trade and he had enough work to keep him busy six days a week. My mother stayed home to raise me so that I would become the young lady they both wanted me to be. They sent me to the local public school because that was the law and they never disobeyed the law. They didn't drink or smoke, rarely ate sweets and seemed to take pleasure in deprivation. Even Christmas was a subdued affair, except for the warmth and generosity of my grandmother Ida, my father's mother. My parents would have preferred a visit to church and a simple dinner but my grandmother always hosted us, covering her house in decorations and presenting a table laden with delicious food. If I close my eyes, I can still conjure up the taste of her home-made custard with a dash of brandy that she poured over the rich, spice-filled Christmas pudding. I always went home with more presents from her than from my parents. They favoured practical gifts like a scarf or a new coat. She spoiled me with toys and, as I grew older, perfume and books.

When we shared the occasional Sunday lunch with her, she would usually cook a roast lamb – the meat a little tough and dry but always good with gravy.

But when she tried to serve my father gravy, my mother would refuse for him.

'That's strange, you always liked gravy before, John,' my grandmother would say.

'Not anymore. I've told you that,' my father would reply.

It was the same when it came to dessert or any kind of sweets. My mother refused on behalf of me and my father, leaving my grandmother confused and upset.

'You always liked dessert before, you always enjoyed a beer before, you always liked a chocolate with your tea before.' The poor woman.

When I helped her wash up after lunch in the kitchen, she would always give me a secret portion of dessert that I finished quickly, relishing every mouthful.

My parents went to church on Sundays, but mostly preferred prayer at home. I was told to pray when I woke up, before I ate anything, and last thing at night. I was supposed to confess my sins to God at every opportunity.

I grew up understanding that God was always watching and that he was mostly disappointed in me.

I thought school would be a great adventure. I imagined making friends and experiencing something different to my own small world. But my mother sent me to my first day of kinder-garten dressed in a uniform two sizes too big with my hair styled the way hers always was – in a matronly bun. Ridiculous on a five-year-old in a baggy uniform.

I was an immediate target. I had no friends but I loved actu-ally being in class and being allowed to go to the library. From the time I could read a sentence, I sat happily alone at lunchtime, reading books in the library but I never took them home, not wanting my parents to question what I was reading.

I savoured the books my grandmother bought me for Christmas and birthdays, reading them over and again and then hiding them at the back of my wardrobe in case my mother decided to throw them out, something she did once, teaching me a lesson about keeping what I valued safe and hidden.

My parents did not read novels. They rarely watched television, and if they did, it was usually the news. At night my father would read the newspaper and my mother would sit next to him doing crossword puzzles. They were young but seemed decades older in their behaviour.

Twice a week after school, my mother had a bridge game with some women in the neighbourhood and I was handed over to my grandmother for the afternoon. She lavished me with the love and kindness I was missing, as she filled me up with treats.

There was an explanation, of course, for why my parents lived such an austere lifestyle, why they needed me to listen without complaint, why it was important that I never disobey them.

They had both spectacularly messed up their lives and were hoping to stop me from doing the same thing, hoping to redeem themselves by being the most upstanding citizens in the whole of Australia, never mind that it came with a certain degree of cruelty.

I didn't know this when I was little. I just knew that there were a lot of rules in my house and I was punished for disobeying them. And I knew that it was possible to commit more sins than I could imagine. As I got older, my grandmother let me in on some of the truth. And I began to understand that I was my parents' greatest sin. I was responsible for my mother's fall from grace.

'How come you're my only grandma?' I remember asking her once. I was around ten at the time and I noted that most of the children in my class spoke of more than one grandparent.

'Your mother's parents were...' She sighed, patting her hair back into place, even though her tight, short curls never really moved. 'Well, they were a different kind of people. They raised her to be a good girl and they wanted a lot for her, as every parent does. They were a very religious family. Your mum's dad was a pastor at church. I'm not sure which one but I know it was very strict. No dancing, no drinking, no television. So many rules, you can't imagine.' She was making me a snack at the time and she handed me the plate, stroking my hair after she set it down on her kitchen table.

'Your mum was supposed to marry a young man in the church who was training to be a pastor himself. That was the plan. But she fell for your dad. He went over there with his boss to rewire the church and I remember he came home and told me he'd met a lovely girl.'

She sat down at the kitchen table with me, her ever-present cup of tea in front of her. 'Her parents weren't happy. They told her not to see him and she should have listened. I mean, I know you can't tell young people what to do. It always goes wrong and they, well, they slipped and her parents just couldn't take it. They cut her out of their lives, called her all sorts of names.'

I didn't know what 'slipped' meant. I pictured my mother falling over and her parents being angry. I knew that if I dropped something or accidentally broke a glass, I was always punished for my clumsiness with hours in my room, so that idea made sense to me.

'What names?' I asked, and my grandmother seemed to realise she was talking to a ten-year-old. 'Oh, listen to me prattling on. You only need one grandparent, me, and I love you enough for a thousand grandparents.'

I didn't quite understand it until I was older but my mother fell pregnant with me accidentally and felt she had to keep me, and my father felt he had to marry her, and that trapped two people together who were really unsuitable for each other.

*I think they really only bonded over their mutual dislike of
their only child.*

*I brought them little joy with my attention to my schoolwork.
I did well and was praised by teachers as being polite and enthusiastic.*

*'Don't go letting that woman's words of praise go to your
head, young lady,' my mother told me after a parent–teacher
conference when I was only eight years old. Sitting next to my
mother as the teacher talked about how well I was doing, I had
felt my face flush with pride. 'You're no better than the next
person and I'd better not ever hear of you stepping out of line.'*

*I understood from an early age that my mother hated me, and
while I do know why she hated me, I don't understand why she
continued to hate me for the whole time I was living with her. It
wasn't the 1950s – it was the 70s and 80s when I was growing
up. She had a choice to return to work and forge a path for herself,
but instead she chose keeping me in line as her career. And my
father just went along with it. I'm sure he must have tried, in the
beginning, to defend his mother but I know that my mother
conducted a continuous campaign to make sure his loyalties lay
with her. Sometimes at night I would get out of bed to go to the
bathroom and stand silently outside my bedroom door, listening
to my mother talking, catching phrases like, 'going to ruin our
child,' and 'has no idea of what kind of life we need to live,' and
'undermines me all the time.' I began to make sense of what she
was saying when I was ten and then I began listening when I
could. I knew she could only have been speaking about my
grandmother and I know my father's silence meant that he was
taking it all in, listening and accepting that his mother was not a
good person. I am sure it went on from the moment my mother
found out she was pregnant with me. I think the fact that I was
allowed to see her at all meant that he was still holding on to a
tiny shred of his past life. I am so grateful that he did.*

When I was older, maybe thirteen, my mother spent a week

in bed and that's when I was made aware of just where her antipathy for me came from.

I was not told anything except 'just let your mother rest', so of course I asked the only person who would talk to me.

'What's wrong with her?' I asked my grandmother, who had come to take me away for an afternoon.

'It's the same thing that happened when she had you,' she explained. 'She was very sad for a long time and it was all made worse by the fact that her father wouldn't see her, and then, just as she was getting better, he died. She never got to see him after he stopped speaking to her, and I know from your dad that she always hoped to reconnect.'

'So it's my fault she gets sad?' I asked my grandmother.

'Oh no, love, no it's not,' she reassured me but I could hear the hesitancy in her voice.

I think that in my mother's mind, her father's death and my birth were connected forever. When she looked at me, she saw not what she'd gained – a daughter – but all the things she had lost. She lost her chance at the life she was supposed to live and connection with her family.

I think my father really loved her and that's why he tried so hard to become the kind of man her family would find suitable. I can imagine that my mother dreamed of seeing her parents again one day and having them approve of her perfectly behaved daughter and of how strictly she and my father adhered to all the things she had been taught as a child. But she never got the chance to do that. And while I don't understand her dislike for me, I will always understand her need to have her parents acknowledge that she was living an acceptable life. I've never stopped wanting the exact same thing.

I only remember being hit, actually slapped, once. Mostly I was locked in my room, shut out of their affections, belittled, warned and disciplined if I showed even the smallest amount of independence of spirit.

What happened shouldn't have come as a surprise to them, and yet I think what they most felt when I started acting out was... shock. They didn't understand how all their rules and regulations had failed them.

They still don't understand it.

SEVEN

GRACE

I wake extra early in the morning, my body filled with energy for the new day. The first thing I do is send a text to Cordelia.

Good morning, darling. I hope you have a wonderful day.

She replies the way she always does.

Stop contacting me.

The words will never lose their sting. My beautiful girl, with blonde hair and chocolate brown eyes, has not spoken to me since what I have taken to calling 'the incident'.

In therapy, I pointed to 'the incident' as the cause for my daughter wanting nothing to do with me, but my therapist said, in that quiet measured way he had, 'I think if you are truthful with yourself, Grace, you will admit that what happened was the last straw for Cordelia, rather than the entire cause of your estrangement.'

'Hmm,' I replied, which was what I did when I wanted to tell Dr Gordon to go screw himself.

It takes me over an hour to ready myself for the day. I want to look perfect. As I inspect myself in the mirror, I realise that my hair needs to be recoloured. My natural colour is threatening to come through and I can't have that.

I'm sure if I went back to my natural colour, I would see a lot of grey. But other than that, I don't believe I look fifty-two years old. I am, as my new hairdresser likes to say, in absolutely fabulous shape. It's genetic luck, I believe – because after everything I have done to my body, there's no way I should look to be in my forties, rather than my fifties.

The sky is a vibrant blue as I board the train, the heat rising off the platform in waves. The journey home will, no doubt, be somewhat odious as the carriages fill up with people sweaty from the heat and a whole workday, but now there is only the smell of perfume and aftershave and chatter about weekend plans. It's only Tuesday but summer makes people yearn for the weekend even more.

Six years ago, I would never have imagined travelling on a train to work. I had a car and driver. Bert would pick me up outside my house every morning at 8 a.m. He always had the morning paper and a coffee – almond milk, shot of caramel – waiting for me. Bert was nearly eighty and only worked for me because it kept him interested in the world. I worry about him now but I also feel like I disappointed him. I disappointed a lot of people. I hope he's found someone else to drive for. I would have found him a new job if anyone had taken my calls after it happened. It's so easy to simply remove someone from your life these days. Their name comes up on your phone so you can refuse the call and then you can block and delete them there and everywhere else as well. I feel like the whole business community did that to me. And it's only since I got out of the clinic that I've had the strength to remind some of them of what they owe me.

I feel like my family blocked me as well and I still, no matter what anyone says, don't believe it was all my fault. I know who to blame for everything that has gone wrong in my life. I definitely know who to blame.

At 8.30 I am standing in front of the receptionist, Melody, who is flicking through a magazine. Ava told me office hours begin at 9 a.m. but Melody is here so she should be working.

'Good morning, Melody,' I say, and she looks up from her magazine, raising her eyebrows. 'Ava told me your name. I'm Grace, as I told you yesterday, and I am starting today as Ava's assistant. I assume her office is unlocked?'

'Um... yeah but you can't go in there,' says Melody. 'Ava isn't here and she won't be—'

Before she finishes her sentence, the lift in front of reception opens and a man emerges. He looks to be in his fifties with a full head of thick grey-brown hair, artful stubble and blue eyes.

'Collin, this is Grace,' says Melody quickly. 'She's Ava's new assistant and she wants to go into her office but I said that she has to wait for Ava.'

Collin looks me up and down; a shine in his eyes indicates his interest. 'Right, Ava mentioned she'd found a new assistant. I hope you're going to be able to help her. She's really a little,' he waves his hand, 'all over the place right now.'

From the website I know that the CEO of Barkley Education and Training is a woman named Patricia Riley. She is away a lot because she is trying to sell the company and their products overseas. She is also, I read, working on opening an arm of the company in London. The day-to-day business is run jointly by Ava Green and Collin King, and I know, without even having to think about it too hard, that if a new arm is opened in London, Patricia will have to put either Collin or Ava in a posi-

tion of power, assuming she chooses to be the one who opens
the new arm of the company.

I smile at Collin. 'It's lovely to meet you,' I say. I have not
done a deep dive on him but I glance down at his hand and see
no sign of a wedding ring. 'I'm going to do my best to help.'

'Great,' he says, reaching out his hand, 'nice to meet you
too.' I let him grasp my hand in a firm handshake.

'I'll wait for Ava in her office,' I say, and without waiting for
anyone to say anything I move away.

I know there will be forms to fill in and all sorts of information to get before I can properly start the job. But right now, I
could at least have a general tidy up.

The office is in as much chaos as it was yesterday. I place
my bag on a chair and start by opening the blinds and clearing
away the half-empty coffee cups. I am careful to only make tidy
piles of the papers as opposed to moving them. Ava will want to
take me through things.

Just before 9 a.m., I make a cup of coffee in the kitchen with
milk and no sugar. I know she takes her coffee with milk but I
am unsure about the sugar so I place that and a packet of artifi-
cial sweetener on a saucer with a teaspoon.

And then I go and wait by the lift.

Ava is three minutes late, burdened with files and a laptop
and her bag.

'Good morning,' I say as the lift doors open and I reach for
the files, which she hands me.

'Grace,' she says, and though she smiles I can see that she's
had a frustrating morning. Her blouse is misbuttoned and her
hair pulled back into a short ponytail, not a good look.

I follow her to her office, where she stops by the door. 'Oh,'
she says, 'you tidied.'

'I didn't move anything, just neatened it until you tell me
exactly what you want me to do,' I say, a little unsure now.

'And you made me coffee,' she says as she drops her things onto a small grey sofa in her office.

'Of course,' I say.

'Thank you.' She nods and then she wipes her hand across her cheek. She's had a tough morning and a little kindness goes a long way.

'Shall we get started?' I ask after she's taken a sip of her coffee – no sugar or sweetener, I note.

'Yes,' she says. 'There's a lot to do.'

'I know there is,' I say, and Ava has no idea that I'm not just talking about work.

EIGHT

AVA

Grace is quick and efficient, intelligent and, it seems to Ava, almost immediately able to anticipate her needs.

They spend the first few hours of the morning organising Ava's office, filing and stacking paper into piles in order of how they need to be dealt with. It is how Ava likes to run her office, but since her last – admittedly not great – assistant left, everything has overwhelmed her. The fact that she is permanently exhausted doesn't help either.

'I must be the messiest person you've ever worked with,' she says, lifting a pile of papers as she searches for the roster for the trainers from two weeks ago.

'You were simply in need of an assistant,' says Grace. 'People can only handle so much by themselves and you've been doing everything.'

'I have,' agrees Ava, feeling validated.

'It's almost lunchtime,' says Grace, 'would you like me to get you something to eat? I saw a lovely café downstairs.'

'Oh, I hadn't realised, but actually, I am hungry – are you sure you don't mind?'

'That's my job,' Grace says, smiling, and Ava sends a silent prayer of thanks up to the heavens for Grace's arrival. Her office feels like it's under control again and by extension, her work life.

There is a knock at the door and Ava and Grace look up.

'Well, look at you girls getting on with things,' says Collin.

'What can I do for you, Collin?' asks Ava, immediately feeling the churn of dislike she has for the man. He seems to glide through his day doing not very much but he's always on the phone to Patricia, singing his own praises. He has a large network of friends from school and gets introductions into the largest, most expensive private schools with ease. He is part of the 'old boys' club' of private schools, his road in life smoothed before him by his parents, who were both lawyers. Trusting him and responding to his interest in her when she first started working for Barkley was a huge mistake and one Ava has never forgiven herself for.

She has felt every step of her climb up the corporate ladder, from the time she was in her last year at an under-funded public high school and decided to do a business degree till now.

She has worked her way up in the company from the position of receptionist, which is where she began despite having a business degree. She knows that Collin has resented each promotion she has received and that he's now incensed to find her on the same level as he is. The patronising tone he always assumes with her is infuriating, but the last time she brought it up he merely grinned at her and said, 'Come on, Ava, you're imagining things. I thought we knew each other better than that. We do, don't we?' The way he was looking at her made her shudder so she simply walked away.

'I imagine that calling grown women girls is something frowned upon in the business world these days,' says Grace lightly.

Collin laughs but there is some uncertainty to his laughter.

'Sorry,' he says, 'it looks like you women are getting on with things.' As if that is any better.

'Collin, what do you need?' asks Ava.

'I just wanted to let you know that I've managed to get the principal of St Augustine on board. It's a big school, Grace, very prestigious. I'm going to call Patricia about it. Did you want me to let her know about anything for you? I know the trainers are taking up a lot of your time.'

Ava shakes her head. 'Nothing, but well done, Collin. Very well done.' The words are insincere and Collin knows it.

'Well... old friend on the board, you know,' he says, waving his hand.

'Isn't life easier when one doesn't have to work too hard to meet the right people?' says Grace and she offers Collin a glorious smile.

Ava can see Collin's confusion. Grace is very attractive and he's not sure how to react to being insulted by an attractive woman, and he's not quite sure he's been insulted either. Ava wants to cheer. She struggles to put Collin in his place and finds herself taking on all the most difficult jobs, like managing the hundred-plus trainers they have, because she can't say no to him. She can't say no to him because she didn't say no to him ten years ago when they first started working together. They have the same title but she still feels like Collin is her boss, and she thinks it is possible that he is paid more than she is, something he has hinted at.

Patricia has let both of them know that she will be the one running the arm of the company she is planning to open in the UK and that one of them will be made CEO of Australia, and with every fibre of her being, Ava wants that job. One of her almost daily fantasies is that Collin simply disappears one day and she never has to deal with him again.

'Right, well, carry on,' he says and leaves.

'Well,' says Grace, 'he's nice-looking.'

'Yes, but...' says Ava, not wanting to bad-mouth a colleague on Grace's first day in case Grace thinks that's the kind of person Ava is.

'But not someone I'd want to have over for dinner,' says Grace and Ava laughs.

'You're amazing,' she says.

'Thank you, now lunch,' says Grace with a smile.

Ava finds her purse and gives Grace the company credit card. 'Buy for both of us,' she says.

'Are you sure?'

'Absolutely. I love the chicken salad but they have lots of other choices.'

'Maybe you should lie on the sofa for ten minutes while I get lunch,' says Grace gently.

'Is it that obvious that I'm exhausted?' asks Ava. She would take offence if she had the energy but the words seem to be meant kindly.

Grace nods. 'I saw the photo of your two little ones. It's hard being a working mother.'

'Amen to that,' sighs Ava, even as she experiences a tiny sting of alarm. Since Emily left and her desk has piled up with papers, Ava has kept the photograph in her top desk drawer, which means that Grace opened the drawer when she was alone in the office. *She was obviously just tidying or looking for something*, she assures herself, immediately dismissing any niggling worry.

'I'll be back soon,' says Grace and she leaves the office, closing the door behind her with a soft click.

Ava looks at the sofa. She should carry on working but... without thinking about it anymore she lies down on the small sofa, curling up on her side. She'll just close her eyes for a few minutes. Grace will be back soon enough.

It feels like only seconds have passed when she feels a hand on her shoulder and opens her eyes. For a moment she has no idea where she is and then she sees Grace. 'Oh,' she says, sitting up and wiping at her mouth, embarrassed to have been caught so fast asleep. 'How long have I been asleep?'

'Only fifteen minutes, which is the perfect amount to feel refreshed and not groggy,' says Grace, and Ava realises that she does feel that way. If she naps in the afternoon on a Sunday, she usually wakes feeling more tired than when she lay down, but now she feels wide awake, ready for work. 'Your salad is on the desk.'

'Thank you.' Ava goes to sit behind her desk and opens the salad, digging in with the fork next to the bowl.

Grace turns to go. 'I'll leave you in peace,' she says.

'No, don't go,' says Ava, 'sit down, eat with me. Tell me about you.'

'Not much to say really,' says Grace, sitting down and opening her own bowl of salad. 'I'm not married and I don't have children. I've always been quite dedicated to my work.'

'Oh,' says Ava, unsure if she should express sympathy.

'But tell me about you,' says Grace. 'How old are the girls?'

Ava takes the photograph out of the drawer and puts it on display, where she likes it to be when her desk isn't covered in paperwork. It's one of her favourites because it was taken on a hot summer's day just after both girls got out of the pool, and Finn somehow managed to zoom in close enough to see not only their gorgeous smiles but also the tiny droplets of water on their hair. They looked like mermaids. Finn takes the most beautiful pictures of their girls. Their friends always ask him to take pictures at birthday parties and Ava once suggested he could make quite a good living out of it, but Finn shut her down with a laugh. 'As if I would compromise myself with a job like that,' he said.

'Hazel is five and a real handful, and Chloe is three and she's quiet but determined,' says Ava as she gazes at the picture, feeling her heart swell with love for them.

'They sound adorable. Do you have a nanny or are they in school?'

Ava finds her last bite of chicken salad hard to swallow as she thinks about this morning and finding Finn passed out on the sofa, his hands covered in dried paint. He occasionally works all night when he is feeling inspired, and she knew there was no point in trying to wake him. It was easier to simply do everything herself.

Only after she had dropped the girls at school had she glanced in the mirror and realised that she hadn't even brushed her hair properly, quickly tying it back in an unattractive ponytail it was too short for. When she arrived at work, her heart was racing with anxiety and her gut churning with anger at Finn. But then Grace was waiting for her and there was a fresh coffee on her desk and somehow it all seemed easier after that.

'Hazel is at school and Chloe is at preschool. My husband, Finn, is an artist and he takes care of the girls during the day, when they're home... Well, he's supposed to.' Ava blushes at the overly personal share.

'They're beautiful children,' says Grace, dropping her green eyes to her empty salad bowl. She stands and picks it up and Ava's as well. Ava tries to remember the last time anyone, even Emily, picked up an empty plate or cup for her. 'Now I'll throw this out and we can get back to it.'

Ava goes to her window to look out into the city. The sky is a deep blue and she knows that out of the air conditioning, it's incredibly hot, the pavements burning and the air thick. But she also knows, with a little spark of joy, that she will get home before 6 p.m. today because of everything she and Grace have achieved. Maybe she can take the girls for a quick swim. Summer has flown by and she feels like she's worked through most of it.

'Right,' says Grace as she walks back into the office, 'let's sort out these trainers, shall we?'

By the end of the day, Grace has managed to book twenty trainers into different hotels so they can visit schools across the country. Ava feels like they've done a week's worth of work in just one day.

At five minutes past five Ava says, 'That's enough for today, I think. You've been absolutely brilliant, Grace.'

'I'm so glad you're happy,' says Grace.

'Any plans for the evening?' asks Ava as they get ready to leave.

'Plans?' replies Grace. 'No, no plans.' There is something in the way she says it that makes Ava think that Grace must be lonely. She remembers Grace telling her she is not married and has no children.

Life sometimes feels very chaotic to Ava but she will be surrounded by her family when she gets home. And she knows that if she went home to an empty house or apartment every day, it would not be something she would enjoy.

'Well, I'll see you tomorrow,' says Grace.

'Yes, thank you for your work today. It all feels so much better.'

'I'm glad. I'm here to help you in any way you need me to.' She nods and leaves the office.

Ava takes a quick look around in case she has forgotten anything, admiring the neat desk with an organised stack of papers to go through tomorrow.

Everything is in its place and she couldn't be more grateful for her new assistant.

NINE

GRACE

I stride along the hot street to the station, trying not to find the people in my way irritating. There is a relaxed atmosphere in the air – it feels like the whole of Australia slows down over summer. People are less stressed, the heat making everything feel heavy and slow.

I used to be one of those people although I mostly worked through the summer. I worked through my weekends as well. That's something I regret now but it's just another in a long line of things I regret. Instead of allowing myself to ruminate, I make a list of things to be grateful for. *I'm grateful for the job, grateful Ava believed Liza, grateful I had somewhere to go today and something to do, grateful Ava likes me.*

I stand on the platform, waiting to get on a train as hot air blasts through the station. I am not really looking forward to getting home but at least I have a working air conditioner.

I could have rented something nicer but the place I have chosen feels like the kind of apartment an assistant would rent. It's right that I live in this particular building. My downstairs neighbour works in a supermarket, which I only know because she leaves dressed in a uniform. It is a place for those who are seen but not seen, essential but never really noticed.

I chose my apartment because of its proximity to the rehabilitation facility. I'm not going back, never going back, but for some reason I feel the need to be close to it just in case. I drive past it on my way to the grocery store, and each time I do, I remind myself that I will never let my life spiral out of control again.

When this is done, I will find somewhere nicer to live. The one thing I have been left with is money. But that old adage about it not buying happiness is completely true. I have a substantial amount of money in my bank account but nothing else. I have lost everything else. I have lost my company, my house, my daughter, my husband and my reputation. I sold my company for way below its value but it was still a large sum of money. Liza Hong, the woman who bought it from me, agreed to provide a reference for me if anyone called. Liza and I have known each other for years, both working in the same industry, and we had a mutual respect for each other as businesswomen and colleagues. I lured her away from another company to come and work for me, and it felt as though together we would be able to take on the whole world.

Now Liza owns my company and all she feels for me is sympathy. I loathe being pitied. But I have to tolerate pity for now. Liza is also sceptical of my reasons for wanting to work as an assistant instead of simply retiring and living off the money I have.

'Why throw yourself back into the business world, Grace?' she asked when I called her after I left the clinic. 'It's not about money, and after everything that happened, surely you don't want to start again?'

'I can't explain it, Liza,' I told her. 'I want to work, and if that means starting at the bottom, fine. Just tell whoever calls that I was a great employee.'

'But why take such a menial job?'

'I have my reasons,' I told her, and I do.

'What if you get caught in the lie?'

'Then I'll lose my job and be back where I am now. I'm not asking you to critique my choices. I'm asking for your help. You owe me that.'

'Fine,' she sighed.

And to her credit, she obviously gave me a very good reference. Ava didn't bother to call Geoff but I will wait for a bit before I tell him to stop answering the phone as I have instructed.

The train ride home is, as I thought it would be, fuggy with sweat and body odour. I lean far away from my travelling companion, a large man with a damp shirt. I try breathing through my mouth but the thick smell of body odour is everywhere. It is a relief to get off the train. You can feel that summer is ending. The evening air has lost its heavy heat and is now just lovely. It will be warm for many weeks during the day still but the nights will gradually cool over the autumn months.

I'm not hungry but I know I need to eat so I stop at a sushi restaurant that I've eaten at a couple of times, because they are busy so their food is fresh. At home, I enjoy the crunch of perfectly prepared vegetable rolls and the salty hit from the soy sauce. The food at the clinic was stodge, filled with sugar and starch, and I could only ever eat a small amount of it.

I was there for six years. Six long years. It was necessary for me to stay, not just to kick my drug of choice but also to receive the therapy that would make me acceptable to the outside world. I learned a lot about myself, and what I realised is that the one thing that can never be taken from me is my determination to be who I want to be. Dr Gordon talked a lot about forgiveness and moving forward and I agreed with him about all of it. I told him I was no longer angry, no longer plotting revenge, was only going to live my life in peace, spending every day trying to make up for my mistakes. I was determined to make Dr Gordon like and believe me and I succeeded because here I am, eating sushi and working for Ava Green.

After dinner I clean again, allowing the restoring of order to calm me. I furnished the apartment with cheap, mass-produced furniture. There is nothing beautiful about any of the pieces I chose, from the grey sofa covered in a hardy fabric to the small timber table surrounded by cross-back chairs in painted white. When I leave, I will leave it all here for the next lucky or unlucky tenant.

I try to prevent my mind going back to the home where I lived with my husband and child but it's a struggle. This is one of those times when I would give anything for a drink, anything to feel the cool burn of the alcohol going down my throat, and know that it would only be a short time until I was numb and woozy. I remember the relief of the first sip that always came with the knowledge that soon my mind would slow and the terrible, churning thoughts would quiet.

I lay my outfit for tomorrow on the bed, choosing shoes and a belt to go with the pale blue dress. I have seven acceptable work outfits to rotate through for my working week so that I don't need to do the washing every day. They are all nicely made but nothing compared to the clothing I used to own. All those beautiful fabrics and designs are gone now. I will one day buy such clothing again, but for my current purposes, all I need are serviceable items. My mother used to say, 'A lady always looks her best,' and she was always well turned out with her hair neatly done and her nails manicured. And a frown on her face.

At the clinic my therapist and I discussed mothers a great deal. He was a nice man with a pleasant face but an air of weariness as though he was tired of the burden of so many damaged people's problems. You wouldn't think a therapist would actually use the clichéd phrase 'tell me about your mother', but he did.

'My mother was strict but wanted the best for me,' was all I could manage. I wasn't really there to talk about my problems. I was there to get through the years and get on with my life.

I raised Cordelia differently to how I was raised, not that she remembers any of it now, or perhaps she just chooses not to. My daughter is focused on the things I did wrong, on my one spectacular failure. She doesn't remember the bath times I was there for when we made soap bubbles together, or the school sports days I moved heaven and earth to attend. She's forgotten the stories I read and the ice cream sundaes we made together before snuggling up on the sofa to watch a movie.

I close my eyes and picture my lovely girl, see the smile on her face on the day she finished her final exams at school, feel the hug she gave me and smell the light floral scent she always wore. She had, by then, started asking me to curb my drinking. She had started casually pointing out that it was too much and then gone on to tell me about the health issues that came from excessive consumption, and then she had gotten angry and told me I was going to die and leave her with no mother. 'You fell asleep on the sofa again, Mum,' she would say, or, 'Do you really need to have that much wine in a week?' or, 'You know alcohol is a poison and you shouldn't be having it every single day.'

I always told her I was fine, that it was under control, but she knew it wasn't. She had some idea why I had started drinking in the first place, but she believed it was a crisis of my own making because her father was a very convincing liar. She thought my paranoia was driven by my drinking and she never believed any of the things I told her.

I never listened to any of the things she was saying either. I was mired in my own misery and no one could get through to me, but now Cordelia doesn't want me to speak to her and I wonder if she would be happy if I did die. I hope not. I still love her with all my heart. I know if she could just understand why everything happened, she would forgive me, but she has to allow me to speak to her before I can explain.

The triumphant hug she gave me the day she finished her exams is the last time she hugged me, the last time she agreed to speak to me. She was eighteen. Six years is a long time to go without talking to your child. Every day my whole body aches for her touch and I will never get used to it.

Without thinking, I get the bottle of vodka out from the freezer in the kitchen.

I twist off the top and inhale deeply, the medicinal smell penetrating my lungs, filling my senses. And then I close it back up again, twisting the top tightly.

'You see,' I say aloud. 'I'm not an alcoholic.' The words are my comfort and my truth. I was not an alcoholic. I am not an alcoholic. What I am is someone who was driven to the bottle by utter despair. *Isn't that what every addict would say?* I hear Dr Gordon ask me but I wave away his words. I know who I am.

Satisfied that I am ready for tomorrow, I sit on the sofa and text Cordelia.

I hope you had a good day, darling.

She responds very quickly.

You need to stop contacting me.

I think she waits for my texts. She hates me and wants nothing to do with me but I am her mother and she needs to know that I am there, waiting for her forgiveness. She hasn't blocked my number and that would have been very easy to do. We are still tied together, my child and I, and she still needs to know that I think of her every day. I think it comforts her and the poor girl needs some comfort. Her life has also changed in the most shocking way. After it happened, after the trial was over, the only thing she could think to do was flee the country. She went to London for some time but I know she's back in Australia now, living in Melbourne, something I only gleaned from looking up the name of a café pictured in one of her Instagram posts. I don't know why she has chosen to go there because she doesn't have a lot of friends in Melbourne but perhaps Sydney was filled with too many bad memories. I know she is with her boyfriend and I also know that he's not good for her. She's never shared anything about her relationship with me but I follow her on Instagram, under another name of course, and I've seen the way he responds to her posts. Whereas her friends compliment her photos, he seems to favour a level of mocking sarcasm that I don't like.

On a photograph she took of herself as she was deciding between two dresses, her friends gave general opinions basically stating that both the green floral full-length style and the shorter blue one were gorgeous, but he said, *My darling Cordy, don't you have enough dresses?* She hates to be called Cordy. He followed the statement with a host of laughing emojis, as though she is a joke.

On a picture of her standing in front of her new office at the design firm where she works, he commented, *Never thought that degree would get you anywhere, babe, but look at you now.* Again, he followed this with his favoured laughing emojis. I've never met him. But I don't like him.

I think for a moment before I compose my reply to Cordelia. It is unfair that she blames me for everything, and part of me wants to howl at the injustice of it all, to point out in a long list everything that was done to me before I did anything in retaliation. But that will achieve nothing. I desperately want my child back in my life and so instead I reply the way I usually do.

You know I can't do that. I love you and I know you're angry with me. I understand.

I wait so long for her reply that I start to think she is done with the conversation, but then she does send me a message, hurtful and vicious and filled with all her pain.

Good God, what is wrong with you? You killed my father. You should be in jail. I hate you.

I'm not quite sure how to answer that so I send her my stock standard reply that I have been sending for the last six years, every time she brings it up.

I love you and I'm sorry you're in pain.

I never meant for him to die. He was Cordelia's father and a girl needs a father, even after she becomes an adult.

I believe it was not my intention. I only meant to do what he had done to me.

I only meant to burn down everything he loved and believed in, in the same way he had burned down everything I loved and believed in.

It was an accident.

I think.

TEN

AVA

The first week and a half of Grace's employment flies by and Ava's new assistant is everything she hoped she would be. Grace gets in earlier than she does every day, and every day she is waiting for Ava as the elevator doors open.

The trainers quickly realise that they can ask Grace for help on the practical things like booking into hotels and so Ava's phone is not constantly pinging with texts from them, which gives her time and space to concentrate on other things, things that she hopes will impress Patricia, like bringing in new business.

Her home life still feels out of control and she finds herself longing for the office, where everything is neat and tidy and Grace doesn't question her judgement.

When she arrives one morning furious and stressed because Finn had promised he would wash Hazel's school uniform and then neglected to do so, leading to Hazel having to wear the same uniform for a fourth day in a row, stains included, Ava can't help complaining to her assistant.

'I just don't understand... I asked him about it twice and he actually told me it had been done, he told me the uniforms were clean,' she grumbles as Grace sits waiting patiently for Ava to tell her what she needs done that morning.

Grace clucks her tongue. 'I've worked for lots of mothers and I know that no matter how many hours you put in at the office, there are always many more hours when you get home. It's so much to ask of a woman because once we only had to stay home and have babies, but now we have to have babies and work and take on the whole mental load of running a family. Women's liberation is wonderful but it seems to me that all it has really meant for us is that we have more work to do. I don't have children but many of my friends do and I have seen how difficult it is for them. Their children are older now but when they were young… it was very hard.'

'Well, I mean, I wanted kids,' says Ava, feeling guilty for bad-mouthing her husband. 'I think Finn was happy without them but he adores the girls and he's so good with them, he's just not practical.'

'Which makes it very hard for you,' says Grace, and even though Ava hates herself for saying something negative about her husband, she can't deny that it feels good to have someone understand. Complaining to Lucy about Finn always felt disloyal but somehow because Grace is someone she doesn't know very well, it takes the sting out of her crossing a line in her marriage.

A little over two weeks after she hired Grace, on a balmy Thursday morning, when the lift doors open, Ava knows that Grace will be standing there, waiting to greet her. She knows that there will be a fresh cup of coffee sitting on her desk and that there will also be a list, made by Grace, of the most important things they have to get through today. Last week, Grace suggested they each make their own lists and then compare in the morning, and that way, everything is handled and nothing forgotten. Ava's work life is calm, serene and ordered in a way that it has never been before. It hasn't been long but it feels like she and Grace have worked together for ages already.

She's even had the time to call two prestigious all-girls' schools and get an appointment to spend time with the principals so she can pitch their programme.

The doors slide open and Grace is standing exactly where Ava expects her to be, her arms open to take Ava's laptop bag from her.

'Good morning,' Grace says warmly. Today she is dressed in a fitted grey skirt with a cream blouse. Ava has begun paying extra attention to her clothes in the morning when she has the time, and this morning ran relatively smoothly because Finn was awake and told her he could handle breakfast and drop-off without her.

'Are you sure?' she asked him, surprised.

He shrugged his shoulders. 'I know you think I don't see how difficult these mornings can be but I do. I'm letting the canvas sit for a bit so I won't be working at night for a day or two, so I can be up to help in the morning. I want to help you, Ava. I may not always get it right but I try. I try to get it right...' It was an odd thing for Finn to say, so odd that Ava had no idea how to reply. In his pocket, his phone buzzed. He took it out and looked at it, shook his head and put it back in his pocket.

'Something wrong?'

'Not at all,' he said. 'Now you just take your time getting ready and I'll sort everything out,' he said as he packed the lunch boxes with healthy food.

Ava smiled and rewarded him with a quick kiss, jubilant at being able to shower and dress without the anxiety over time tapping at her. Today she is dressed in a fitted sleeveless black dress, and her hair and make-up are done. She feels every inch the professional.

'Morning, Grace,' she replies.

'Ah, Ava,' says Collin, who is standing by the reception desk. 'I just wanted to chat with you about your appointment at Redwood High.'

'What about it?' asks Ava, jutting her chin out, instantly suspicious and immediately regretting telling Collin about the appointment to meet Ms Vale, the principal.

'I wanted to let you know that I ran into Amber Vale last night at dinner. She lives close to where I do and we both favour the same little Italian restaurant. She and I had a lovely chat about the programme and she's agreed to give it a go, so there's no need for you to meet.' His smile is a level of smug that Ava would like to smack off his face.

'Collin...' she begins, unsure what to say because the heat of anger is burning through her.

'How lucky that Ava set that up for you,' says Grace.

'Well... she didn't exactly—' begins Collin.

'Coincidentally, Ms Vale only just called and left a message for Ava about coming in to speak at their careers day as an example of a woman forging her way ahead in the business world.'

Collin flushes and Ava wants to cheer.

'Well, I would think—' he says.

'That it's better for a woman to speak at an all-girls' school and I agree with you,' says Ava, finding her voice and squashing her anger at Collin. 'Have a good day, Collin,' she says, turning away from him and following Grace to her office.

Once she is seated behind her desk with the door closed, she says, 'Is that true?'

Grace sits down as well and hesitates for a moment. 'I know they have a careers day coming up next week because it was on their website when you asked me to do some research. I can call them and offer you as one of their speakers.'

Ava shifts in her chair. She doesn't approve of outright lying but she knows that all Grace was doing was protecting her.

'That's probably a good idea,' she says, 'but, Grace, it's best not to—'

'Lie, I know. I do apologise but he's...' Grace waves her hand and Ava nods. They don't need to say anything.

Ava takes a sip of her coffee and then a deep breath. 'Right, I can see you've made a list and so have I,' she says, opening her computer to find her own list. 'Let's see what needs to be done right away and then you can call the school and see if I can come and have a chat to the girls. It's a good idea to speak to them and I can talk to Amber Vale about the programme as well.'

Once their lists are completed, Grace leaves the office and Ava opens her email to check on what's come in over the time she and Grace have been working. There's one from Patricia, the CEO.

Hi Ava,

Things are going really well in the UK and I should be in a position to sign a lease on some offices this week. I know you and Collin are both aware that my move to the UK means that I will need to appoint an Australian CEO to oversee operations. So, this is just a heads up to let you know that I will make this decision in the next two weeks.

Best,

Patricia

Ava's heart sinks. Both she and Collin knew this was coming but now that it's official, it feels very real. She is in direct competition with Collin for the top job.

Right on cue, Collin pops his head into her office. 'Seen the email?' he asks.

'I have,' says Ava.

'May the best man win and all that,' he says, offering her a Cheshire cat grin.

'Or the best woman,' says Ava, smiling tightly.

'Yes, of course,' he says and leaves, obviously disgruntled at her not giving him the reaction he wanted.

Ava sighs, glad that it's close to lunchtime. She needs a walk, even though it's broiling outside.

Grace is not at her desk. She finds her in the kitchen making a cup of tea. 'I'm going for a walk,' she says.

'Okay,' says Grace and then she looks out at the corridor to see if there is anyone coming. 'Is Collin married?' she asks.

'He is,' says Ava. 'Why?' But Grace doesn't respond.

If Grace has a crush on Collin, it will not be a good thing. Relationships don't belong in the workplace.

If Grace does have a crush on him, it may affect her working for Ava. 'He's been married for twenty years,' says Ava, and Grace nods.

'Will you get lunch out?' asks Grace.

'I may. Can I ask why you're interested in Collin?'

Grace stares at her and Ava wishes she had taken the time to phrase the question more tactfully.

'No reason,' says Grace with a smile.

And while Ava would like to push her on this because there must be a reason for the question, she knows she can't. Grace and Collin are around the same age. It's quite possible that she is interested in him.

'He's married,' Ava repeats, hoping that Grace understands what she's saying because she knows that Collin doesn't care at all that he has a wife and children, and that's something Ava knows all too well.

ELEVEN

GRACE

'I understand,' I reply and Ava stares at me for a moment and then nods and leaves. I am grateful to be alone for a bit.

I sip my tea and mull over what I know about Collin. He's a very good-looking man. It's been a while since I noticed or even thought about men at all.

I am too young perhaps to remain alone forever but I cannot imagine ever being with someone again.

It is better if I remain single, I think, at least until I have done what needs to be done.

Melody flounces into the kitchen, pushing past me without saying anything to open the fridge and grab a yoghurt.

She pulls off the top and grabs a spoon, leaning against the counter while she eats.

I glance around quickly, making sure I haven't left a mess, and then I go to leave the kitchen.

'Collin's cute, isn't he?' says Melody. I know she's talking to me because no one else is here.

'I suppose,' I say.

'I've seen you looking at him,' she smirks.

I'm not quite sure what kind of a response she's looking for so I simply watch her as she spoons yoghurt into her mouth.

'Are you married?' she asks.

'No,' I reply.

'It must be hard to be single at your age,' she says, mixing up the yoghurt.

'It's fine,' I say. 'Everyone is different.'

'That's for sure. If I was as old as you and single, I don't think I would cope.'

'Well...' I begin.

'But you seem to be coping very well. Have you got a cat or something? If I was single at your age, I would definitely have a cat. Collin thinks you're pretty.'

'Oh,' I say.

'For an older woman, and you are, attractive I mean. And... like you have one of those faces that I feel like I've seen before.' She studies me as she licks her spoon slowly.

'Well,' I say, 'you certainly have never seen my face before.' I can feel my heart speeding up as she looks at me.

'Maybe,' she says but I don't reply.

I turn and leave the kitchen to go back to my desk.

'If I was your age and single, I would get a cat,' she repeats, and she laughs but I ignore that too.

Are she and Collin involved in some way? Is she jealous because he told her he thinks I'm pretty?

I want to laugh at her for being insecure but I know better than anyone that men will betray you without even thinking about it. I have a moment of sympathy for Collin's wife, a woman who may or may not know that she's married to someone who seems to be flirting with the office receptionist and maybe even doing more than that.

I wonder if she suspects anything, and if she does, if she's going to do something about it.

I open my computer and push thoughts of Melody away. I am sure Collin and his wife are perfectly happy.

But then, until one terrible day, so were my husband and I.

TWELVE

AVA

Ava leaves the building, taking deep breaths of hot air when she's outside. The heat hits her in the face and she immediately regrets her decision to leave the cool office, ducking quickly into a café, where the air conditioning is on high. She orders a coffee and a sandwich and finds a table at the back, opening her phone and giving herself permission to mindlessly scroll cute puppy and children videos for a few minutes.

Fifteen minutes later she has finished her avocado salad sandwich and is feeling able to tackle the rest of the day. Time away from the office always helps.

She checks her lap for her paper serviette and, realising it has fallen on the floor, bends down to get it. When she sits up again, the café door swings open and Collin and Melody walk in, his hand on her back as he guides her to a seat.

She watches as they lean towards each other over the small café table, whispering, and then she stands, meaning to go and make herself known, greet them before leaving the café. But as she gets closer to their table, a woman with a whiny toddler in her arms blocks her view, and in between the words 'I wanna ice cream, wanna ice cream', she hears Melody speak.

'I don't know if this is the right thing to be doing,' the young woman says, and as Ava moves past the table, Collin replies, 'Trust me, it's the only way to get what we want.'

With her heart pounding, she is out the door and on the street walking through the heat and back to the office. What were the two of them talking about? What do they want? To be together? Are they sleeping together? It's possible. Of course it's possible, even though Melody is half his age and it's highly problematic if they are sleeping together because of the power imbalance between the two. Melody surely knows it's wrong but Collin spends an inordinate amount of time talking to her, leaning over her desk. Just the way he did when Ava first started at the company. She remembers what it was like to bask in his attention. His blue eyes have a magnetic quality and Ava can remember how carefully she used to dress every morning, checking her image in the mirror of her small bedroom in the apartment she shared with her mother, trying to imagine what she would look like to Collin.

'You're getting very dressed up for a receptionist job,' she remembers her mother, Pam, saying to her one morning.

'They say you should dress for the job you want, not the job you have,' Ava told her. 'I want to manage the whole company.'

'Oh, Ava sweetheart, I know that you're capable but you mustn't miss out on the things that make life worthwhile. A husband and children are what you should be looking forward to.'

'But what if that's not all I want, Mum? I don't just want to be a wife and mother. I want more for my life.'

Her mother looked so distraught for a moment that Ava immediately felt bad for saying anything. 'It was all I ever wanted,' her mother said. Ava grew up knowing that her mother had been desperate for more children but it never happened, and then of course her parents got divorced when Ava was eleven. Her mother has remained single ever since.

Ten years ago, sitting behind the receptionist desk, Ava would answer calls and direct people to the right person, but she knows that part of her was always alert to Collin's presence, always waiting for him to walk by.

A Christmas party from a decade ago comes back to her as she walks back into the office building. A night when she was enjoying the free-flowing alcohol. She hadn't met Finn yet and she was very drunk.

Barkley Education and Training was a much smaller company then with half the number of employees it has now. Ava had only been working on reception for a few months and she was desperate to prove that her business degree had more value. Patricia had hired her but barely glanced at her as she came and went. The one person who had been kind to her was Collin. He would stop and chat with her every morning, just exchange a few words, and he'd even bought her coffee once.

The building where the company was housed needed a lot of work, but it did have a huge roof terrace with views over the harbour. The Christmas party was in full swing and Ava was on her fifth cocktail when Collin approached her.

Ten years ago, Ava was lithe and blonde, her big blue eyes mentioned by every man she met. Her hair hung down her back and for the party she was dressed in a tight sparkly black cocktail dress that was just a little too short for a company event.

'Don't you look ravishing,' Collin said, offering her one of his beautiful smiles. She had been attracted to Collin from the moment she saw him but she knew he was married. In fact, his wife was standing on the other side of the terrace, talking to Patricia.

'Thank you,' said Ava, curtsying and giggling.

'We've got some gifts for the staff,' he said. 'Will you come downstairs and help me get them?'

'Oh presents, yay,' laughed Ava, feeling an agreeable wooziness as she followed Collin to the elevator that would take them down to the office.

He stood close to her, and she could smell the whisky on his breath and the earthy smell of his aftershave. 'You know you're one of the most beautiful women here,' he murmured.

'And you are...' she began and then he leaned in and kissed her and somehow it seemed a good idea to keep kissing in his office. He had a large sofa there, big enough for them both to lie on.

Once it was over, Collin adjusted his pants and tucked in his shirt. 'I think it would be best if we didn't mention this to anyone. Christmas parties always get a little...' He didn't finish the thought but Ava understood exactly what he was saying.

'Of course,' she agreed. 'Let me just go to the bathroom and then we can get the presents.'

'Oh, it seems they're already up there. I'll see you on the terrace,' he said and he bolted out the door.

Ava instantly knew she had been used. In the bathroom, she washed her hands and smoothed her hair but refused to meet her own gaze in the mirror. She was ashamed of her stupidity.

She wasn't able to look at anyone when she got back to the terrace but as Patricia wished everyone a Merry Christmas, she couldn't stop herself glancing around, and she caught Collin's wife staring at her.

Ava looked away first, her shame intensifying as she thought about what her mother would have said about her sleeping with her boss. She worried, momentarily, about being fired before she realised that there was no way Collin would share the story. He was married and Ava was single. He was her boss. He would keep the whole thing quiet.

He stopped talking to her beyond issuing instructions when they all returned to work after the new year break, and Ava felt a wave of shame wash over her every time she saw him.

Perhaps today she would report him for what he did and for

the way he treated her afterwards, but she had gone willingly enough.

Collin never leaned over her desk again but, in a weird way, that actually worked in Ava's favour. She began to concentrate at work, to do research that she thought would help the company and to present that to Patricia, leading to her first promotion. She regrets the encounter with Collin, but not the outcome of it.

In the lift back up to her office, Ava thinks about how Collin treats Melody. Have they had sex yet? Melody has been with the company for nearly a year. Is it more than just one encounter?

If Collin and Melody are having an affair, she needs to tell Patricia.

Grace is sitting at her desk just outside Ava's office, her gaze fixed on her computer screen where the names of the trainers are listed. 'Can you get Principal Adams on the phone for me please, Grace,' Ava requests, knowing that she needs to get on with her afternoon. Grace nods, immediately searching for the principal's number.

In her office, Ava sits down behind her desk and mulls over the problem and then it occurs to her that this is exactly the kind of thing that would make Patricia pass Collin over for the promotion. It's not a good look and there's no way Patricia would jeopardise the company's reputation.

It would be wonderful to have Collin working for her or, even better, simply gone so she doesn't have to ever again confront the one stupid mistake she made ten years ago.

She feels like she's been handed a bomb and the only question now is whether she is prepared to use it to get what she wants. And is it a bomb at all or is she just making more of how friendly they are than is necessary?

What were Melody and Collin talking about? What are they prepared to use to get what they want, and could what they want be Ava losing out on the CEO position?

'I've got Principal Adams from Edgeworth High on the line,' says Grace through the intercom, interrupting Ava's spiralling thoughts.

'Thank you,' she says and she lifts the phone, hits the right number and greets the principal. She needs to tread carefully.

Sex is a landmine in the workplace and not one she wants to make the mistake of stepping on. Accusations of an inappropriate relationship without proof could easily blow up Ava's career instead of Collin's.

'Principal Adams,' she says, 'thank you for taking my call.'

She concentrates on her call, leaving the problem of Collin and Melody for another time. When Patricia has to make a choice, Ava wants her work to speak for her. And she just has to hope that's enough.

At the end of the day, Grace and Ava finish tidying the office so everything is ready for the morning.

'Anything you need me to work on overnight?' asks Grace.

'No,' smiles Ava, 'you do quite enough work during the day, thank you.'

'I'm so glad you're happy,' says Grace and then her phone buzzes in her pocket and she takes it out and looks at it. 'Damn,' she mutters softly.

'What is it?' asks Ava without thinking that Grace may resent the question.

'They're fumigating my building for termites next week. I've never found one but apparently people on the floor below me have. I thought it would mean someone coming in and just spraying but apparently they tent the whole building and use some nefarious poison. I need to find somewhere to stay for five days.'

'Oh, that's awful,' says Ava.

'Yes, but it needs to be done. I'll just have to pay for a hotel. Perhaps I can find something close to this office building, although they tend to be very expensive in this area.'

'Yes, we're close to the city,' agrees Ava.

'I'll find something,' Grace says with a shrug.

They pack up the office in silence, getting their bags and walking to the elevator as an idea runs through Ava's head. Finn will be angry, but so what? She's the one who pays the mortgage.

They ride the elevator down together. Grace is getting off at the first floor to walk to the station but Ava's car is parked underneath the building.

'See you tomorrow,' says Grace as the doors open on the first floor.

'Um, Grace,' says Ava, putting her hand on the door to stop it from closing.

'Yes?'

'I have a room. I mean, it's like a small apartment above my garage so it's a separate entrance and everything. It's perfect for one person. We had a tenant but he moved out four months ago and Finn is supposed to find someone new but... well, I'm happy for you to take it for the time you need it. It's furnished and everything and it's completely separate...' She stops speaking, knowing she's babbling.

'That would be amazing,' says Grace, 'thank you so much, but are you sure? I would have to pay you rent.'

'That won't be necessary. It will only be five days.' Ava smiles, delighted to be able to do something nice for Grace.

'That's so kind of you,' says Grace.

'Great, we'll discuss tomorrow,' says Ava, letting the door go. Grace nods and waves.

In the car, Ava once more finds herself going over what she heard Melody and Collin discussing. Are they sleeping together? She shudders, pushing the idea of them together away, and then turning on the radio to distract herself as she remembers her own encounter with Collin again. Despite her worries over what she heard she reminds herself that it's been a really productive day. Things feel more under control than they have in a long time.

She has really found the perfect assistant and it feels like Grace is someone she can be friends with as well as colleagues. She can't wait to get to know her better.

THIRTEEN

Dear baby girl,

Children raised the way I was can go one of two ways, I think. They can either turn out exactly like their parents or do a complete 180. No prizes for guessing which way I went.

When I entered high school, I was even more acutely aware of how restricted my life was. I used to sit alone at lunch and watch other girls chattering and laughing and envy them their lightness, their freedom. My resentment of my parents began to show itself in the usual ways. I still did well at school, aware that education was my way out of my parents' house, but I began answering back, sneaking sweet treats into the house bought with money my grandmother gave me, and refusing to attend church on Sundays.

'What do you mean you're not coming?' my mother asked me when I told her the first Sunday I decided I would no longer go to church.

'Just that; I'm fourteen and I don't want to go anymore. You go.'

'You get up off that bed, young lady, and get yourself dressed right now,' she snarled, 'or there will be consequences.'

'What consequences? Will you lock me in my room? Fine, I'm used to it. Will you deny me food? I'm used to that too. Will you stop me from going out with my friends? Don't worry, I don't have any because everyone thinks I'm weird, and I am weird because you're so weird.'

My mother took three steps towards me, her teeth bared and her face puce with fury, and slapped me across the face. 'You have no idea what I gave up for you to exist and I regret it every single day,' she hissed. I was used to cruel words but she had never hit me before. I felt my eyes grow hot with tears but blinked them away and looked at her, an uncommon feeling coming over me. It took me a moment to realise what it was. It was triumph. I had got to her. I had made my mother lose control, and what she hated more than anything in the world was to lose control. It's why she didn't drink or eat anything sweet. It's why she exercised every day and kept such a tight hold on me.

She knew what happened when she lost control because the evidence of that was staring back at her, with my cheek turning scarlet. And if she lost control, she lost everything that mattered to her.

We continued to stare at each other, my mother and I, and then she turned and left the room, closing the door and locking it from the outside. I didn't care. As far as I was concerned, I had won.

That was just the beginning for me. My mother never hit me again but I kept taking steps to push her there. I cut off my long hair to a shoulder-length bob like a lot of the girls in my year had. I began hanging out after school, just loitering along with other students, hoping for an invitation to join a group. I took up drama classes and started wearing make-up to school, all of it old and given to me by my grandmother. I started going to her house whenever I could. She never turned me away despite knowing how angry it made my mother. Instead, she fed me and loved me and gave me money for new clothes. 'Now you don't tell your mum and dad about this,' she would say, pressing ten dollars into my hand and accepting a hug from me as thanks.

I gradually turned into someone who was still weird at school but was acceptable, even with my good grades.

If my grandmother hadn't died, I would probably have moved in with her and gone to university and lived a normal life.

But when I was fifteen, I came home one day from school to find both my parents sitting in the living room. I thought I was in for yet another lecture because I was getting one every second day by then from either my mother or my father. Seeing both of them together was new.

'Sit down, we have news,' my mother said, gesturing to a fabric armchair covered in garish green. She looked... happy. Her cheeks were pink with excitement and her eyes shining. In contrast, my father was looking at his shoes. I should have realised how unusual it was for him to be home early but it never even crossed my mind.

'Your grandmother had a stroke,' said my mother.

'Oh, no,' I gasped, tears immediately filling my eyes. 'Is she at the hospital, is she okay? Can we go see her?'

'She's dead,' my mother said, the word a triumphant spit of cruelty.

'No,' I said, 'she can't be.'

'She is. The funeral will be soon. I hope you can conduct yourself in the proper manner,' my father said, standing up and leaving the room.

'Perhaps you need to reconsider your attitude now that she's no longer around,' my mother said.

No hugs of consolation in my family.

I leapt off my chair and ran for my room, throwing myself down on my bed and giving in to a terrible force of teary grief. I was devastated.

Her funeral was held in our local church and it was packed with people who knew her. Friends from the street where she'd lived sat next to the group of women she'd played bowls with and the people from the local nursing home where she'd volunteered. The priest made a speech about how much she had helped all those she knew, how kind and giving she had been, and then my father got up and recited a few facts about her, his face stony with lack of emotion. I had wanted to say something but my parents had both refused and I was so devastated by her death that I'd simply accepted their decision. I was weighed down by grief, understanding that I had lost the one person who had truly loved me. I had no idea how I would survive without her.

At the graveside, my mother whispered to me as the coffin was lowered into the ground. 'It was stress that killed her. She was always so worried about you.'

'That's not true,' I said loudly, making everyone turn away from the mahogany coffin and look at us.

'You drove her mad,' said my father, loud enough for only me to hear.

'That's what happens when you disobey, when you don't behave,' my mother said.

I felt this knowledge settle over me, understood it to be the truth and blamed myself for her death just as they wanted me to. I had lost control, disobeyed my parents, and I had paid with the loss of the only person who I truly loved. My mother had done the same thing and lost her own father, her family and her position in society. I think she revelled in my loss.

I retreated after that, settled back into doing what I was told, spoke little, ate less, went to school and came home again. I had no one and nothing.

Sitting in church one Sunday, I was slouched over when my mother poked me in the back. 'Sit up straight,' she whispered fiercely, and I pushed my shoulders back as a little girl in the pew in front of me giggled. Her mother touched her gently on the head, saying, 'Quiet now, darling,' with an indulgent smile.

I had never had that, would never have it, and I wondered in that moment if it wouldn't be better if I had simply not existed at all.

It is a terrible thing for a child to grow up without that love. It made me constantly question myself and my place in the world. There was nothing I could do or say that would make them love me.

One night, I woke from a nightmare where I was lost in a forest, thick trees ropy with roots all around me, dark leaves leaning down to touch me. I was calling for my grandmother even though I knew she would not come. I woke with my heart racing, and as I took deep breaths to calm down, I realised that I would need to save myself. No one was coming to save me or help me or love me. I would need to love myself enough to get away from my parents, to make a life alone. I could never have predicted how that would happen, but that's the way of the world, baby girl. The moment you think you have a plan and a way forward, everything changes.

FOURTEEN

GRACE

It's Sunday morning and the sun is streaming through the single sliding-glass door that leads to my apartment's small balcony. I have a chair out there but it's not really a pleasant place to sit. The view is of another old building and, at the side, an alleyway where they keep their bins. I will be moving into Ava's garage apartment today and I'm looking forward to the large old trees and lush grass of Ava's suburb.

It was so much easier than I'd expected it to be.

I knew about the apartment over the garage. The day before my interview I drove past the house and saw the feeble sign in the window of the small apartment. I googled it and couldn't find it listed for rent anywhere. Perhaps Ava and Finn were just hoping that someone would see the sign and enquire?

If she hadn't offered it to me, I would have told her that a friend had given me a place to stay. The building where I have rented an apartment for six months is old, with red brick and timber window frames. It doesn't have a termite problem. If Ava asks, I will be able to explain in detail the process for tenting a whole building to treat it for termites. I've done my research.

It hasn't taken me long to pack a suitcase and a bag to take to Ava's place. I told her that I would arrive in the afternoon. I have to admit that one of the worst things about my current situation is the yawning weekend days with nothing to occupy myself.

I know that in the months leading up to my stay at the clinic I would sleep late on the weekend, always waking with a thumping head and spending the rest of the day groggily trying to make it through.

Cordelia was eighteen and off with her friends most of the time, studying or partying, one of the two. The house felt cold, even on the hottest summer's day, without her there. But I don't blame her for staying away. I blame the people responsible for my drinking, for my despair, for my downfall.

I take a cloth and wipe the counters in the apartment, letting memories flood over me, letting the most terrible day of my life come back to me. They hit hard, making my knees weak and bile rise in my throat.

I grab the vodka from the freezer, twist off the top and inhale deeply, and then I sink to the floor of my small kitchen. You can bury a memory deep down in your psyche but it will never stay there. Without warning it will rise through the dirt of your subconscious to confront you, and I know, after my time in the clinic, that it is best to let it happen, to let it come and to sit with it. Trying to stop it is what made me turn to alcohol. I can't do that anymore.

I am back in the old office, my beautiful office with a city view, and with my assistant Tamara, working through all the problems that came in every day across my fifty salons.

'Right, that's done,' I remember saying to her as we fixed a glitch in the computer system that was preventing online bookings. I glanced at the time. 'It's after four,' I said. 'I need a coffee, what about you?'

'Absolutely,' she agreed, offering me one of her dimpled smiles. 'I'll go.'

'Don't use the kitchen, go downstairs to the café. I think we've earned a treat as well – get me a Florentine,' I said, handing her the company credit card, and she smiled again, saluting me.

'Best idea ever, boss,' she said and then she left the office.

My business took up one floor of a small building in the city. It was a new building, slick with concrete and lightly tinted glass. The rent was enormous but I was easily able to afford it. My personal office was a place of calm and order with a whitewashed timber desk and a white leather sofa on a plush grey carpet. A small bronze plaque from each of my fifty waxing salons lined the walls, and on nights when I worked late and worried over the time I was spending away from home, I would run my hands lightly over the engraved lettering – Wax to the Max Bondi, Wax to the Max Sydenham, Wax to the Max St Ives – marvelling at all that I had done.

Tamara had been working for me for two years. She'd been in my home for dinners and she'd travelled with me to beauty fairs overseas so we could source new products for my salons. She had begun working for me straight out of university, eager to use her marketing degree. She was pretty, not beautiful but pretty, with blonde hair and a dimpled smile and the freshness of youth on her skin.

Years have passed since then. She's still pretty now but the blush of youth is gone.

I am keeping tabs on her the same way I am doing with a lot of people. I watch her on Instagram, read her posts.

I often think about everyone I worked with. I am watching some but not all of them. I wonder what they say about me when they speak of me or if they even speak of me at all. When it happened, my story was a cautionary tale, told in restaurants and pubs. But I'm sure it's all faded from memory now.

I sniff the vodka again, letting the memory bruise me once more. When Tamara left the office that day, I sat back in my chair and closed my eyes, anticipating the rich taste of dark chocolate mixed with cornflakes and nuts. I was tired but it was an exhilarated tired because we had solved a problem that had been plaguing us for some weeks. I had no idea that in a matter of minutes my exhilaration would disappear as I was made to understand that my whole life was a sham.

It came down to a simple mistake. Surprising how often that happens in life – something small leads to something enormous, the flapping of a butterfly's wings to the tsunami.

I see myself as I was that day. I was wearing a navy-blue dress with a matching jacket, teamed with black stilettos. My hair was done in a chignon, with not a single tendril out of place, a style I had practised until I could do it quickly and perfectly.

I look back at myself now and cannot believe that I had no instinct, no clue as to what was about to happen to my life. I had no idea that I would never look as put-together, as effortlessly in charge, as I did that day.

The phone on the desk pinged with a message and I looked down. A twist of fate, a coincidence, a small mistake and a whole life was changed.

Tamara and I had phone cases that looked similar, almost identical, and that was the start of the butterfly's wings, *flap, flap*.

I didn't think, I just picked up the phone and read the message, assuming it was mine. *Flap, flap* went the butterfly's wings, and a wave that would drown my life was unleashed.

In my kitchen, I lean my face over the vodka again, sniff, and then I touch my lips to the rim. But I don't drink. I am not an alcoholic. I don't drink but instead I let the memory of the text I saw on a phone that I instantly knew wasn't mine, return.

Hey sunshine girl, can't wait to see you xx

The sender was improbably called 'your stars and moon,' sickening and silly and even more so because I knew exactly who it was. I couldn't unlock her phone so I couldn't check the number but that didn't matter because I was already certain.

To anyone else reading, it was just a text from a man Tamara was involved with, just a sweet text, but I knew who it was from immediately and without question.

Because I used to be his sunshine girl, before my business grew so large, before Cordelia was born, before he began to mock what I did with my time rather than support it. I was his sunshine girl.

We met on an icy winter's day at university. Grey clouds overhead made two in the afternoon seem like much later as I walked into my lecture for statistics. I was cold and irritable and I slumped down into the first empty seat I came to, and then I looked at who I was sitting next to, catching the gaze of a brown-eyed boy with chestnut hair, and I smiled.

'Aren't you a ray of sunshine?' he said, smiling back. And from then on, I was his sunshine girl and I thought I would be always and forever. It wasn't perfect but no marriage ever is.

Hey sunshine girl, can't wait to see you xx

I stared down at the words, the noise of the constantly ringing phone outside my office disappearing.

It could have been a coincidence of course. It's not exactly an original term for a loved one. And while I sat at my desk with her phone in my hand, I hoped and prayed it was. Not just because it would otherwise mean that my husband was cheating, but because of who he was cheating with. I paid her salary. I spent every day with her. I liked her and spent time building up her self-esteem so that she would thrive in the workplace. I was a good boss and I believed I was a good wife. But if this had happened, I was obviously a bad boss and a bad wife. I knew that Robert did not think me the best mother so when I added all that up, I was a failure – three for three.

Why would she have done it otherwise? She was young and there were more than enough men on the apps she was using that she sometimes discussed with me. Why do it?

When she walked in holding two cups of coffee she said, 'I forgot my phone. I must need this more than I thought.'

'You got a message,' I said. 'I thought it was my phone.'

Her gaze went to my phone lying on the desk in a matt silver case, just like the one she had.

'I read it.' It was all I needed to say.

She knew. She put down the coffee slowly and then held out her hand for her phone, opening the screen and checking the message when I gave it to her.

'Oh, that's just a friend of mine,' she said, giggling nervously.

I looked straight at her, met her gaze and I knew she was lying in the way that you sometimes know. My whole world crumbled.

'Right,' I replied. 'I need...' And then I stopped speaking, my feelings overwhelming me, almost suffocating me. I stood and grabbed my bag and left the office, getting into my car to go home but I didn't go home. I drove around aimlessly for some time, the phrase, *Hey sunshine girl, can't wait to see you*, repeating in my head, willing tears to come because at least that would be a relief from the awful heavy feeling in my chest. But I couldn't cry. Finally, I stopped at a bar and enjoyed the relief of a few drinks.

With each sip of my vodka tonic, I heard my mother's disapproval – *sorrows are meant to be faced, not drowned* – and my father's disgust – *only the weak and the pathetic turn to drugs and alcohol.* I heard Robert's voice – *you love that business more than anyone, more than me, more than Cordelia* – and I heard Cordelia's voice, loudest of all: *Why can't you come, Mum, why? Everyone else's mum will be there. I'm more important than the conference. I am.*

My phone began ringing and I saw that it was Robert so I silenced it and then I put it on the bar and watched as I drank, watched him try to get hold of me over and again. Robert never called me during the day. As a mother, I wondered briefly if he was trying to reach me because of some emergency with Cordelia but I dismissed the thought. His calls came so soon after what had happened and they were relentless. Cordelia had her own phone anyway and hers was the only call I would have answered. In between there were calls from Tamara, from Liza, from a salon. I ignored them all for the first time in more than a decade.

I sank my sorrows until I couldn't see straight and then I drove home, my vision blurry, my head pounding. I'm lucky I didn't hurt myself or anyone else.

That came later.

I remember stumbling into the house at 1 a.m., not caring about how much noise I made as I climbed the stairs to our master bedroom. I expected to find Robert asleep but he was sitting up in bed, the bed with the headboard upholstered in cream silk that I had paid for. His bedside light was on, a book in his hand.

'I guess your little girlfriend called you to tell you that the secret is out,' I slurred.

'Grace, you're drunk,' he said. 'I've been calling you for hours. Where have you been?'

'In a bar, Rob... Robbie... Robert. I saw your text to her, I saw it,' I raged.

'I have no idea what you're talking about. Your assistant called me to tell me she was looking for you. She said you left and didn't return and that there was,' he waved his hand, 'something with a salon, I have no idea. I didn't listen. What on earth is wrong with you?'

He was so filled with sneering judgement, so certain as he sat in our bed, no trace of guilt on his face.

'You're sleeping with her, with Tamara,' I spat. I waved my arms around, my stomach churning with alcohol. I hated that he was in the room I regarded as my sanctuary from the world. I had chosen the mixture of white and cream so carefully, loving the hushed feel the thick carpet and raw silk curtains gave the room. But now it was spoiled with the presence of an adulterous bastard.

'What are you talking about? You're being ridiculous and you're blind drunk. I knew your alcohol consumption was getting out of control but this is ridiculous. Did you actually drive in this state? You could have killed someone or yourself. Get into the shower and then go to sleep.' He slid down in the bed, turned off his bedside lamp and closed his eyes as if he was simply going to sleep on an ordinary night.

I lurched towards him and slapped him on the shoulder. 'You don't get to... lie about this!' I screamed, slapping him again.

He sat up in bed and grabbed my hand before the next slap. 'Touch me again and I swear I will hit you back,' he snarled. 'You're embarrassing yourself, Grace. Go shower and go to sleep.'

'You're screwing my assistant, you're screwing her,' I sniffed, stepping back and stumbling, twisting my ankle in my high-heeled shoes. I kicked them off, tears streaming down my cheeks. 'How could you, Robert? My assistant? How could you?' My nose began to run and I wiped it with the sleeve of my navy-blue jacket.

'I am not sleeping with Tamara,' he said softly, his voice touched with concern for me, and I had a moment where I thought, even in my confused and drunken state, that he might be telling the truth, that I had taken a simple text and turned it into something else.

'You're lying,' I tested.

Robert sighed and rubbed at his eyes as though I exhausted him. 'This is how you get, Grace. You have a few drinks and you become paranoid and belligerent. Why are you trying to destroy everything when you have what you want? Why make up stories?'

'I'm not... not,' I hiccupped, 'making it up. You called her your... sunshine girl and I...' My stomach twisted violently and I dashed to the bathroom, making it to the toilet just in time to empty the contents of my stomach.

I was crying as I finished and Robert came into the bathroom. 'Oh, Grace,' he said, 'look at you. Clean yourself up, for God's sake.' And then he closed the door and left me there.

I threw up again and again until there was nothing left but bile and despair inside me. And then I got into the shower and stayed there for as long as I could.

When I finally got into bed, Robert was fast asleep.

'You're a liar,' I whispered.

His eyes sprang open. 'And you're a power-crazy drunk.'

'I want a divorce,' I spat.

'Fine by me. I look forward to not having to deal with you and to enjoying the spoils of war. Half your company belongs to me. Think about that, Grace.' He slid out of bed and grabbed his pillow. 'I'm not cheating. You're making things up to destroy our marriage and I don't care if you do anymore. You don't care about me or Cordelia. The only thing you love is that stupid business of yours, and I will take half of it and destroy it.'

He left the room, leaving me with my pounding hangover and anxiety holding my heart.

Back in my little apartment I shake the memory away and put the cap back on the bottle. I pick up my suitcase, stashing my vodka inside as I remember the words I uttered that night when he told me he was going to take everything I had built from me.

'I won't let you,' I whispered into the air. 'I'll kill you first.'

I would live to regret that threat.

FIFTEEN

AVA

Ava moves the daisies around in the vase so that the white and orange mingle equally.

The flowers are just a small extra touch. Grace will be here soon and she wants everything to look perfect. Hiring Grace seems to have been the only thing she's done right in a long time.

Last night she told Finn about the email from Patricia and he did not react the way she'd expected or wanted him to.

'It's official now. One of us is getting the top job,' she told him after the girls were in bed.

'Right, that's going to make things awkward.'

'Yes, I'm worried that it will be him and that he'll rub my nose in it every day.'

She has never mentioned what happened with Collin when she was a receptionist. She never wants Finn to have to think about it on the odd occasion that he and Collin meet, like staff Christmas parties. But she lives in fear of the man bringing it up.

'Didn't you say that you're better at managing people than he is?' asked Finn as he poured himself a glass of water.

'I am. I mean, I take care of all the trainers but he's better at bringing in the business, simply because he has more time and he's sneaky. He went behind my back and spoke to the principal of a school I had a meeting set up with.'

'That is sneaky.'

'Yeah, he said he just ran into her at a restaurant but I don't believe it's a coincidence. I should never have told him about the meeting, but we're supposed to be on the same side.'

'It may have just been a coincidence unless Collin actually stalked the woman,' said Finn slowly. 'I don't think you should read anything into it. And maybe...'

'Maybe?' she asked.

'Maybe it would be better if he was the CEO. It's a lot more work and a lot of travel around Australia and Asia. Patricia will be busy with the UK and that means that you'll have to take over everything she's been doing. It will mean a lot more time away from home.'

'And a huge pay rise,' snapped Ava as she finished wiping down the kitchen counter.

'But time away from the girls.'

Ava stopped cleaning, immediately weighed down by the boulder of guilt that always sat on her shoulder. 'This may be my one shot, Finn. It could really change our lives. We could pay off the mortgage a lot quicker, take a vacation every once in a while...'

'And it will mean that I'm on daddy duty a lot more and I just... I think you work hard enough as it is. Collin will be a good boss.' He looked away as he said the words, as though he didn't really believe them.

'You have no idea about that, he's awful,' hissed Ava.

'I think that's an exaggeration,' replied Finn, looking back at her.

'It's not... I'm...'

'Look, I have to go upstairs. I want to get some work done

tonight. It's up to you, of course, but I think this will negatively affect our family life. Patricia travels two weeks out of four. And she has endless dinners out to attend. Right now, Collin does some of that, and if you're in charge, you'll have to do a lot more of it.'

'How would you know that?' asked Ava.

'Oh, um... I'm sure you mentioned it. I have to go or I'll get nothing done,' he said, leaving the kitchen.

Ava finished cleaning as she dissected the conversation, searching for even a tiny bit of support from her husband in his words. Finn is interested in her work up to a point but she has never discussed Patricia's schedule with him. And how does he know anything about what Collin does and does not do? She's never told Finn how much Patricia travels. She's never worked it out herself beyond knowing it's a fair amount. Maybe Finn just picked the amount out of thin air. Wherever he got the information, it's probably close to the truth. Although she would set her own schedule, and would never want to travel quite as much as Patricia, getting the promotion would mean a lot of time away from her daughters, and even when she's gone on quick interstate trips, she's missed them every moment she's away.

But Finn could have at least tried to be supportive.

Ava went to sleep mulling over everything Finn had said and woke up this morning already resentful of him.

'Grace is arriving today,' she told him at breakfast. 'I want to make the apartment look nice for her, can you help me give it a clean?'

'She works for you, not the other way around,' Finn said.

'She's still a person and I want it to be nice for her, Finn. I would clean for anyone.'

'And the flowers?' he asked, gesturing at the bouquet on the kitchen counter. She had placed them in a vase to put in the apartment.

'I like her,' Ava replied. 'Are you going to help me or not?'

'I'll take the girls to the park, get them out of your hair,' he said.

Ava had known he wouldn't want to help clean and he liked the large park a few blocks away from their house. It was equipped with soft matting and an intricate climbing frame as well as a protective fence that surrounded the play area. The girls loved it and Finn was free to sit on his phone while they played.

The apartment had come with the house and a tenant, which had seemed fortuitous at the time they'd bought it, six years ago. The huge mortgage was daunting despite Ava's salary and her belief that she would only move up in the company. At the time Finn had been taking regular commissions as well, something Ava had thought would continue until Finn announced that if he wanted to become a serious artist, he needed to concentrate only on his work. He stopped taking commissions when Hazel was six months old and Ava went back to work. Ava had been supportive at the time, believing that Finn putting together a show and selling his beautiful work was only months away. But because Finn did the bulk of the childcare and Ava worked, he hadn't quite painted enough canvases to warrant a show, and he was very particular, so many of his paintings were instantly declared not good enough and abandoned.

Their previous tenant, Jed, who was studying to be a chef and just starting out in the restaurant trade, had left to take a job at a restaurant in Melbourne. Having him living in the apartment meant they had some extra money coming in to help. Ava really wanted someone else to move in as soon as possible.

The apartment had been built for the teenage son of the last owner and rented out when he moved away. It's well done with a nicely tiled bathroom and shower and a reasonably sized kitchen with a black stone benchtop. It's big enough for one person to be very comfortable in because it has a separate bedroom and living area. Grace won't be here for long, and as soon as she moves out, Ava will have to take on the task of finding a tenant. Finn was going to do it but it's not a priority for him and she's tired of nagging him over everything. Some days it feels like all she does when she speaks to him is give him a list of tasks to accomplish, tasks she has asked him to take care of over and again.

This morning, after the girls had left the breakfast table, with the cleaning of the apartment on her mind, she again listed all the things that needed to get done in the house.

Finn listened impassively as he sipped his coffee. 'You know in the same amount of time it takes you to tell me to change the bed linen and do the recycling, you could actually do those things yourself,' he said.

'You're right, I could do it all, but it's not fair. I shouldn't have to keep asking, Finn,' she said. 'Why can't you do things like that, and like getting us a new tenant during the week when I'm at work?' She stood up from the table, picking up the breakfast plates and loading them in the dishwasher.

'Ava, I know that I don't earn the money you do right now, but I've nearly got enough work for a show and then I will be bringing in some cash. You know Hector is just waiting for me to have enough pieces to show in his gallery. That's my work and that's what I do during the week in addition to taking care of the girls. And I really wish you wouldn't continually minimise what I do and my work. I really wish you would stop criticising me with every breath you take.'

'Okay fine, I'm sorry, Finn,' she said, holding up her hands. 'I'll sort it all out.'

'That's not what I'm saying, Ava. You're making this about domestic bullshit but it's more about how you speak to me and what you say to me. I know you view me as a screw-up and sometimes I view myself that way as well, so you don't have to worry that I'm not thinking about things as much as you want me to.'

'I don't view you as a screw-up.' Ava sighed.

'Oh, please. I know what you think,' he replied. 'And maybe you're right, maybe I am just... just that.'

Ava squeezed her eyes shut, knowing that the girls were playing in the living room and that if she said what she wanted to say, it would only lead to a huge argument. And also knowing that Finn wanted her reassurance, something she didn't feel like giving at the moment.

Instead, she went to pack the bag so Finn could take the girls to the park.

It has been quite peaceful to clean the small, neat space rather than tackle her big, chaotic house. She has cleaned everything thoroughly, even the shelves in the wardrobe, and now she looks around, making sure it's all perfect. The window is open, letting in the hot February air, and for a moment she considers closing it and switching on the air conditioning but she wants it to feel and smell fresh.

A text on her phone alerts her to Grace's arrival and she opens the door of the apartment and waves down at Grace, who is standing in the street in front of her car.

Grace waves back and hurries up the bright blue painted timber stairs.

'Oh, this is lovely,' she says, looking around.

'Are you sure?' asks Ava. 'If it won't work for you, you can tell me.'

'No, no... I love it,' says Grace, moving around, ducking into the bedroom and the bathroom. 'It's so much nicer than a hotel room. But are you sure I can't pay you rent?'

'It's only for a week,' says Ava. 'I have to find a tenant for it afterwards.'

'Why don't you let that be my job, then? I'll advertise and screen applicants and bring you the best few so you and your husband can choose someone.'

'I couldn't ask you to do that,' says Ava, even as a warm rush of relief surges through her at the idea that this might be one less thing she has to deal with.

'But you didn't ask, I offered, and it's the least I could do. It's so kind of you to give me a place to stay for the week.' Grace smiles and nods as she speaks and Ava understands that the offer has been made with genuine intention. Grace seems like one of those people who will say, 'Let me know if I can help,' and actually mean it, instead of saying the words and hoping the person will politely decline any help at all.

'Then I will gratefully take you up on your offer,' Ava says. She feels like she's achieved something even though nothing has been done yet.

'Mummy, Mummy,' she hears from the driveway.

'That will be Finn and the girls, come and meet them,' says Ava, and she turns and goes down the stairs from the apartment to the driveway.

Hazel and Chloe are standing with Finn, neither of them wearing hats, their cheeks red and their faces decorated with the chocolate ice cream they love so much.

Ava bites down on her lip, not wanting to admonish her husband in front of Grace.

'Goodness me,' says Grace, 'you look like you've had fun in the sun. I bet you've both got very pretty hats.' There is something in the way she says it that points out the girls' red cheeks and their dirty faces without actually having to say anything. Ava is at once embarrassed and vindicated. It is not unreasonable for her to be angry at Finn.

'Yes, we forgot the bag with snacks and hats,' says Finn sheepishly.

The bag I packed for you to take before I began cleaning. Ava swallows the words before she has a chance to say them. She hopes that Grace doesn't think she's a bad mother. A small niggle inside her makes her question allowing Grace to stay. Her home life and her work life are suddenly intertwined. It was an impulsive decision but there's nothing she can do about it now and it's only for a week anyway.

Finn offers Grace a dazzling smile and his hand. 'I'm Finn, and Ava tells me that you've sorted out her office beautifully.'

Grace extends her hand and Ava sees a slight flush along her cheeks. Finn is charm itself and even though Grace must be at least ten years older than him, she clearly cannot help being affected.

'I'm Grace,' she says, and then she looks down at the girls, 'and you must be Hazel and Chloe. I'm looking forward to getting to know you.'

Hazel holds out her hand the same way her father did and shakes Grace's hand. 'I'm looking forward to getting to know you too,' she says in her best grown-up voice.

Grace laughs. 'I can see the world is not ready for young Hazel Green.'

Ava glows with pleasure at the compliment. Hazel is headstrong and stubborn and difficult but Ava is continually cautioning herself to resist the urge to stamp out these traits. It's what her mother tried to do with her, wringing her hands every time Ava talked back. Her mother is bewildered by her rise in the corporate world. She only went back to work after the divorce when Ava was eleven and then she hated every moment she had to sit behind a desk as a secretary.

'Children are the greatest gift in the world,' she always said. 'If I could have had a household full, your father would never have left us. Aim for that, Ava. Aim for a household full of children and a man who stays.'

Ava knows that if her mother had been able to stay home with her, she would have succeeded in stamping out the very qualities that Ava needs in the business world. Her childhood was a little lonely but she is grateful that she had time and space to hold on to who she is. Her mother's absolute love for her has never been in question but Ava has always had the sense that her mother felt she somehow failed her only daughter. 'I wanted to give you the best life possible, not subject you to being in a single-parent family,' her mother often said. 'You deserved so much more than this.'

'But you have given me the best life, Mum,' Ava would comfort her. 'I know you're here for me.'

Her father remarried soon after the divorce and now Ava does have a whole lot of half-siblings, but she sees them rarely. Her stepmother preferred that Ava's father forget about his first family and he has managed that very well in the way that only men seem to be able to do.

Ava sighs, letting thoughts of her father go. She has her mother's love and support and that's all she needs.

'I want to swim, I want to swim,' says Chloe.

'Yep, yep, let's go,' says Finn. 'Good to have you here, Grace, let me know if you need a hand moving in.' He smiles and, once again, Grace flushes slightly.

Finn the fabulous flirt is how Lucy has always described him because he is. *Flirting isn't cheating*, Ava reminds herself. And it's not. Flirting is innocent and everyone does it. Even Ava finds herself smiling and cocking her head when she's trying to close a deal with a male principal. It's human nature to notice good-looking people and Finn is very good-looking, as is Grace, although she seems to prefer a very understated look.

'Right, I'll go and collect my things,' says Grace.

'Do you need any help?' Ava offers.

'No, it's just a suitcase and some groceries. You go and enjoy the afternoon with those lovely girls.'

Ava nods and hands Grace the keys. She goes to check that the girls are wearing sunscreen and their swim hats. It's another broiling day and she hopes neither of them got terribly sunburned. The park has a sun cover but it was irresponsible of Finn to forget the bag.

Once she's satisfied that the girls are protected, she goes to the kitchen to make lunch for everyone and finds herself humming as she works.

Grace is sure to find them the perfect tenant, and having a tenant again will help with the bills and the mortgage. Her good deed in offering her assistant a place to stay for the week has been immediately rewarded.

As she chops up fruit, she congratulates herself on hiring Grace. What she needs is a 'Grace' at home as well. If she does get the top job, the extra money might mean she's able to hire someone. It will benefit both her and Finn, no matter what he says. She's sure he will be happy to have more time to work.

In the pool the girls shriek and splash, and outside the cicadas buzz loudly and Ava has a moment of contentment. All the little stuff that Finn leaves undone can be sorted by someone whose job it is to keep the house running.

Tonight, she will speak to him and let him know that, despite his reservations, she definitely wants the top job and they will find a way to make it work.

Things are going to get better from now on, Ava can feel it.

SIXTEEN

GRACE

I am happily unpacked and enjoying a plate of brie and artisan crackers in the apartment over the garage on my first evening when there is a light knock at my door.

When I open it, it is to find Hazel with a grin on her face. 'Mum says we're having a barbecue and do you want to come to dinner please and thank you.'

I can't help laughing at the child as I nod. 'I would love to, thank you.' She is such a beautiful little girl and I only have to look at her father to see where she gets her looks from. I hope that as she grows, she will not allow all the attention her looks will get to sway her from becoming the person she's going to be. I can see a very bright future for her indeed. From everything I know about Ava, I am sure Hazel will be encouraged to conquer the world by her mother.

'It starts soon cause Dad says it's getting late and me and Chloe need to give him a bit of a bloody break.'

'I will be down in a second,' I say. 'Thank you very much, Hazel.'

She nods and goes down the stairs, jumping from tread to tread.

I had prepared for this eventuality. I wouldn't want to take a bottle of wine but I have bought a lovely box of expensive chocolates for Ava and two small bags of chocolate coins for the girls.

I do a quick check of my hair and make-up and make my way downstairs. It's only just after five but I imagine that a Sunday with two young children can feel very long. Cordelia is an only child, and on a Sunday, when I wasn't working, I enjoyed every moment I spent with her as we went to a movie or visited the zoo. But I was mostly working. That's the truth. Dr Gordon thought it was important that I constantly admit the truth to myself, and I know that more than once I had to hold back from screaming that, when I looked at the people who surrounded me, I knew I wasn't the only one lying.

I take a deep breath before I walk through the open front door and follow the sound of voices into the house.

Ava is bustling around the kitchen, throwing together a salad.

'Oh, you shouldn't have,' she says to me when I hand her the chocolates. Hazel and Chloe stand right next to her in anticipation of their own gifts, which they are delighted with.

'Now, no eating them before dinner,' I say with a quick look at Ava, who nods. I wouldn't want to overstep.

'I wasn't sure what you eat but Finn is making chicken and corn on the cob,' says Ava placing the salad on the dining room table.

Sliding glass doors are open to the garden and I follow Ava outside where Finn is standing in front of the barbecue in shorts and a tight T-shirt that rides up, revealing a taut stomach when he lifts his arms a little.

The smell of roasting meat fills the air and I swallow quickly. I haven't been able to eat meat for six years. 'I'm vegetarian,' I say, 'and salad and corn are perfect, exactly what I would have for dinner if I was cooking.'

'Great,' says Ava, looking relieved.

Dinner is a slightly awkward affair as no one is quite sure how much they can ask. Our relationship should be confined to the workplace, and my being here has taken things into the personal realm. I take control of the situation by quizzing Finn on his work and it's immediately obvious the man enjoys discussing it.

'Ava tells me you're an artist,' I say. 'What's your favourite medium?'

'Well, I mostly work in oil paint but I also love to use charcoal. Sometimes a piece works better with the depth and variety of shading that charcoal allows.'

'And what do you like to paint?' There are paintings hanging all over the house but I haven't looked closely enough at any of them to determine if they were done by Finn or not.

'I love faces,' he says. 'I like angles and shadow, the way a person's face tells me who they are and what their story is.'

I nod eagerly, noting that it must mean the portraits of the girls are all by him. He is very good.

I would ask him what he sees when he looks at me but I bite back the question. I may not like the answer.

'And do you take commissions?' I ask even though I know the answer to this. I have looked him up, and although he has a website, he explicitly states that he is not taking commissions right now. I have no idea why not but perhaps he feels it would be beneath his talent to paint someone's grandparent or child. If I were Ava, that would upset me, especially when she works so hard. I have a vague idea of what her salary must be and I also know the price she paid for this home. They must be financially stretched, as many families are. Why would Finn not be doing everything he can to bring in extra money?

'I do sometimes, but not for a bit. Right now, I'm working on a portrait of my great-grandfather. He lived in Ireland and he was a farmer...' Finn carries on speaking and I nod while observing Ava, who is cutting up food for the girls and wiping sticky hands and getting water when they ask for it. Every now and again she puts some food into her mouth. 'I hold down the fort around here and paint when I get the time, and Ava gets to go out into the world and be with grown-ups all day long,' Finn finishes.

I nod and smile and then risk a glance at Ava, who flushes slightly at this comment. Of course I know that Ava is a woman struggling to balance everything in her life. I remember being that woman once.

I remember staying up until four in the morning when Cordelia had a temperature one night, checking on her every twenty minutes as I waited for the medicine to do its work and then going to wake Robert and begging him to let me get a few hours of sleep before my meeting at the bank where I was rene- gotiating my business loan. The next night when Cordelia was fine and I was dragging myself exhaustedly through dinner, I heard him on the phone to his mother explaining how tired he was because he had to work and take care of a sick child. His mother hated me, found me arrogant, and was only too keen to listen to how her son was suffering being married to a woman who had no idea how to put her family first.

'Isn't she lucky to have you,' I say to Finn now, who nods his approval of himself.

The corn is delicious with butter and herbs and soon enough dinner is over. Ava gets up to start cleaning.

'I have an idea,' I say quickly.

'Does it involve eating those lovely chocolates?' laughs Ava.

'No,' I say, 'those are just for you, but perhaps as a thank you for this lovely dinner and for letting me stay, you will allow me to give you some time off.'

'Oh?' says Ava, not quite sure what I'm suggesting.

'Why don't you leave the clean-up and the children to me, and you and Finn take yourselves out for a drink somewhere?

It's still early and I'm sure Hazel will be able to tell me exactly what to do and you can have an hour or two, just you and your husband.' I hold my breath while Ava considers this and I can see she's going to refuse. She doesn't know me that well after all.

'I can tell her what to do, I can, I can,' says Hazel, desperate to be in charge of an adult.

'That sounds like a great idea,' says Finn as he leans back in his chair.

'Well...' says Ava and I can see her wavering.

'You have my number and I have yours, and I'm sure you could use a break. You work so hard.'

'Yeah, come on, let's go for a drink. We haven't done that for ages.' Finn stands as though the decision has already been made. I notice he makes no attempt to pick up anything off the table.

'Only if you're sure, they need to be in bed by eight and—'

'I'm sure, and I think all children need a bath and a story, and Hazel will be more than up to the task of telling me what to read.'

'Okay, okay,' agrees Ava. She is still uncertain but there is also the tug of some much needed time away. If she had hired me from a babysitting site, she would have interviewed me once and then given me a try, assuming that my references had been checked. As it is, we have already spent many hours and days together, and she has checked my references.

'Wonderful, just put everything down and out you go. It's not much to clear away.'

'Yes, come on, Ava, let's go,' says Finn.

It takes a few more minutes of negotiation and Ava explaining everything the children need to me and her showing me a list of emergency numbers on the fridge before they are out the door and I am alone with the children.

I never babysat as a teenager. The only child I have ever

taken care of is Cordelia and, of course, things are different with your own child.

The three of us clean up after dinner, even little Chloe helps, carefully carrying one plate at a time into the kitchen. Hazel is bossy almost to the point of being rude, instructing me on what to do, but I don't take it personally. She's five and I know that the world will tell her soon enough to be quiet and to be polite, to be nice, to be agreeable and keep her opinions to herself.

'Now what?' asks Hazel, once everything is clean.

'Well,' I hesitate, 'maybe we could... bake something?' Children love baking. Cordelia used to adore it, standing by my side and throwing chocolate chips into cookie batter with a certain level of seriousness. She grew into a very good baker by the time she was eighteen. I have no idea if she still does it. I feel a strong ache over my heart at how six years may have changed my child, at how much of her life I have missed.

The only thing I do know is that she is with the wrong man.

Garth Stanford-Brown is a lawyer in a large firm and he's nine years older than Cordelia. I follow him on Instagram as well and his posts are filled with pictures of himself in his graduation robes, celebrating case wins, playing football. He is the star of his own show and he wants Cordelia to be less than she is, to blend in instead of stand out. That's why he mocks her on her social media accounts. Basically, Cordelia has chosen a man just like her father but with considerably more intelligence and money.

'Yes,' says Hazel, bringing me back to the cheerful kitchen that needs updating but is perfect for children with its cream melamine doors and blue stone countertop, 'we can make cupcakes. Mum has a box in the pantry and she said we could do it on Saturday if she had time. But she didn't cause she was doing the washing and doing the washing and then she had to go to the grocery store and Daddy said she never bloody stops for a minute.'

'Well, we have time tonight so let's do it. What about you, Chloe?' I ask her much quieter sister, who simply nods.

We grab everything we need and I notice that the pantry has sticky shelves as does the fridge. I'm itching to wipe them down but that might be a step too far. I've already tidied the living room on the basis that the children's toys were everywhere and I am babysitting the children so that's fine.

I am patient with the girls as they throw ingredients in the bowl and eat chocolate chips because we are making chocolate chip cupcakes. It was the one thing I always had time for with Cordelia, a precious half an hour where I would not answer the phone or worry about work. Robert never joined us so it was always our time.

'It must be fun having Daddy home with you every day,' I say to Hazel, who shrugs and then puts another chocolate chip in her mouth.

'If you eat them all, our cupcakes won't be very nice,' I say with a smile. 'What do you do with Daddy when you're not at school?'

'We go to the park and we go to the shops and sometimes we go to a restaurant with Sami's mum and we have milkshakes. Chloe likes strawberry – right, Chloe?' Hazel asks her sister, who nods enthusiastically.

'Sami's mum?' I say, hoping for more information.

'Yeah, she's nice and Sami is in my class and every day after school Daddy and her talk and talk and talk and me and Sami and Chloe play on the climbing frame at school even though Chloe is not allowed because it's only for big kids.'

'I'm big,' protests Chloe, holding up three fingers to show me just how big she is.

'You are,' I agree, 'and I bet you're very good at the climbing frame.'

'Does Sami have a daddy?' I ask Hazel. I have no idea if Sami is a boy or a girl. It's a name that could be either.

Hazel leans towards me and whispers as though someone may be listening, 'Sami says his dad runned away.'

'Oh,' I say. So, Sami is a boy and Sami's mother is alone. I wonder if Ava has ever thought to question her children like this.

Certainly, I never thought to question anyone in my life like this. I assumed Robert and I were a team, that our marriage was based on a solid foundation of love, trust and friendship. I assumed Tamara liked and respected me.

I shake the thoughts away and try to concentrate on what I'm doing with the girls.

'Right, all done,' I say to them, and they both stand back while I slide the cupcakes into the oven. 'Now it is time for bed,' I say, 'and in the morning, when Mum says it's okay, you can both have a lovely cupcake.'

'But I want one now,' says Hazel.

'Me too,' agrees Chloe.

'Well, they will take some time to bake, and Mum said you need to be in bed by eight. It's seven now and you still need a bath and a story. And if you aren't in bed on time, then Mum will not ask me to babysit again and we can't bake cupcakes.' I shake my head sadly.

Hazel considers this for a moment. 'Okay,' she says, 'but you have to leave Mummy a note that says we can have one.'

'I will, I promise,' I say. 'In fact, we can write one right now.'

Hazel has just begun learning to write but she is already quite adept. I help her with spelling and some letters and soon there is a note on the counter: *Cupcakes for after breakfast!!!* I study the wobbly letters and take a deep breath as I remember teaching Cordelia to write, guiding her small hand. I don't think I appreciated the time enough. What I wouldn't give to go back and start again.

'Now bath and bed,' I say.

'Bath and bed,' agrees Hazel, 'and I can show you which story to read.'

'Yes, bath and bed,' repeats Chloe.

Hazel talks me through the bedtime routine, even reminding me to put toothpaste on her toothbrush. It takes longer than I imagine it should but finally both girls are tucked up in bed, eyes closing after a long day in the sun.

I leave them and go back downstairs to the kitchen, where I finish cleaning up, and then, because I cannot sit still for too long anymore, I begin organising and wiping the shelves in the pantry. Ava might consider this an overstep and I'm sure it is, but I can't seem to help myself. Order calms me, tidying calms me.

When I come across a dusty bottle of wine in the pantry, I wipe it down carefully and replace it, but then I stop tidying and just stare at it, knowing what relief it would bring.

But after the relief would come the guilt and the shame. I regret what I allowed alcohol to do to me. It cost me my child and I will never forgive myself for that. But I cannot go back in time. I can only move forward.

Upstairs I hear a cry as though a child has woken from a nightmare and I leave the past behind as I make my way to Chloe's room to pat her back and comfort her back to sleep.

It's just me and these two beautiful children. I can't imagine anything better.

SEVENTEEN

AVA

Ava watches Finn talking to the bartender, trying to mentally separate herself from her position as his wife and just observe. Finn thinks she imagines he's flirting with other women.

Maybe she does? Maybe he just can't help being charming and sweet to everyone he meets.

They are at their favourite little wine bar, where a young brunette woman is serving. She's pretty in a wholesome way with big blue eyes. Finn may not think he's flirting but the bartender certainly does. She is blushing and stumbling over her replies as Finn asks, 'And what year is that from?' as she shows them choices of plum-red wine.

'We'll both have a glass of that, thanks,' interrupts Ava, pointing to the bottle the woman is holding, and then she looks at the price and recoils slightly. Fifteen dollars a glass.

It's not that they can't afford the occasional babysitter for evenings out like this, but that finding one requires energy that Ava simply doesn't have. Finn's parents will come if she asks them but Ava always gets the sense that they have a very busy social life they are reluctant to give up. They like taking care of the girls during the day, which helps Finn but not Ava. Her mother, Pam, is happy to babysit but it comes with a price. If Pam comes over, Ava has to make sure the house is clean, the laundry put away, the fridge full of nourishing food. Last time she came over was when Ava and Finn were attending a wedding, and every phone call between her and her mother for weeks afterwards started the same way.

'I hope you've managed to get that stain off the carpet,' her mother would say. Or, 'I stopped at the grocery store and saw they have apples on special and I noticed that you don't seem to have any fruit for the girls. Would you like me to get you some?' Or, 'I didn't want to say anything but the shelves in your cupboards are very sticky. I know you're busy but it's important to have a clean house for children to grow up in.' She meant well but she unwittingly added to Ava's mother guilt.

Getting her mother to babysit was emotionally expensive and Ava preferred to meet her at a park or a café so she could spend time with the girls without Ava feeling on edge. Pam is an adoring grandmother and the girls are lucky to have her. 'Thank you for letting me see my precious angels,' her mother always says when they say goodbye to each other after a visit. Her phone is filled with pictures of the girls and she will proudly tell everyone they meet, 'These are *my* granddaughters.' It's lovely to see and Ava hates to get upset at her for just wanting what's best for the girls. It's easier to be able to put the worry of her messy house out of her mind and just enjoy the time together.

Tonight is not supposed to cost a lot of money. It's supposed to just be a quick drink, and if they have two each, it's costing them sixty dollars. Ava earns a good salary, very good, but prices in Sydney just get higher every day and she's always conscious of being the only breadwinner.

The bartender fills two glasses and, with another smile at Finn, moves away to serve her next customer. The wine is delicious with a hint of dark cherry taste.

'I met with Chloe's teacher at preschool on Friday,' says Finn.

'Why? I didn't know there was something scheduled.'

'There wasn't, but I just like to let them know who I am, get to know the teacher, discuss my kid in more depth than I did on the first day, you know. I did it with Hazel as well.'

'Isn't it Celia?' asks Ava. Finn shakes his head and sighs as if Ava should know this. But she had assumed that since Chloe was attending the same preschool Hazel did, the teachers would be the same. On the girls' first day of school, she had taken Hazel to kindergarten and Finn had taken Chloe to preschool. When Finn has frustrated her beyond what she thinks she can endure and she fantasises about leaving him, she always reminds herself of these practicalities and of how hard it would be to raise two young children and work full time.

If that doesn't work, she thinks about how devastated the girls would be to no longer have their father in their life every day. But mostly she reminds herself that she loves her husband, despite his irritating quirks.

'What's her name? Is she nice?' Ava asks as she wonders how pretty the new teacher is and then she chastises herself for this.

'Olivia and yeah, she seems really lovely. She's in her twenties and she has an amazing face, you know, like big green eyes and high cheekbones,' he says as he gestures to his own face. 'I asked her if I could draw her. She seemed keen.' Finn takes a sip of his wine.

Ava also takes a large gulp of hers, holding it in her mouth for a moment to let the slight acid kick remind her to think before she speaks.

'I don't think that's a good idea,' she says after she swallows.

'Why?' he asks.

'She's... Chloe's teacher and it would be unprofessional,' she says.

'Your assistant is staying in our garage apartment,' he responds.

And here they are again. Tit for tat. She's not sure when they moved into this space but it seems that whatever she says, Finn has a comeback for. It's never a discussion, but rather a comparison.

Finn, it's exhausting to have to clean up after you cook dinner.

It's exhausting to cook dinner after a day of taking care of our children, Ava.

Finn, can you please take out the garbage? I've got a headache, work was so stressful today.

Being home with these two was stressful, especially since Chloe has a cold.

Finn is better at the game than she is and she usually ends up giving in. 'I know, it's just... just don't, okay?' She cannot give him a logical reason.

'Sometimes I think you don't take my work seriously,' says Finn, finishing up his glass and signalling the bartender for another. 'Two please,' he says when she comes over, and Ava adds another thirty dollars to the bill.

'I do,' she says. 'But there are other people for you to draw. And also...' She wants to stop herself, wants to not have the conversation because they've had it too many times to count, but somehow, sitting alone with him, without the possibility of interruption, she can't stop herself from saying the words. 'I think maybe it's time you thought about getting a part-time job. I know that you need time to work but with the interest rate rises on the mortgage and everything else... maybe you could start taking commissions, just one or two, because even a small amount would help...' She stops speaking, disconcerted by the way he looks at her.

'It's funny how you want me to be everything, Ava – like not funny ha ha, but funny weird. I take care of the girls so you can work, don't I? If I get a job, who will take them to school in the morning?'

'I take them to school most mornings, Finn,' she says, the words stated without emotion.

'Yeah, throw that in my face,' he says. 'You let me know I'm a loser at every opportunity. Why can't you ever just be happy?' He drinks down his second glass of wine quickly as he looks around the wine bar, and Ava struggles for some way to talk to him without upsetting him. They sit in silence for longer than she would like but everything she wants to say seems wrong.

'I may just use the bathroom and then we can go. I want to get some work done tonight,' he says, standing up.

He moves away from her and Ava gulps her glass of wine, hating that she has to rush it and that she has spoiled this precious time off. *Why can't you ever just leave it?*

Finn has left his phone sitting on the bar and when it vibrates, she looks at it. A message flashes across the screen and disappears. She thinks she sees the word 'love' so she picks it up and unlocks the screen but it doesn't work. She tries twice more before she sees Finn coming towards her and she quickly drops it back onto the bar. Finn has changed his unlock pattern on his screen. They have always known each other's patterns because Finn has a habit of forgetting his. But he's changed his and not told her.

When did that happen?

'Ready?' asks Finn.

'Yes,' she says, standing up.

In the car on the way home, she tries to think of ways to ask Finn about his phone that won't make her seem like she's being paranoid or controlling but nothing seems right.

The house is quiet. Grace is sitting on the sofa watching a cooking show on television.

'You're home early,' she says when she sees them. 'The girls were an absolute delight and I hope you don't mind, but we baked cupcakes.'

'School night,' says Ava tightly, 'and not at all. I'm sure they loved that.' And then because she doesn't want Grace to think she's being rude, 'It was so lovely of you to babysit for us. We had a nice quiet drink and we don't get that very often.' She can see a question in the woman's eyes despite the nice words.

'I'll see you at work tomorrow then,' says Grace and she moves towards the door.

'You might as well drive in with me,' says Ava, wanting to offer something more. 'I have a parking space.'

'Oh,' says Grace, 'that would be lovely, thank you. You're being so kind.'

'It's no problem at all,' and she offers Grace a genuine smile.

'Goodnight, then.'

'Goodnight,' Ava replies, 'and thank you again.'

In the kitchen the dishwasher is humming, the surfaces sparkling clean, and there are cupcakes cooling on the counter.

Ava hears the door to the loft where Finn works slam shut. There will be no more talking tonight.

She picks up a cupcake and bites into it, savouring the still-melted warm chocolate chips.

She has nothing to worry about, she's sure. Finn is not that kind of person.

Instead of thinking about it anymore she grabs the girls' lunch boxes from their bags –something she should have done on Friday afternoon. She throws out the wrappers they have stuffed in there and wipes them out so they are ready for tomorrow.

She goes into the pantry to find the muesli bars they both take to school every day, flicking on the switch before stopping and staring.

The shelves are rearranged, clean, ordered.

Grace obviously did this. A shiver runs through her as she

explores the feeling of being exposed. Her pantry was an absolute mess, not something she wanted anyone but family to see, not something Finn would ever think to arrange or clean or agree to clean if she asked him, and something she was definitely going to get to when she had the time.

But now it's done, tidy like her desk at work, like the living room and the kitchen, like someone else lives here instead of Ava.

If she and Finn had not just had an awkward car ride home in silence, she would run up the stairs to talk to him about this.

But even if she does say something, he will only tell her it's her own fault for allowing her assistant to live in their house. *She's your assistant*, Ava can hear him saying, *she was helping you*. And she knows he would probably be grateful that someone else did the work.

Ava can't find the right amount of gratitude inside her. This is her kitchen in her house where her husband and children live and another woman has cleaned for her, and not a woman paid to do the job, which is somehow different.

But you do pay her and she said she was happy to assist you in any way she could. Isn't this just an extension of that?

Logically Ava knows that this is true but she can't make herself relax about the idea. Shaking her head, she packs what she can in the girls' lunch boxes and then she takes a cup of tea to bed with her, where she goes through any emails that have come in over the weekend.

And then she finds herself scrolling through home organiser videos on Instagram, watching as professionals come into people's houses and clear out their cupboards. By the time she has scrolled her way through half an hour of the same kinds of videos, she has convinced herself that she's overreacted to what Grace did. The woman was just trying to help and it's not a big deal. There are plenty of people whose pantries look much worse than Ava's did.

Grace will be gone in a few days anyway and Ava's pantry will revert back to its usual chaotic state. Just like the rest of her domestic life. She should enjoy Grace's help while she has it.

Satisfied, Ava turns off her light and rolls over to go to sleep. Finn will not come to bed for hours and she knows that this is partly her fault. She should not have said anything about him getting a job.

If she hadn't, it would have been easy to ask him about the pattern on his phone. It's probably just that he forgot the old one and didn't want to bother Ava.

Her eyes close on that idea as she drifts into sleep, comforted that she's making more of things than she should. Everything is fine. Just fine.

EIGHTEEN

Dear baby girl,

Things don't stay the same. Whether they are good or bad, the only certainty in life is change.

For me that happened when I met him. I was fifteen.

His name was Luka and he arrived at my school with dark brown hair, pale green eyes and an expulsion from his last school hanging over him like an exotic cloud.

I had never met anyone like him before. He didn't seem to care that he was in disgrace, but rather shared the information with anyone who would listen. 'Pulled the fire alarm and the whole school went mad,' he laughed. He didn't pay attention in class when he was supposed to, instead reading magazines right in front of the teachers. He was in detention virtually from day one and I was watching him, not just with newly arrived teenage desire but with envy as well.

I had spent the year before I turned sixteen colouring inside the lines, keeping my parents happy, keeping my teachers happy, terrified that something would go catastrophically wrong if I did anything different. Because it had gone catastrophically wrong once. My behaviour had killed my grandmother, the one person in the world who'd loved me unconditionally.

Luka seemed to have no idea that his behaviour could cause the world to shift off its axis.

One parent–teacher night, a month after he arrived, I sat next to my stern-faced parents as they listened to my English teacher sing my praises. 'She's so creative and her grasp of the texts is excellent,' Mrs Williams told them.

'Well, isn't that what's supposed to happen?' my father asked.

'She should not be lagging behind the top students,' my mother said.

'Oh,' my teacher flushed, 'but she's third in the class and...'

I tuned out and looked around the hall where all the teachers had set up tables. At each one there was a student and one or two parents. My eyes landed on Luka's family. He was sitting between his mother and father, both of them casually dressed in jeans. I watched our science teacher, Mr Baker – a strange little man with a pair of glasses on his head and another one hanging around his neck – speak. I couldn't hear what he was saying, but he was obviously explaining that Luka had failed the last science test. I knew he had. Luka looked unconcerned but then nothing ever seemed to worry him. But what floored me was that his parents didn't seem that bothered either. Instead, his father, a large bearded man, shrugged his shoulders and then ruffled his son's curly hair, earning a lopsided smile from Luka, and then they stood up to move on to the next teacher and his mother wrapped her arm around his shoulders and smiled.

I didn't understand how such love and acceptance were possible. If I had ever failed an exam, I would have been locked in my room for days. And yet here was Luka, messing up his life at every opportunity but still cloaked in his parents' love. It made me angry and sad. What was wrong with me? I understood all the reasons my mother had for not loving me, but I felt that there must be something more, something inherently unlikable, unlovable about me. I could never ask her about it because I knew the horrified reaction I would get.

I went home that night more confused about the world and my place in it than I had ever been.

I never imagined he would speak to me but one day, after lunch, he walked back into class and placed a caramel chocolate bar on my desk. They were sold by the canteen but I was never allowed money for the canteen. My mouth instantly filled with saliva at the idea of the sweet treat. Since my grandmother had died, they'd been few and far between. I never had money to spend.

'You look like you need a treat,' he said.

'Oh, I couldn't, I...' My cheeks flushed as I stuttered.

'You're not on some idiotic diet, are you? You don't need to be.'

I shook my head, taking refuge in silence.

'Go on,' he said, and even though the teacher had just walked into the room to begin the lesson, I grabbed the bar and ripped open the yellow plastic covering, taking a quick, huge bite. Luka started laughing and I closed my eyes as the sticky sweetness flooded my senses.

'More where that came from, wait for me after school,' he said.

'Sit down, Luka,' thundered the history teacher, and he sat.

I knew my parents would be angry. I knew I would be punished but there was no way I would not be waiting for Luka after school. Our last class was sport, where the boys and the girls separated. We were doing gymnastics, something I usually enjoyed, but all through the class I messed up, falling when I should have tumbled and missing and tripping when I should have skipped. Showering afterwards, I tried to get myself to accept that he wouldn't be waiting for me, that it was just some cruel joke on his part. I understood cruelty for no reason. I could deal with that.

But when I walked out of the girls' change room, he was right there, waiting for me.

'Want to get a milkshake?' he asked.

'I don't have any money,' I said.

'I've got some, let's go.'

I wish I could explain the wondrousness of that first afternoon with Luka, baby girl. We ordered two different flavours of milkshake at the café he took me to and swapped halfway through. I can't remember everything we talked about but I do remember him telling me that his parents were artists who believed he would achieve his potential when he was ready. I know that I talked about my grandmother a lot and said little about my parents except to tell him they were strict.

I know that he walked me halfway home and kissed me when I said I needed to be alone from there so my parents didn't see.

And I know that when I walked in my front door and my mother was sitting in the kitchen with her arms folded, fury colouring her face, I didn't care. It was two hours past the time I was usually expected home and they had no idea at all where I'd been. I'm sure that my mother had only imagined I was doing something wrong. She was absolutely correct. I had been told that I must never go near boys as they were 'filthy creatures with only one thing on their minds and that's to ruin a young woman's life'.

'You...' she began.

I looked at her and for the first time in my life I felt pity for her and for the way she lived her life. 'I know,' I said casually, 'I'm going to my room and you're never going to feed me again until I die,' and I flounced out of the kitchen and slammed my bedroom door.

I didn't get dinner that night, of course, but the next morning when I came into the kitchen to make my breakfast, no one said anything.

I ate in silence and then packed myself a lunch and left. Not a word was spoken.

And I knew I had won.

I never let them tell me what to do again. And they hated me for that right up until the time they kicked me out.

NINETEEN

GRACE

In bed I toss and turn. Ava and Finn did not look like the couple of hours away from the house had done them any good at all. In fact, it looked like they'd had an argument. What a shame.

I also worry about the work I have done in the kitchen. It was an overstep and there's no way I should have done it. I found an old packet of cigarettes hidden on a top shelf and put it back carefully where I found it but whether Finn or Ava hid it there, it was obviously not meant to be seen. I have invaded their privacy. Perhaps I could say it was something Hazel suggested and we made a game out of it? No, that's not fair to the little girl.

I want to make Ava's life easier, so easy that she trusts and relies on me, but perhaps I am moving too fast. Next to my bed I watch the numbers on the digital clock I brought with me flip through the night and into the next morning. I wish frequently for the icy hit of the vodka that I know would soothe me to sleep. But that's not open to me anymore. I know I could have a drink and no one would know, no one would even suspect. It's not like anyone is keeping tabs on me but I have to maintain control until I know that I have achieved what I came here to do.

Sleep eventually comes at close to three in the morning but I am up early, before seven, and ready for the day so I go downstairs to wait. The kitchen door that leads to a small courtyard is open with the February heat already in the air.

Ava is in the kitchen with the girls, her hair wet and her face make-up free as she struggles to pack lunches, make the girls breakfast and unpack the dishwasher. I know I should just leave her to it. She wouldn't want me to see her like this but I can't help myself.

'Can I help?' I ask and Ava turns quickly, seeing me, and I watch her cheeks glow red. I have caught her in chaos. 'I'm ready to leave and I have nothing to do. Let me help,' I say.

Ava's shoulders drop and she nods her head. 'Maybe you could do Hazel's hair, she wants a French braid.'

'Of course,' I say and Hazel hands me her hairbrush and then turns around.

'Do you know how to do one?' she asks.

'Oh yes, I used to do it for...' I catch myself just in time, 'for myself and my friends when I was younger.'

'How old are you now?' asks Hazel.

'Fifty-two,' I say.

'You don't look it,' says Ava as she finishes unloading and reloading the dishwasher.

'Thank you,' I say as my hands move automatically through Hazel's dark hair. It's silky-soft and has the clean scent of baby shampoo that I remember so well from when Cordelia was little. I even remember the day she told me she wanted to try a different shampoo. She was seven and I was still buying her the same baby shampoo I had always used.

'I want the one with flowers on the front,' she told me, referring to an advert she had seen on television. We are never given warning for the last moments of childhood but I remember throwing away the last empty bottle of baby shampoo and how sad that made me feel.

'All done,' I tell Hazel and she runs off to admire herself.

Between me and Ava we soon have the children dropped at school and we are on our way to work. I want Ava to trust me, to like me. I can feel that I am very close to achieving this goal.

'Um, Grace,' she says and I know what's coming.

'You're upset about the pantry,' I say.

'Well... it's...'

'Can I be honest with you, Ava?'

'Of course.'

'I was feeling... unsettled last night because I was in a new space and I've just started this new job. And I guess... it just calms me down to organise things... It really helps and I knew as I was doing it I shouldn't but somehow...' I stop speaking, and shrug.

'Don't worry about it,' says Ava, 'really... I'm actually quite grateful.'

'You're so kind,' I say.

Ava smiles in reply and we sit in silence for a short time, not quite awkward but not easy either.

One way to build trust with someone is to tell them about yourself, to tell them something personal and painful.

'My mother used to do the same thing, organise shelves and cupboards when she was anxious,' I say.

'I understand. Everyone copes in their own way.'

'They do,' I agree and then I shake my head and touch my eye. 'I miss my mother so much.'

'I'm sorry,' says Ava, 'when did she die?'

'Five years ago. She and my father owned a café that specialised in organic meals in the Blue Mountains. When Dad died of a heart attack, my mother didn't have the heart to continue the café and closed it, and then she suffered a stroke soon after that.'

'Oh my goodness, so close together,' Ava says after hearing my sad story.

'They loved each other very much.' I wipe a non-existent tear away. My parents are still alive, living in a nursing home in Sydney. I don't visit and they don't care that I don't.

I haven't seen them for more than six years. All through my life I have had periods when I did not see them, starting when I was only a rebellious teenager, infuriating them with my mistakes. Every time I went home, it was always with the hope that they would finally simply accept me. They kicked me out at sixteen but I didn't let that stop me from staying in school. I went back home to visit at eighteen when I had gotten into university. 'A woman like you will need a job,' my father said. 'No man will want you with your attitude.' I don't know what I expected. Congratulations? We're proud of you? Why is it abused children cannot stop hankering after their parents' love?

I went back to visit again when I was twenty-five and I took Robert to meet them. 'Are you prepared for what marriage to my daughter will be like?' my mother asked him, producing much laughter around the table, where a spare tea had been laid. Dry sandwiches sat next to rock-hard scones with a tiny pot of jam for everyone to share. I was mortified, especially since Robert came from money and his family had, by then, been treating me to lavish dinners both out at restaurants and in their home.

I went back to introduce them to Cordelia and finally it seemed that I had achieved everything they wanted for me. I was a wife and a mother, acceptable in society's gaze. I was a working mother so that was a slight problem but my mother managed to keep her thoughts to herself when I came over. She doted on Cordelia, delighting in playing pretend housewife with her. I knew better than to ask her not to teach my daughter to iron. She wasn't doing any harm, I reasoned, and it was more important that Cordelia have a relationship with her grandmother. Robert's mother encouraged her to shop and have expensive lunches. Neither of her grandmothers encouraged her to study hard and achieve. The kindness that I had always been searching for from my parents was easily given to Cordelia. My mother even started keeping sweet treats in the house for when she visited. She never offered me a chocolate when we came over and once, when I boldly took one, she said, 'Women of a certain age tend to put on weight,' and then she looked me up and down as I tried to suck in my stomach. I was running a growing company by then, a wife, a mother and by all accounts a successful human being, but in my mother's eyes, I was always failing in some way.

And then, of course, it all went so terribly wrong and I knew, before I even entered rehab, that my parents would never want to see me again. I do hope Cordelia is still in contact with my parents. I don't want to see them and I know they have no interest in me but I think it would be heartbreaking for them if Cordelia no longer spoke to them. I still care, no matter how hard I try not to. Human beings are infuriatingly complicated.

'Were you ever married?' Ava asks, pulling me back to our conversation, which I'm glad of. She quickly says, 'Sorry if that's a personal question.'

'It's fine and no, I was engaged once but Michael died.' If Cordelia had been a boy, I would have named her Michael. I really like the name.

'Oh,' she replies, waiting patiently for the rest of the story. And what a story it is – all ready and prepared for whomever might ask the question.

'He was my high school boyfriend and the love of my life. We were planning on getting married, and then when he was nineteen, he suffered a heart attack during a game of rugby. He had hypertrophic cardiomyopathy, which is a thickened heart muscle. No one knew he had it and he just suddenly collapsed and before anything could be done, he was gone.'

It was a terrible tragedy. It didn't happen to anyone I know but it was something I read on the internet as I was scrolling through Facebook and I had to stop for a moment to consider the fickle nature of fate. I had only just had my phone privileges returned at the time – my phone being something I needed to earn with an acceptable level of participation in my own recovery and remorse for what I had done. I was thrilled to have my phone back but disheartened to know that I would still need a lot more time before I was declared rehabilitated and allowed to leave the clinic. Even worse was the idea that few people actually wanted to hear from me. My first text to Cordelia was met with a furious reply.

Hello darling, I have my phone now. I wanted to let you know. We have a lot to talk about. I hope you will allow me to explain. I hope you will consider forgiving me.

How dare you? After everything you did. You ruined my life. Don't contact me ever again.

There was no way I was going to respect that wish. I'm simply not capable of it. I contacted her once a day, and in between, I scrolled other people's sad stories.

The story of the young man who'd died suddenly of a heart attack helped me put my own situation into perspective for a short amount of time. And it's proved useful now.

'You poor thing, how awful for you and his family,' says Ava.

'His mother still blames herself to this day. But I think mothers always blame themselves and they shouldn't. How could she have known?'

I watch Ava as I say this and I can see her making a mental note to ask the doctor to check her children's hearts at the next visit. I was like that with Cordelia when she was little. If I read or heard about some condition that had killed a child out of the blue, I would immediately make an appointment to have her checked out for the possibility she had it. Robert thought it was funny. He called me neurotic. I suppose I was. I try to avoid thinking about Robert but he appears without warning these days, and he's always judging me. I can feel him criticising me from the grave. It doesn't matter. He can judge all he likes. It is Cordelia that I need to find a way back to; Cordelia that I miss terribly. Hard to imagine that after all the care I took to raise my lovely girl, I managed to eviscerate our relationship in one year.

'And do you have any other family?' Ava asks and I have to think quickly.

'I have an aunt in London. We were very close before she moved and she's not really well. I am hoping to see her in my next vacation.'

'I love London,' says Ava as she pulls into the parking garage.

When we have parked, I get out of the car and go up first because we have agreed that it will be better if our living arrangement is not public. 'It's not anyone's business,' Ava said and I agreed. It suits me. When I've done what I need to do, I don't need anyone knowing that I lived with Ava, even for a short period of time.

The elevator doors open and I can see Melody slouched behind the reception desk, her eyes on the phone she has next to her on the desk.

'I always feel it's so important that the first person someone sees when they enter a business is engaged in their work and ready to greet a customer,' I say to her instead of saying good morning. Melody rolls her pretty blue eyes, heavy with fake lashes. 'No one comes here this early,' she says.

'Still, it's important,' I say.

Melody stands, grabbing her phone off the desk. 'I may just get myself a coffee,' she says and she walks away, leaving the desk unattended at the exact time Ava walks in.

'Everything okay, Grace?' she asks.

'Oh yes, I'm just waiting until Melody returns with her coffee. She has a tendency to leave the desk unattended and I hate to think of anyone walking in and seeing no one here. I have noticed it a number of times and I've only been here a few weeks.'

'Did she ask you to watch the desk?'

'Oh no, she told me not to bother because no one comes in here this early.'

Ava frowns and we both wait for Melody to return, which she does, a smile on her face and her eyes on her phone. It's a wonder the girl doesn't trip over something.

'Melody,' says Ava, and the young woman looks up, her full lips already in a sulky pout. 'I would prefer it if you didn't leave the desk unless you have asked Grace or James to take over for you.'

Melody gives her a curt and rather rude nod and sits down, and Ava and I make our way to her office. I have a small desk and chair outside the office but we like to begin our day going through everything that needs to be done.

'She never takes her eyes off that phone,' I say when we are seated and I am ready to begin making notes.

'I've noticed that too,' says Ava. 'I may just send her an email about that.'

'I can draft it for you if you like,' I say and Ava nods.

'Great, now let's get on with what we need to do today.'

Ava is well put together this morning, her hair neatly styled and her face made up. The blouse she was wearing this morning had a Nutella streak from Chloe's hand but I mentioned it before we left the house so she changed, and because she knew I was with the children, she took some extra time with her appearance. She looks calm and in control. Just the way I used to look before it all fell so spectacularly apart.

. . .

The day passes quickly enough with endless conversations with trainers about flights and motels and general debriefs over how things have gone. Collin pops his head into the office near the end of the day to let us know he's leaving for Melbourne for a quick visit.

'Patricia is flying back to Australia for a few days for her niece's wedding and she asked me to come down and see her,' he says, smirking.

Ava keeps her head down, her concentration on the document she's reading, but no one can miss the tensing of her shoulders. 'That's good.'

'Yes,' says Collin when nothing else is said, 'I have a feeling we have much to discuss.'

Ava nods, a furrow appearing between her eyes.

'Where did you say they should stay when visiting Bendigo?' I ask her even though we have just discussed this.

'See you tomorrow then,' says Collin.

'Have a good flight,' replies Ava.

'Odious man,' I whisper once he's gone.

Ava looks at me and then she offers me a genuine smile. 'So it's not just me, then?'

'Not at all.'

'I think Patricia is going to offer him the Australia CEO position,' she says, biting down on her lip, and I can see how much that idea pains her.

'You don't know that,' I try to comfort her but it does look that way right now.

Ava shrugs. 'It's impossible to do it all, especially with the girls. Collin has a wife and kids but they barely affect his work.'

'It's different for men,' I agree and I remember an argument with Robert eight years ago.

'There is more to life than your work, Grace. You may think

you're doing everything you can to be here for Cordelia but she feels that you're not. You were supposed to be there at the play tonight and instead I had to go alone. It was her final production for the year.'

'It was an emergency,' I told him. 'We were in the middle of stocktake and the system crashed. I had six staff members helping me and we had to get it done. I couldn't just leave them to it.'

'Not good enough, Grace, simply not good enough. I had to leave my dinner early so I could go and be there for her. My work is important, Grace. I don't just run a string of silly salons dedicated to removing hair.'

Today I would have laughed at him. Today I would have informed him that my string of salons paid for Cordelia's private school and our beautiful house and the cleaner who kept it immaculate. I would point out that his work in 'the growth of greenspaces in the city' was important but by no means the thing that was keeping our family going. But then, all I felt was guilt, terrible, heavy mother guilt that I had let my daughter down. She had understood from the moment she had the dates for the play that her father would not be there but would be having dinner with the premier of New South Wales. That was important – even though hundreds of other people would be there and it was unlikely that Robert would even get to speak to the man, let alone pitch his business. He had paid for the privilege of the dinner but none of that mattered. My stocktake was not important. I thought I would be done. I thought I would easily make it, but I didn't. And I felt awful and she hated me for it and he hated me for it as well.

'I'm sure that Patricia knows who does the hard work,' I say in an attempt to cheer Ava up but she simply shrugs.

'I don't think so. I work and work and it's better now that you're here but mostly I feel like I'm dropping balls all over the place. I'm not good enough at work, and at home I'm not a good enough mother or wife.' She looks down at her hands, twisting her wedding ring on her finger, and I get the feeling that she's spoken aloud without meaning to.

I nod my head, understanding exactly what she's saying. 'I think you are doing a wonderful job everywhere,' I say softly and she looks up at me and smiles.

'Thank you, Grace, that means a lot.'

I know I am not the one she wants to hear those words from. She wants to hear them from Patricia, and from Finn, and even from her children. I remember what it feels like to want to hear those words, to need to be acknowledged by those closest to me.

At the end of the day when we are finishing up, I remind Ava about the email to Melody. 'Oh yes, but I just need to check up with a supplier who has promised a shipment of books for weeks now.'

'I can send it, just something that asks her not to look at her phone or leave the desk. I can use your email.'

'Perfect, just send it to me to check before you send it.'

I send Ava the email a few minutes later.

Hi Melody,

Just a quick reminder about not leaving your desk unattended, and I know our phones are our lives but it would be good if you could keep yours in your bag when on reception.

Thanks so much,

Ava

Ava is on the phone to the supplier but she gives me a thumbs up.

And then I delete that email and send Melody my own.

Hi Melody,

This email is to inform you that we are concerned by your performance at work. Time away from the desk without asking for someone to cover is not acceptable.

Furthermore, we request that personal phones are put away during office hours. This lapse on your part has been noted many times.

Please consider this your first warning,

Ava.

Australian employment law requires three warnings before an employee is fired. Ava will thank me for this later, I know she will.

TWENTY

AVA

On Monday night, the girls are tired after a long, hot day and Finn disappears as soon as dinner is over, to work. He was distracted during dinner, checking his phone constantly. He left Ava with the clean-up and even asked her to do story time.

'But they love it when you do story time,' protested Ava.

'I'm working on something new, Ava, something amazing, and after this, I only need one more and then I'll have enough for a show,' he said but there was something in his posture, in the way his eyes flicked from side to side as he spoke, that made her question what he was saying. Was it just an excuse to lock himself away from his family?

But she wasn't able to deny him the time, cautioning herself not to let one changed lock pattern on a phone make her question everything he says. She even indulged in a fantasy about a sold-out show and ongoing work for Finn as she cleaned up the kitchen.

Bath time with the girls takes longer than it should, but then it always does when they feel that Ava is stressed and rushing them.

Both Hazel and Chloe complain that she's 'not doing good

voices' when she reads them a story so she compensates with two stories. Finally, at 10pm, she is in bed. Her phone pings with an email and she considers ignoring it but picks up her phone and takes a look.

It's from Collin. He loves to send emails late at night as if to prove how hard he's working. But he probably indulged in a long lunch and a leisurely dinner before taking some time at his computer. Irritation flares inside Ava as she reads his email.

Go easy on Melody, she's only young. You're from a different generation and you don't understand that their phones are their lives.

Ava is instantly insulted and admonished.

We're a business, Collin. She can go on her phone at lunch like everyone else.

She waits for a few minutes, hoping that the email exchange will end there, but Collin likes to have the last word.

While Patricia is away, I would prefer if you consulted with me before you send my employees emails about their conduct. You were young and free once, Ava. I remember you were.

'Prick,' mutters Ava. She knows exactly what Collin is saying. He's rubbing her nose in it already.

His smug email and the idea that he already knew he was the new CEO for Australia plague her all night.

Obviously, Melody went running to Collin as soon as she got her friendly email asking her to stay off her phone. Collin spends at least twenty minutes a day hunched over the reception desk, 'chatting' with Melody. He's so much older than her that Ava can't believe the young woman allows it. Ava has thought about bringing it up with Patricia but Melody seems to be enjoying their chats and it's all out in the open so she has no idea what she would say exactly. *I'm worried he talks to her too much.* That sounds weird. Bringing up her own mistake with Collin would be disastrous for her. And she can just imagine if she accused Collin of having an affair with Melody without proof. She would be fired.

She allows herself ten minutes of musing on how to prove that something is going on, even imagining presenting Patricia with evidence and then watching as Collin is reprimanded and maybe even fired. But then she reminds herself that she has no way to verify if anything is actually happening between the two of them. She has an idea and she can't go blowing up everyone's lives with just an idea. She makes a decision to start watching the two of them carefully. Maybe even noting when they are both out of the office at the same time, like when they were in the café together, whispering to each other about something. This thought leaves a bad taste in her mouth. It makes her feel grubby but she can feel she's losing this competition with Collin, has probably already lost it.

On Tuesday morning, after a lot of tossing and turning, Ava cannot help but feel grateful to see Grace, once again, standing at her kitchen door during the breakfast rush. Finn was still fast asleep when Ava got up.

The kitchen that was so perfectly clean and tidy on Sunday night has already settled back into chaos.

'French braid, French braid,' yells Hazel when she sees Grace.

'Of course, get your brush.'

'Me too, me too,' exclaims Chloe, jumping up and down.

'Absolutely.' Grace beams and Ava wants to tell her she

doesn't have to get involved, but the woman looks genuinely happy to be with the girls so she nods gratefully and finishes everything off before dashing upstairs to fix her own hair and make-up.

In the car on the ride to work she and Grace discuss Ava's presentation at Redwood High School's careers day this afternoon.

'I'm worried they're going to find me boring,' says Ava.

'Nonsense,' says Grace, 'you're a woman running a company and raising a family. What could be more interesting?'

'Not running it yet,' says Ava.

'No,' agrees Grace, 'but it's not over until it's over.'

Ava is cheered by this, and at work she parks the car and gives Grace a few minutes to go up first, scrolling through her phone to check if she's missed any emails.

When she gets upstairs, Melody stands as soon as she sees her. 'Good morning, Ms Green,' says Melody.

'Morning,' Ava replies, 'and you know to call me Ava.'

'Just trying to be professional.' Melody smirks and Ava shakes her head, walking away.

Outside her office Grace is on the phone to one of the trainers and Ava can hear that the young woman is worried about being late because she's on a bus that's stuck in traffic. Grace is speaking in a low and soothing tone, letting the woman know she'll sort it out with the school.

There is a coffee on her desk and the office is neat and tidy, and Ava slumps into her chair and takes a deep breath, letting go of her exhaustion. She thinks about Finn, who is probably still sleeping. *Will he ever have enough work for a show?* And then because it's been in the back of her mind since it happened, she turns over the problem of him changing the lock pattern on his phone. There was no way she could speak to him last night but she will make sure she has the conversation tonight.

'Right, I've sorted that out,' says Grace, coming into the office. 'I've pushed it back an hour and the school are happy to accommodate.'

'Thank you,' says Ava.

'What shall we start on today?' asks Grace, and Ava pulls herself back to work so that everything that needs to get done will get done. Her personal life will have to wait, but then it always has to wait.

'Melody went to Collin to complain about the email I sent her,' she tells Grace, and she is gratified when Grace lets out a short bark of laughter.

'What a child,' she says and suddenly the whole thing doesn't seem serious at all. 'If she can't learn to accept some constructive criticism about how she does her job, she will not survive in the corporate world,' says Grace.

Ava shakes her head. 'That should be true but she's very pretty and that gets you quite far, with or without skills or ability.'

'It does,' agrees Grace, 'but at some point, you can't just get by on charm and looks alone.'

'I hear that,' says Ava.

'I've worked in a lot of places and I've seen what happens when a young woman thinks her looks will get her what she wants. They do to a certain extent but there's always trouble afterwards. Sometimes they get involved with men who have seniority and it all goes very wrong. Workplace affairs are always a terrible mistake.'

Ava swallows. 'I know... I...' she begins and then she stops. There's no way she's going to confess her own dalliance with a much older man to Grace.

'I worked for someone once whose husband cheated on her,' says Grace. 'He was an older man and his mistress was just starting out in the industry where he worked – the affair changed everyone's lives and not for the better.'

Grace stares at Ava intently and Ava feels like Grace knows something about her, can see inside her to her own transgressions.

'What happened?' she asks, unable to stop the question.

'Oh, well, you know how these things work,' says Grace, waving away the question. 'His wife took it very hard, I believe.'

Ava feels sweaty in the frigid air conditioning. 'I'm sure the young woman regretted it,' she says.

'I'm sure she did but she destroyed a family.' Grace shrugs. 'And these things always have a way of coming back to bite you, karma and all that.'

'I may just... use the bathroom,' says Ava.

She stands and goes to the bathroom, locking herself in a cubicle and putting her head down on her knees.

Her clumsy encounter with Collin from years and years ago returns. Once again, she experiences the humiliation of seeing him the next day and knowing he had seen her naked.

She had been mortified and it took months until she could look Collin in the face again. He'd seemed completely unaffected by the whole thing, which somehow made it even worse.

But when she began climbing the ladder, she felt that something was shifting inside Collin. He had been in a senior position to her once but he wasn't anymore. She has been wondering about him and Melody, and despite it making her feel like a bad person, she has been wondering if she could use their relationship to hurt Collin, if they are having one. She has conveniently forgotten that Collin has something on her, something that he could use if he told the story the right way. It's a different time now and she knows she would be believed and supported but it could still damage her reputation and cause people in the company to see her in a different light. No matter how much things change, they also remain the same in many ways.

Could he actually use one transgression to end her career

here? It would be insufferable to work for him, awful to have anyone know what happened. If he was the CEO, he wouldn't even have to fire her. He could just tell one person – Melody maybe – and the information would spread through the company and Ava would be the one disgraced.

She doesn't know why this hasn't occurred to her before. Should she go to Patricia first? Is she just imagining that Collin will use it? Won't he be hurt more than she is? Unless he says that she instigated it, that it was all her and he's just a man who couldn't resist. Women are blamed no matter what they do. She had been drunk, wearing a short dress, willing. None of that should matter when it comes to blame but it all would – of course it would if people started talking.

Collin is going to use that night against her, she can feel it, and she knows that she needs to stop it happening.

Standing up, she goes to the basin, washes her hands and fixes her hair in the mirror. She's not going to let him. She's not going to let him get to her or take a position that she has right-fully earned from her. No matter what she has to do.

She makes her way back to the office and sees Collin standing at reception, talking to Melody. Should she warn the young woman? What would she say? It's so complicated. She and Collin have had nothing more than a business relationship since that night.

As Ava watches them, Melody turns to look at her and then flicks her dark hair over her shoulder, leans towards Collin and whispers something.

They both laugh and Ava abandons any idea of saying something to Melody. It's not her job to talk to the young woman, but if she does become CEO, she will certainly put a stop to whatever it is Collin is doing. She'll put a stop to everything she doesn't like in this company. She has Grace to help her do it.

TWENTY-ONE

GRACE

There is something different about Ava after she returns from the bathroom, something bothering her. It seems my mention of the affair has worried her. I find that interesting. What is she hiding?

'If you can just get on with next week's schedule, that would be great,' she says and I dutifully get up and leave her office for my desk.

When I sit down, I hear a soft click behind me and I realise she has closed her door. I liked to keep my door open when I was running my company, liked to be able to see everyone bustling around the office and for them to know that they could come to me with anything.

Liza and I had offices next to each other and we would be back and forth all day. I believed Liza and I were friends. Perhaps we were in some way. When she got divorced, I was a shoulder for her to cry on, someone she could come to at any time to report on what was happening.

The day after I had seen the text on Tamara's phone, I didn't go into work. Instead, I stayed home, nursing a hangover.

I waited until Robert had left for work and Cordelia had left for school before getting out of bed.

I felt hideous but I showered and dressed and then went down to the kitchen, images of Robert and Tamara in bed together making me feel sick. I called Liza.

'I need you to fire Tamara,' I told her.

'What? Why?' she asked and I explained about the text, about confronting my husband.

'Grace, that's awful... Are you absolutely sure? Because you said Robert denied it and so did Tamara.'

'I'm certain enough, Liza, and it's my company and I want you to fire her.'

'But what reason will I give her? How can I explain? Do you want me to say something about the text?'

I was silent as I made myself a cup of coffee, finding my almond milk and adding just a quick shot of whisky in the hope that it would help me think straight.

'I don't care what you tell her. You'll figure it out,' I said.

Liza sighed and I could picture her in her office, staring out at the view with her perfect, silky black hair sitting on her shoulders and a pen in her hand. I could hear the clicking sound of the plunger on the pen as she pushed it continually, something she did when she was frustrated.

'Grace, this may come back to haunt us. I can't just fire her because you suspect her of an affair with your husband. Surely you have to see that sounds... strange.'

'Liza, I know it's the truth.'

'You have no way of proving it, Grace. What if she goes to the Fair Work Commission? You can't simply fire someone because of this. What if you're wrong?'

I sighed, taking a sip of my coffee and feeling the settling burn of the whisky as it hit my stomach. 'Liza, when you told me that Louie was cheating, did I tell you that you couldn't prove it? A wife knows. I know they're having an affair.'

'You sound... I think you need to take some time and really have a chat with Robert. This may all just be in your imagination.'

'Fire her,' I barked and I ended the call.

But Liza didn't. She wouldn't. She sent me an email stating that I had no proof and that Tamara would be well within her rights to sue us for unfair dismissal.

I'll move her on to receptionist work for a bit. Give you two some space. But you need to sort this out with Robert.

I screamed long and loud when I got that email. I was tempted to march into the office and grab Tamara by her hair and fling her out on the street, but I had consumed quite a few whiskies by then.

I shake my head, letting go of my thoughts of the past and concentrate on my work. I don't want to make any mistakes. Once the schedule is done, I leave my desk and go and make myself a coffee. Melody and Collin are in the kitchen. I don't say anything, just offer them a tight smile and busy myself making my drink.

Whatever conversation they were having stops while I am in there.

But as soon as I leave, there is a burst of raucous laughter and I want to turn around and fling my hot cup of coffee in Melody's face. I hate the idea of people laughing at me behind my back. That was the worst thing about being cheated on, the humiliating knowledge that Robert and Tamara were laughing at me as they screwed each other.

I drop my coffee on my desk and go to the bathroom, where I close myself in a stall and try to get a hold of my emotions. The desire for a drink is a physical need, crawling up from my toes, but I don't need a drink because I'm not an alcoholic and I will be fine.

I'm willing to bet that if I confronted Melody, she would say they were laughing about something else, but I know what the truth is. Just like I knew about Tamara.

The day I told Liza to fire Tamara, I spent hours searching for evidence, looking through our credit card statements first. I found charges for flowers and restaurants and a weekend away. The problem was that Robert did occasionally buy me flowers and I knew he went out to dinner with friends and I remembered him talking about a boys' weekend away. I couldn't remember any of the dates. I couldn't categorically point to a charge and say that was when he'd been with Tamara. Robert was good at covering his tracks.

But I knew, I just knew, and nothing would sway me from the belief in his adultery.

Over the weeks that followed, he continued to deny it and I continued to push for him to leave the house and grant me a divorce. He asked me to go to therapy with him and I did go once, but when we sat in front of the woman, he laid it all out for her and even though I kept explaining that I just knew, she told me that she thought I would benefit from some therapy by myself. 'Paranoia can be very damaging for a relationship, especially coupled with excessive alcohol consumption,' she said primly, crossing her long legs and smiling in Robert's direction.

I felt like I was going slightly mad.

And unfortunately, the only way I could get through the days without dissolving into a heap was with some help from my friend alcohol.

I tried to only drink in the evenings when Robert and I pretended everything was all right in front of Cordelia. My daughter knew something was going on and when I was especially drunk, I would lay it all out for her, trying to convince her that her father was cheating, needing her to be on my side. It is those moments that I am most ashamed of when I think back to that time.

Soon drinking at night wasn't enough, as each day I went into work and saw Tamara on reception. We never spoke and Liza told me she was angry about the demotion even though she was still earning the same salary. I hated seeing her, and a wine or two at lunch helped me buzz through the afternoon. But as it always goes with these things, my consumption continued to escalate.

Two months after I found out about the affair, I was arriving late to work, falling asleep at the office and barely functioning when I was awake. I was inebriated most of the time. Every conversation with Robert led to him accusing me of being an alcoholic and of being paranoid and delusional. He stayed out late 'working' or 'just getting some space' but I knew he was with her. And I knew I would catch him because a week after I had seen that text, I hired a private detective. I hadn't expected it to take him so long to get proof, but eventually he came through.

Three months after I had hired him, I had my evidence. Pictures of Robert meeting Tamara at a restaurant in the middle of the day like they didn't care who was watching. Pictures of them sharing a meal, sipping glasses of wine, animatedly talking. And of the two of them clinched in a hug at the end before they parted.

That night I waited up for him to come home and then I flung the pictures at him. He looked through them impassively.

'She called me to talk about the way you're treating her at work. She's tried talking to Liza but she's getting nowhere. She's a young woman and she's incredibly distressed and she thought that since you were accusing me of cheating with her, I would be able to make you see sense. But no one can talk to you anymore, Grace. You're insane.' He dropped the photographs on the floor and went off to sleep in the spare room, and I picked them up and ripped them to shreds. No proof would be enough. Gaslighting. That's what we call it now and it goes on all the time, but when you're in it, there is no way to counter it. Maybe I was wrong? Maybe I was paranoid? Maybe it was the alcohol? I went back and forth even as I continued to tell Robert that I only believed one thing.

'I don't care what is or is not happening,' I told him the next morning. 'Our relationship is over. Please leave the house and I promise I'll be fair.'

Robert laughed at me, actually laughed at me. 'I will not leave, Grace. Half the house is mine. Half your business is mine. I'm not going anywhere. You're the one who should leave. You need to be in therapy, you need help to give up your addiction to alcohol. You need treatment.'

I was standing in our perfectly white marble kitchen at the time, holding a cup of doctored coffee in my hand, and I remember flinging it at him with intense force. It hit him in the chest, the mug falling to the floor and smashing, a brown coffee stain covering his pale grey shirt.

He touched his fingers to the stain and lifted them to his nose. 'Whisky?' he said. 'At this time of the morning?' He smiled and shook his head. 'Oh, Grace. Poor, poor Grace.' And then he left to change and go to work.

Cordelia started avoiding me. She was in her final year of school and busy with friends and activities. She took to studying at the library after school and going straight to her room if she came home and saw I had already been drinking. She lost weight that year, my poor child. The stress was too much for her and I will never forgive myself for that.

Liza took over more and more of my duties at work. And still I had to see that little bitch every day when I walked into my office – my office and my company.

'You need to get yourself together, Grace,' Liza told me one night after she found me asleep on the sofa in my office. 'You can't go on like this.'

'I shouldn't have to,' I spat. 'I should be told the truth. Tamara should go and Robert should leave my house.'

'I've spoken with her,' Liza said gently. 'I didn't want to bring it up but I asked her and she says she doesn't even know what you're talking about. She has a boyfriend. She's not sleeping with your husband. Something is wrong, Grace, and you need to get some help.'

'What I need is for Robert and that little bitch to die so I never have to see either of them again!' I yelled.

Liza shook her head and turned to leave my office and then she stopped.

'Oh,' she said.

Tamara was standing in the doorway, staring at me, her face pale with shock.

When Robert died two nights later, Tamara was one of the first people the police interviewed and she had a lot to say.

'I'm leaving now,' says Ava and I nod my head, pulling myself back to my day as I realise that I have whiled away more than an hour lost in thoughts of the past.

'Of course, good luck with the talk,' I say as I admonish myself to stop letting my mind wander.

I spend the rest of the day struggling to concentrate and I'm grateful that Ava is out of the office for most of the afternoon. She returns from her talk buoyed by the reaction from the girls and Amber Vale and I try to muster as much enthusiasm as I can. I'm very relieved at the end of the day when she says it's time to go.

Our car ride home is mostly silent, each of us lost in our own thoughts, and I am grateful for that. I thank her for the lift and take the stairs up to the small apartment when we get home.

'See you in the morning,' she calls and I wave as I go.

I never wanted to have to think about the past again. I

thought I had put it all firmly in a box at the clinic, locking away everything that had hurt me and everything I'd done because of that. But memories refuse to stay locked up and, in the apartment, I take the bottle of vodka out and inhale until I feel high on the fumes. But I don't drink. I won't drink.

TWENTY-TWO

AVA

Ava wonders at Grace's silence on the car ride home but she is soon swept up in the dinner routine. Once the girls are asleep, she cleans up as she thinks about how to speak to Finn about his phone. She would love to just leave it, but she can't let it go.

Determined, she goes up to the loft, where Finn has his studio. Ava rarely bothers him while he works but she can't wait another day to talk to him.

'Okay if I come in?' she calls, knocking lightly.

'Fine,' comes his reply but she can tell from just that one word that he is angry about being disturbed.

'What do you need?' he asks.

Ava had wanted to talk a little and broach the subject in an offhand way but she can see that Finn is not in the mood for a chat. He is standing behind a canvas that is almost life-sized, his paintbrush in his hand. Ava looks around the loft, where they have left the floorboards rough and bare and there is only a small window for air. The place is too hot in summer and cold in winter but Finn loves it because it's just his space.

'Ava, what do you need?' he asks again, impatiently.

'I didn't know you'd changed your phone pattern,' she says.

'You should probably tell me what it is in case you forget it again.'

She keeps her tone light, non-confrontational.

'You're not actually snooping in my phone, are you, Ava?' Finn says, dabbing lightly on the canvas and then stepping back.

'No, I...' She's not sure what to say. 'I wanted to use it at the bar the other night and I couldn't get in, so I thought—'

'Why? You had your own phone.' He sounds relaxed, not angry or accusatory, merely curious.

Ava shrugs. It was a stupid idea to ask the question.

'Can I see?' she asks, hoping to just move on, and before he can say anything she goes around the side to look at the canvas. It's a huge portrait of a beautiful woman's face, dark eyes and olive skin with a tiny scar near her eyebrow. 'She's beautiful. It's very good. Who is she?'

'You don't usually come up here,' says Finn in reply.

'Do I know her?' she asks. 'She looks familiar.'

'Sami's mother, the little boy in Hazel's class. They were in preschool together. You must have met her at least once. Or maybe not, I usually do the parties and things. I need to finish, if you don't mind.'

'I thought you were working on a portrait of your great-grandfather,' she says, glancing around the studio, seeing the large canvas next to a wall, half finished. Finn's art supplies cost an absolute fortune but he thinks nothing of abandoning a project halfway through if he is no longer feeling inspired.

'I told you a few days ago I was resting the canvas and this one called to me,' he says, looking at her. 'I really don't want to talk right now if that's okay.'

Ava knows there is no way he has just started working on the new portrait. This one looks like it's nearly finished and it's beautiful: the woman's slight smile seems to be filled with a quiet joy and her eyes are focused on someone she has affection for.

Ava wants to ask a hundred questions. *Did she sit for you? How long have you been working on this? How well do you know her? How much time are you spending with her? Is she married? If so, what does her partner think of this?*

A spark of hope flares inside her. 'Is it a commission?' she asks. Because maybe that's what it is. Maybe he dropped his 'no commissions' rule because Sami's mother wanted a picture for her partner.

She knows she has met the woman a few times but whenever she is at school, she is usually rushing to get somewhere or trying to do work on her phone at the same time.

'No, I just like her face, now please...' He gestures with his paintbrush to the door and Ava flushes at being asked to leave like she is an errant child disturbing a parent.

She leaves without another word, stomping down the steps to make a lot of noise. *You are a child*, she scolds herself.

She packs the girls' lunch boxes and finishes in the kitchen and then she thinks about taking a shower but she is too angry.

Instead, she goes into the pantry and feels around on the very top shelf where she keeps an old packet of cigarettes for when she's in desperate need of something different. She's had it for at least five years. Tucking the pack and a lighter into her pants pocket, she opens the sliding door out to the garden and sneaks out as though someone may be watching her.

The air is deliciously cool, and just standing in the darkness calms her down. She makes her way to the garden swing and sits down gingerly, hoping to avoid making the chains squeak. And then she lights up a cigarette and takes a deep, bad-for-her lungful.

'Oh...' she hears and she starts, nearly dropping her cigarette at the sight of Grace.

'I am so sorry, I do apologise,' says Grace. 'I just wanted to feel the night air. I'll go.' She turns but Ava shakes her head.

'No, no, don't worry about it, please. I'm being very bad but

I never do this in front of the children or really at all. It's just been a day. Please, sit down,' she says, gesturing to the swing with its padded green seat cushion, and Grace sits.

Ava takes another lungful of smoke, coughing because she's not used to it. And then, taking a deep breath and finding her eyes filled with unexpected tears, she sniffs.

'Oh, Ava,' says Grace softly, 'what's wrong?'

And she says it so kindly that Ava has to shut her eyes tightly and scrabble in her pocket for a tissue so she doesn't just burst into loud sobs. It's exhaustion, she's sure. She doesn't do well on no sleep. She swallows and sniffs and then blows her nose. 'Sorry,' she says to Grace, 'I'm just tired. Collin emailed me late last night and Finn is...' She stops speaking. She should not share any of her worries with Grace. They barely know each other and Grace works for her, but for some reason, speaking to Grace is easy. 'Finn is painting a portrait of the mother of one of Hazel's schoolfriends.'

'Would that be Sami's mum?' asks Grace.

'How do you... How do you know about Sami?' asks Ava, her heart thrumming inside her.

'When I was babysitting, Hazel said that Finn and Sami's mum talk a lot.' Ava waits for Grace to say, 'I'm sure they're just friends,' or something like that but instead the older woman meets her gaze and is quiet for a moment before she says, 'It must be worrying to know that he's painting a picture of her.'

Ava nods. 'But it's silly, I'm being silly. He's an artist and he paints faces, of course he's going to want to paint faces of beautiful women.'

'May I offer you some advice, Ava?'

'Yes.'

'Sometimes, as women, we have a tendency to dismiss our instincts because we don't want to believe that something could be wrong, and also because if we trust that instinct, we would have to do something about it.'

Prickles of unease run up and down Ava's arms. 'Well, I think... Look, I shouldn't have said anything.' She takes another puff of her cigarette, leaning forward and tapping it to get rid of ash on the grass.

'Of course,' says Grace. 'I may just get some sleep. I'll see you in the morning.' She gets off the swing and Ava feels bad but she just wants to be left alone right now.

Once Grace has left, Ava goes back inside and makes herself a bowl of ice cream to take to bed with her. And even though she tries to stop herself, she looks up Sami's mother on the class list, finds her name and then her Instagram.

Anita Gill is one of those women who is effortlessly beautiful with almond-shaped eyes and long legs. Her dark hair looks as good tied up in a messy bun as it does hanging down over her shoulders. Ava wants to believe that the woman is adept at using filters but all her posts have #nofilter as the first hashtag. She could be lying but Ava knows she isn't. She looks like Finn's portrait of her. She keeps scrolling, looking for evidence of a husband, of a wife, of something to stop her from worrying as she wishes she had asked Grace more about what Hazel said, but the conversation felt too personal and unprofessional.

She spoons some ice cream into her mouth, biting down on a large piece of cookie dough, and then feels the bite lodge in her throat as she stops on a picture of Anita, Finn, Sami and Hazel. It looks like it was taken at the school excursion to the Powerhouse Museum that Hazel went on last month. Ava remembers being grateful that Finn had volunteered to go along because there was no way she could take the time off work. She hadn't yet hired Grace.

In the picture, Finn and Anita are laughing at Sami and Hazel, who are staring up wide-eyed at an aeroplane hanging from the ceiling.

Such a fabulous day with my little boy and his class. Time with him is always precious as I navigate life as a single mother #excursion #powerhousemuseum #gratefulfornewfriends.

Ava enlarges the image, studying it closely. Finn looks so happy. Her eyes move down his body. He is pointing at the aeroplane with one hand and the other is hanging down by his side, right next to Anita's hand, their fingers almost interlocked. *Who took this picture? One of the teachers? Another parent? Is Finn having an affair and does everyone else know?* Even alone in bed, Ava feels a flush of humiliation on her cheeks at that idea.

Grace is right. She doesn't want to know this because then she will have to do something.

She sets her phone down and swallows, immediately putting another big spoon of ice cream in her mouth, despite no longer wanting to eat it.

What now? What do I do now?

TWENTY-THREE

Dear baby girl,

In a story as old as time itself, I fell for Luka and stopped doing everything I was supposed to be doing.

I stopped working in class and coming home on time and listening to my parents. And I started having sex. I was too young but that didn't stop me, and every time I spent an afternoon with him, I felt energised, sure that the whole world was good and anything was possible.

I stupidly assumed that if my parents met Luka, they would like him – because how could anyone not love Luka?

I invited him to tea, only asking my parents if a friend could come over, and they were so shocked at the idea of me having a friend that they actually agreed.

When Luka arrived, dressed in jeans with artful holes and a faded jumper, they were beyond horrified.

'Pleased to meet you, sir,' Luka said, holding out his hand to my father.

My father, dressed in a shirt and tie, even for an afternoon tea, simply turned away.

'You're humiliating yourself,' my mother said, her hand fluttering to her throat, where she was wearing her wedding pearls. Both of them left the room and then I heard their bedroom door slam.

Luka thought it was funny, but I was mortified.

'They'll like me when they get to know me,' he said, grabbing a slice of the rather dry sponge cake my mother had made to take with him as he left.

When Luka had gone, I cleaned up the tea things and spent the rest of the night in my room, seething with anger.

From then on, the only thing that mattered to my mother and father was to keep me away from Luka.

They tried locking me in my room but I climbed out of the window, twisting my ankle as I dropped to the ground. My father nailed my window shut but then I just didn't come home. They tried not feeding me but then I hung out at Luka's house and ate dinner there with his relaxed, kind parents. 'Call us Tina and Jack,' his mum told me the first time she met me.

Even though it was the eighties, Tina and Jack seemed left over from the seventies. They grew their own vegetables and were artists who both worked as social workers during the day to make money. Tina was a potter and the house was filled with beautiful glazed bowls and mugs. Jack was a sculptor, collecting rubbish to turn into his pieces. I didn't understand the twisted sculptures but I told Luka I thought they were beautiful.

They didn't believe in stifling Luka or his impulses and they loved me because I would sit and listen to them talk about the terrible state of the world with rapt attention.

And then one awful night, in the middle of winter, I came home to find a small suitcase by the door.

'Are you going on a holiday?' I asked my mother cautiously when I found her in the kitchen, chopping up onions.

'No,' she said. Her hands continued moving, and I noticed that there were tears on her face. Chopping onions always made her cry.

'Oh,' I said. I was cold and tired and just wanted a hot shower and some time in my bedroom. I loved Luka and loved being with him but sometimes I needed a little space just to read or to think about him – ironic, I know.

'I may just go shower,' I said.

'No,' she said and then my father came into the kitchen. He was holding my stuffed rabbit – a toy that I had been given as a baby and that I always kept on my bed.

'What are you doing with that?' I asked.

'You need to leave,' he said, handing me the faded grey toy. 'We've packed a bag and there's a hundred dollars in there. You need to leave our house now.'

'But I'm sixteen,' I protested. 'I'm at school, you can't—'

'We can!' shouted my mother, dropping the knife she was using on the melamine counter with a clatter. She spun around to face me and I could see the slight sheen of dried tears on her face. 'We can do whatever we want. You can legally be on your own. You don't obey the rules. You don't work at school. You don't go to church, and you sneak off like a filthy whore to be with that boy. That lazy, good-for-nothing boy.' Her eyes filled with disappointed rage.

'If you would just try to get to know him—' I began to protest, but my father stopped me by grabbing my arm and dragging me to the front door.

He shoved me outside in the late afternoon chill, threw my case at me and yelled, 'It's him or us. You decide.'

'Wait, give me a chance,' I cried. But the door slammed in my face.

I walked all the way to Luka's house. I had to stop and open the case to get my coat out as the time grew later and it got colder.

But finally, I got there and sobbed as I explained.

'You can stay here,' Luka said without letting his parents say anything else.

I lived with him and his parents for three weeks before it became obvious that they were not ready for me to be there full time.

One afternoon, as we walked out of school together, Luka told me that he didn't think it was a good idea for me to live with them anymore.

'But I've got nowhere else to go,' I said.

Luka was upset but he told me he had no choice. 'My mum and dad, they're just... like, they don't earn a lot of money and it's hard with another person.'

'But I can get a job, I'll contribute, I promise.'

'Sorry,' he said, shaking his head. 'I also need to think about exams and stuff. I want to get into an art course and I need to work. I just think we're, like, distracting each other.'

I understood that he was using his parents as an excuse. Luka was over me.

I accompanied him to his house and packed up my things. His parents were still conveniently at work.

I was sixteen and I had nowhere to go. I could have gone home but that felt worse than being homeless. So, you see, baby girl, I came from nothing.

You need to know that so you understand the things I did. You need to know that.

TWENTY-FOUR

GRACE

The drive into the office today was spent mostly discussing work. It's Wednesday already and my time living in the garage apartment will soon come to an end. I know that Ava regrets taking me into her confidence last night in the garden. We both work quietly at our desks until lunch and I don't bring up anything we discussed.

I can see she needs some time alone to process.

'I may just go and have a walk for twenty minutes if that's okay with you,' I say to her at lunchtime. The relief on her face is obvious.

'Of course, might as well enjoy the last days of summer,' she says.

Passing the reception desk, I see Melody's eyes on her phone, a smile on her face as she scrolls. She is not on her lunch break. I know because the times are staggered.

'Would you like me to take over the reception desk for a bit so you can deal with whatever you need to on your phone?' I ask and she looks up, her eyes narrowing with dislike for me.

'You know you look really familiar,' she says.

'So you told me,' I reply.

'No, I mean like really familiar. Have we met before?'

The little vixen holds my gaze as I feel my heart race in my chest. She couldn't know. There's no way.

'I doubt it,' I say. 'I'm a lot older than you are.'

'Yeah, old enough to be my mother or maybe even my grandma. How old are you, anyway?'

The question is posed rudely and meant rudely. 'Old enough to know not to be on my phone while at work,' I say and I turn and head for the stairs instead of waiting for the elevator. I need the six flights to compose myself.

I have changed the colour of my hair. I have changed the way I do my make-up and the way I dress. I am older and I have lost quite a bit of weight. There's no way that young woman recognises me.

I am flustered at the café where I go to get myself a sandwich to eat in the park and have to repeat the order twice while the woman behind the counter smiles at me.

'Sorry, late night,' I explain.

'No worries, it will be a few minutes,' she replies.

My phone pings with a text from an unknown number, and when I open it, it's a link to a newspaper article. I am suddenly in need of something to drink.

Maybe it's some sort of scam but I have a feeling it's not. I click on it and read the headline and then immediately close it again. I am not ready. I can't do this now in the middle of my workday.

I take my sandwich to the park close to the office. It's filled with people on their lunch break, some snoozing in the sun. There is a t'ai chi class going on near the bench where I choose to sit and I hold my sandwich in my hand, trying to calm my racing heart, as I watch the elegant, slow movements. I keep repeating a phrase I used when I was at the clinic and in distress. *This can wait until I'm ready to deal with it. This can wait until I'm ready to deal with it. This can wait until I'm ready to deal with it.*

I know that if I had employed that mantra when everything started to go wrong, I would still have my company and, perhaps, Cordelia would still have her father. Instead, I let events take me over, I let what was happening control me, and I lost everything because of it. I can't let that happen again.

Who is the text from? It seems obvious that it must be Melody. The timing cannot be coincidental. How has she found out about me? She doesn't look capable of doing anything other than scrolling through her phone. But perhaps that's the only thing she needs to be capable of these days. The whole world is at our fingertips and hiding is almost impossible.

I take five deep breaths, holding them for five seconds each and then blowing out as though I am blowing through a straw, and finally I am able to eat, although the avocado salad sandwich tastes wrong, like it has too much salt on it. I finish it because I know I need to eat something since I didn't have any breakfast. I didn't go to the kitchen this morning to help Ava, sensing that she wouldn't want me there. We have said too much to each other and the problem of Sami's mother hangs in the air between us.

When I walk into the office, Melody is, once again, looking at her phone. She looks up and offers me a wide grin. 'Thought I knew you,' she says and she winks.

Not a coincidence, then. A threat. It's clear it's a threat. I bunch my hands into fists, stopping myself from lunging at her and tearing her pretty hair from her head.

'I have no idea what you're talking about,' I say.

The phone rings and she answers, sitting up straight and flipping her hair over her shoulder. She thinks she's won something from me but she has no idea. I walk away, anger simmering as I work through the problem.

All I wanted was for her to up her game at the office. Now I'm going to have to destroy her.

I manage to get through the rest of the day using a level of concentration and willpower I have never tapped into before.

By the time Ava and I are ready to leave, I am exhausted with a thumping headache and an aching jaw from tensing for so long. I have avoided Melody entirely.

Ava has been uncharacteristically quiet. I know the portrait is bothering her and she would like to talk to someone about it. She hasn't said much about her mother but I hope that she will give her a call to discuss the problem with her. Just like I hope, every day, that Cordelia will give me a call. Mothers never stop wanting to protect, to help, their children. Cordelia will understand this when she has a child of her own. The idea that I may not get to be there for her when that happens slices across my heart.

If I had told Ava any truth about myself, perhaps I could discuss my lovely daughter with her, but everything she knows about me is a lie and now she has said too much to me and regrets it. We are both wary of the boundaries between employer and employee.

'Ready to go?' she asks me. She looks tired as well, worn down by a lack of sleep and her fears.

'I'm meeting a friend for dinner,' I say impulsively, feeling a jolt inside me at the idea that I have no one at all who would be willing to meet me for dinner.

'Oh, that's lovely,' she says, 'then I'll see you in the morning.'

And I nod and smile like it is lovely.

It's after 5 p.m. but the heat in the city rises up from the roads in waves. Summer is not willing to let go. I walk aimlessly through the streets, where everyone seems to be in a good mood despite it being a workday. The extra light makes workdays seem shorter, I suppose. I walk for an hour, waiting for the courage to open the link again, to read the article so I know exactly what Melody knows about me. I've read it already but a long time ago. I didn't read it when it came out. I wasn't strong enough at first and I had no access to my phone. I read it later and then I read it many, many times.

I was blackout drunk and I didn't mean for it to happen. That's the story my lawyer and I stuck to. It was an accident and there was no way to conclusively prove that it was not an accident. The only clear thing was that I was an alcoholic who had seemed very unwell and mentally unstable to all those around me in the days leading up to what happened.

My lawyer was very good – not sympathetic, not warm, not kind, but very good at her job, for which I paid her very well. I listened to her argue for me in court, to her explaining how remorseful I was for the mistake I had made, and even I believed her. 'This accident', she kept calling it, cementing it in the mind of the jury as such, so that they ruled in my favour.

Finally, my legs signal that I need to take a break and I stop. It's nearly 7 p.m. and the heat has dipped, a light breeze cooling the air. I look around me to see where I am. I am standing in front of a bar and next to it is a Japanese restaurant.

A laugh bubbles up from inside me. The universe has a strange sense of humour. *Here's your choice, Grace. Here's where you decide how to play this*, it seems to be saying. It's not unusual to see a bar next to a restaurant, and I pass many bars on my walk to the train station, on my way to the grocery store. They are everywhere, but right here, right now, I feel like I'm being given a choice: confront the truth of what Melody knows and sit with the terror and discomfort of that, or just make it all go away, even for a night.

People move past me, occasionally glancing at me because I am standing staring at my two options.

At the clinic we discussed what to do in these situations, how to act, how to think, when to ask for help. I suppose I should stop calling it a clinic and start calling it what it was: a psychiatric facility for those deemed not guilty by reason of insanity.

If I choose the bar, Robert wins. He's dead but he still wins. If I choose the bar, Tamara wins. If I choose the bar, Melody wins. If I choose the bar, everyone who rejoiced at my downfall wins. I have worked very hard to be here, to be out in the world with the new identity I have chosen.

I need to win now.

I take a deep, cleansing breath and push open the door of the Japanese restaurant, where I am immediately shown to a table for one.

I order quickly, asking for jasmine tea, and then I sit back and take out my phone. Another cleansing breath calms me and I click on the link.

And there it is, in large black letters, the truth of who I am.

THE SPECTACULAR RISE AND FALL OF
GRACE MORTON

TWENTY-FIVE

AVA

Ava trails her hand in the warm bath water, listening but not listening to Hazel chatter about her day as she and Chloe play in the fruit-scented bubbles.

She missed Grace on the drive home this afternoon, missed talking to her because Grace seems to have the ability to put things into perspective. But she was also aware, all day long, that she should never have said anything to Grace at all.

She called her mother instead as she drove home, listening to her talk about bridge club and her struggles to fix her internet.

'Mum,' she said, interrupting her.

'Yes, darling?'

'Did you and Dad get divorced because he cheated on you?'

Ava had never asked her mother such a direct question, had always understood that the reasons behind her parents' divorce were private. As a child she had accepted 'we're just no longer in love with each other' as the explanation.

'Oh, well...' her mother said, obviously struggling with the direct question. 'I think that all of that was a long time ago and we don't need to discuss it.'

Ava took that to mean that perhaps her father had cheated. She wondered how her mother had found out, and what that had been like for her, but she wasn't able to ask the question. If her mother didn't want to discuss it, that was her right.

'How do you think you know if a man is cheating?' she asked her mother instead.

'Ava, is something wrong with you and Finn?' her mother replied.

'No, no,' sighed Ava, suddenly losing the desire to continue the conversation. Her mother would worry and there was no need for her to worry. Not yet. 'Just something I was talking to my new assistant about.'

'Oh, well, that doesn't sound very much like workplace chat but you know best. When am I seeing those gorgeous girls again? How are they enjoying school?'

It was easier to discuss her children than think about what was really bothering her.

But as the girls play happily in the bath, her thoughts return to Grace and what Ava said to her last night.

The woman seemed distracted at the end of the day and kept rubbing her head like she had a headache, which is not usual behaviour for her. She had returned from lunch looking like something was bothering her but Ava didn't want to pry. They had already had way too personal a conversation about Finn.

The image of Finn and Anita circles in her mind. Are they just friends? And how could she ask Finn about it without him getting angry at her? If he gets angry, he just shuts down.

'Hazel,' Ava says.

'Yes, Mum?'

'How often do you play with Sami after school?'

'Nearly every day. I like Sami. He's good at the monkey bars. And Daddy says, "The bloody afternoons go on forever," and Sami's mum laughs and says, "Oh, Finn, Ava is so lucky to have you."' Hazel cocks her head to the side, imitating with what is sure to be some accuracy. 'Your name is Ava.'

'It is,' confirms Ava.

'Your name is Mummy,' says Chloe.

'I'm Ava and I'm Mummy.'

'Today, after school, we played at the park near our house and me and Sami dug in the sandpit till we got to the bottom.'

'I dug too,' says Chloe.

'And Daddy was talking to Sami's mum and then his phone rang and he was talking and talking so much that he didn't get to see our big hole in the sandpit because a big boy came and kicked some sand into it and Sami's mum told him that it was not a nice thing to do and Sami...'

Ava tunes out as she mulls over the problem of her husband and another woman. They do seem to be leading separate lives at the moment. When she gets into bed, he's usually working, and then in the morning, he's sleeping. Have they drifted so far from each other that he would cheat on her? Finn is obsessed with his work, with having time to work. When is he meeting someone to cheat with? Certainly not with the children there, but he often meets friends in the art community for drinks on a Saturday night. Ava doesn't go because she feels completely left out of the conversation and because babysitters are so expensive. Is that when he's meeting Anita?

'And then I said to Daddy that he must get off the phone and stop talking and talking to Collin,' says Hazel, and on hearing the name, Ava tunes back in to what her daughter is saying.

'Who was Daddy talking to?' asks Ava.

'I told you, Mum. Collin, dollin, smollin, bollin,' she rhymes.

Prickles of unease run up and down Ava's arms.

'You know Collin,' laughs Hazel. 'You know him.'

TWENTY-SIX

GRACE

I stumble along the pavement, bumping into a man holding two shopping bags.

'Watch it,' he says, muttering, 'Drunk idiot,' as he walks away.

'You watch it, you watch it, you watch it,' I whisper repeatedly, my feet aching from being in heels all day and walking so much. I stumble twice as I make my way over uneven pavement slabs.

I am not drunk. But I feel drunk.

I am inebriated with despair.

After reading the article all about myself, I have realised that everything I have planned is going to fall apart and I have no idea how to stop it happening.

It's late but there are still people everywhere, shopping, going to pubs, meeting up with friends. But I am alone.

I stop by a children's playground and make my way to a bench, slumping onto it and removing my shoes, not caring what I look like.

Ava needs me. I knew she needed me the day I met her. She is a woman struggling with balance just like I was, a woman carrying mother guilt just like I was, a woman whose husband is cheating on her – just like mine was. *Maybe he isn't cheating, maybe she's just a friend?* 'No,' I say aloud. 'I know the truth now, just like I knew the truth then.'

I needed help back then but everyone around me seemed determined to cause me pain.

I can see that Ava is surrounded by the same kind of people, from her rival at work to her childish husband.

Ava needs me and I'm here for her. I'm going to make sure she doesn't have to suffer like I did.

I'm going to make sure that everyone else suffers instead.

TWENTY-SEVEN

AVA

She cannot believe what she's just heard.

'And what did Daddy say to Collin?' she asks lightly. It could be another Collin. It's a common enough name. The two men have met quite a few times at Christmas parties and cocktail evenings but there is no reason why they would be speaking.

Hazel sighs as if exhausted by her mother. 'He said, "Yes, Collin, I understand but I haven't noticed anything at all."'

'Really,' says Ava, 'and then what did Daddy say?'

'Don't know.' Hazel shrugs, bored with the conversation now. 'Can we have one scoop of ice cream or two after bath time?'

Ava looks at her daughter and can't help smiling at the mischievous glint in her eyes. Ava had not promised any ice cream but Hazel knows how to get her way.

'Yay, ice cream,' says Chloe, slapping her hands down on the water.

'One scoop,' laughs Ava, pushing what she's heard to the back of her mind. She'll ask Finn about it later. Now she just wants to enjoy her time with her girls. But she struggles to concentrate as she dries the girls and dresses them in their pyjamas. Why would Collin be calling Finn, and what is Finn up to on a Saturday night? Why does it feel like all the men she knows are hiding something from her?

Once Hazel and Chloe are both in bed after one and a half scoops of ice cream with sprinkles, negotiated by Hazel, Ava goes to find Finn in his studio.

'This is getting to be a bit of a habit,' says Finn when she asks if they can talk.

Ava rarely disturbs him when he's working but she's not going to lose another night of sleep over a call that may or may not have been from the Collin she works with.

'Hazel said you spoke to Collin today,' says Ava. 'She may have the wrong name, but did you? Is it the Collin I work with?'

'Yeah, he called me,' says Finn, picking up a cloth to clean the brush he's been working with.

'Why?'

'Truthfully, I don't know. I thought he had somehow confused my number with yours at first and it's not like we've had all that many conversations, but he just wanted to ask if you were okay.'

'Why would he want to ask that and why would he ask it of you?'

Finn shrugs his shoulders. 'I have no idea – maybe he was worried about you. He said he saw you sleeping on the sofa in your office the other day.'

'So?' says Ava, anger running through her. 'I was taking a fifteen-minute break. It's only ever fifteen minutes and it really helps keep me sharp for the afternoon.' *The door was closed. How did he see me sleeping?* She shrugs her shoulders, uncomfortable with the idea of Collin watching her while she is asleep.

'I don't think he was criticising you, Ava. I think he was just worried. He said that you've been a little off your game at work.'

'How dare he,' fumes Ava.

'Ava,' says Finn, picking up a tube of paint to add some to his palette, 'he was just concerned. And you have been really stressed lately.'

'Because I lost my assistant, and whatever concerns he had, there's absolutely no reason for him to call you. How did he even get your number?'

'He...' Finn hesitates. 'I gave it to him at one of the parties. We were talking about portraits and he asked if I would paint his boys and I didn't want to say no so I said yeah and gave him my number and I just hoped like hell he'd never contact me. He must have just been being polite because he never did until today.'

'And did he say anything else?' Ava asks, folding her arms. Tomorrow she's going to make sure that Collin understands exactly how over the line he has been. She is so sick of him undermining her. What exactly is he playing at?

'Yeah,' says Finn, picking up a tube of white paint and mixing it with some red, 'he asked how much you knew about Grace.'

'What?' Ava seethes. 'What has that got to do with him?'

'Look, I have no idea. I told him Grace was lovely and then he asked when I'd met her and I told him about her staying here for a bit.'

'Why did you do that?' yells Ava. 'We didn't want anyone at the office to know.'

'Why?' asks Finn, his eyes on the painting as he moves his brush over the canvas.

Ava would like to grab the brush and throw it across the room. Finn seems to have no idea how strange it is to get a call from the man who is her competition for the top job.

'I'll talk to him tomorrow,' says Ava instead of bothering with an explanation for Finn.

Finn shrugs in reply as if to say that none of this has

anything at all to do with him, then says, 'You should just leave it. He's probably embarrassed he called.'

'I'm certainly not going to leave it.'

'Suit yourself,' he says and Ava turns to leave. 'Ava,' says Finn and she stops.

'Yes?'

'You are okay, aren't you? I know that you're stressed and worried about everything all the time, but you are okay, aren't you?'

Ava sighs. 'I'm fine, Finn. I really want to get the promotion and I have a feeling Collin is going to do everything in his power to prevent it happening.'

'Yeah, well, you know how I feel about that.'

'I do,' says Ava shortly. 'Are *you* okay?' she asks just before she turns to go.

'I'm...' Finn shakes his head. 'I'm fine.'

'Is there something you want to talk about, Finn?'

'No, no nothing.'

Ava waits for a moment to see if he will say anything else but his eyes return to his painting. She leaves him to his work and goes downstairs to clean the kitchen, which she does with a lot of clattering as she conducts a whole discussion with Collin in her head, ending with her telling him to go and screw himself. The trouble is that she has to be careful of confronting Collin about anything since she's becoming more and more convinced that he will take the top job and he will not hesitate to fire her or to make life so difficult for her that she simply resigns. It won't be easy but she has no doubt that Collin would find a way to get rid of her.

Pouring herself a large glass of wine, she decides to treat herself to a long bath.

The only bath is in the girls' bathroom, and she crosses her fingers that both of them are asleep and stay that way so she can have some time. Once the bath is full and she's added some of her own lavender-scented oil, she slides in, placing her phone carefully on the side and taking a deep breath as the warm water relaxes her muscles. Sipping her wine, she tries to clear her head of everything.

Approaching Collin in anger would be a bad move. She needs a proper plan and she hopes that she can discuss it with Grace tomorrow morning. Why does Collin care about Grace at all? They've barely had anything to do with each other.

With her wine finished, she is drifting into a light doze when her phone pings with a text.

Hi Ava, so sorry to bother you but I received the strangest message from the number below. Do you know who this might be and why they would have sent such a message? Grace

Ava looks at the message first, her body tensing in the warm water.

You need to watch your back. You and Ava Green won't be in this company for much longer.

Ava stares at the number Grace has sent, trying to recognise it, but when she can't, she opens her contacts and starts scrolling through, trying to keep the number in mind.

When she finds a matching number, she can't believe it.

Melody.

She texts the answer back to Grace.

This is completely unacceptable. I'll speak to her tomorrow. I have no idea what the hell she is thinking.

Grace's reply comes quickly.

No, she's obviously angry about you telling her to stay off her phone. I've also told her so maybe she feels like I've over-stepped. I think we should leave it and see if she says anything else.

Ava thinks for a few minutes. It's probably a better idea than confronting Melody. Especially since Collin has already told her to back off. A growing unease inside her tells her that things in her company are changing and that everything she has worked for could easily slip away from her.

Okay, we'll leave it, but we need to keep an eye on her.

I completely agree. See you in the morning.

Ava gets out of the bath, her neck muscles already tensing and sending a throbbing pain into her head. When she hired Grace, she felt like she was finally getting back control of her work life, but something is obviously going on and she's been so snowed under with work and everything else that she's missed the signs.

Is Collin setting me up to be fired? Has he enlisted Melody's help? Are they having an affair? Is Finn somehow involved because he doesn't want me in the top job? Is Finn having an affair with Sami's mother?

Ava dries her body quickly and puts on her pyjamas. She's being paranoid. Melody is just lashing out at Grace because she's angry and knows she can't say anything to Ava. But Collin is a problem. He wants the top job, and even though he seems very confident he will get it, maybe that's all an act. He speaks to Patricia a lot and perhaps she has said something to him that has made him think that Ava is still in with a chance for the role of CEO of Australia.

In bed Ava shuts her eyes and tries to will her body to sleep but she is wired, churning with anxiety over her work life and her home life. She wishes she had more of a relationship with Patricia, that she and the CEO did more than just discuss work. She and Collin seem to enjoy having dinner together, but Ava rarely sees her outside of work hours.

Needing to talk to someone, even if it will anger him to be disturbed again, she gets out of bed and makes her way upstairs.

She's reaching for the door handle of Finn's studio when she hears him say, 'Please.' He sounds desperate.

Ava steps right up to the door and puts her ear on the wood, closing her eyes and straining to hear what Finn is saying. *Who is he talking to at this time of night?*

'You can't do this. You promised you wouldn't,' he says. 'Please just leave it now. I have children.' He sounds like he's begging someone to not do something. *Who is he talking to? Sami's mum? Is she threatening to tell me about their affair?* 'No, please, please don't call me again,' he says forcefully and then there is silence so the conversation must be over.

Ava steps away from the door, her stomach bubbling with horror and disbelief. He is having an affair. He *had* an affair? Is it actually possible? Is it over? He sounded angry but also desperate. She doesn't want to believe it and yet it seems to make sense. She could be wrong. She wants to be wrong but then who was he talking to at this time of night?

Her husband has been speaking to Collin, her work rival, and now she thinks he may be cheating on her too. Why else would he mention the girls when appealing to someone?

The girls. What will this do to their lives if it's true? Turning quickly, she stumbles down the stairs to their bedroom, nearly tripping but righting herself in time.

She climbs into bed and switches off the light, lying in the dark with tears in her eyes, knowing that, once again, she will not sleep.

TWENTY-EIGHT

GRACE

On the train ride home, I pull myself together and start formulating a plan. It's late and I will need to get an Uber from the station back to Ava's house, but I don't mind the extra time. When I'm at the station nearest to her house, what I need to do becomes clear.

Once I've sent the message to Ava and she has responded, I feel better, but not much. I keep trying to put things into perspective, to remind myself that little Melody will be sorry she ever tried to threaten me. Will she show the news article to Ava and Collin? Probably. That means I need to get rid of her before she does.

The text message was the first step. I hope Ava won't ask to see the original message, because it doesn't exist but I'm sure it will not occur to her to ask me because she trusts me. When I rewrote Ava's email to Melody, it was just to give her a good scare into behaving in a more appropriate manner in the office, but now I'm glad I had the foresight to send it. It will make getting her fired easier. I only need one more thing and I can get Ava to make the decision. Collin will be a problem. He's obviously attracted to her and will fight for her. I can always deny the article is about me. I can make her out to be ridiculous. *You're basing this on me having the same first name as that woman?* I imagine saying in front of Collin and Ava.

The article has one picture of me, and when I get home, I look at my face in the mirror next to the picture, searching for something that will immediately identify the two women as being the same person.

It's the eyes, of course, the same almond-shaped green eyes. Everything else is different.

The woman in the picture has blonde hair that hangs to her shoulders. She is at least eight kilos heavier than I am now. She is wearing a designer wraparound dress in a vibrant red to match her red lips. Her face is heavily made up, false eyelashes complemented by grey eyeshadow. She sits behind a wooden desk, a computer in front of her and a smug smile on her face. That woman had it all. That picture was recycled from an earlier article about me, from two years before.

I remember that interview. It had been for an article on changes in the beauty industry with a focus on companies leading the way. I was so nervous but incredibly excited.

'You'll be perfect,' Robert told me as he lay on the bed in our beautiful bedroom, a glass of wine in his hand. I knew the journalist would be bringing a photographer with him and I was trying to decide what to wear.

'You look beautiful in all of them,' my husband told me, 'but perhaps go for the red.'

There are moments in your life when you somehow just know that you need to try and remember them because they are rare and perfect. As my husband watched me change outfits, I marvelled at everything I had achieved and at the idea that my achievements would be in print forever. I knew that I would send my parents a copy of the article, and in my giddiness, I wondered if they would call and tell me they were proud of me. But they never did and it was silly of me to think they would.

I remember the journalist who came to interview me for the women's business magazine. He was young, just starting out in his career, and seemed like a boy to me as he stumbled over questions and expressed admiration for my company. He was the same age I had been when I'd opened my first waxing salon with nothing more than a few thousand dollars I had painstakingly saved up from working seven days a week for years. I had only wanted to have something for myself, and I had never imagined that one salon would lead to two and that the company would continue growing.

He was sweet and the photographer was a lovely woman who made sure I liked the photograph she took. I floated through the day, happily answering his questions and introducing him to my staff, who all seemed as proud of the company as I was.

Afterwards I took Tamara and Liza to lunch at an upmarket Italian restaurant, where we celebrated me and my success. It was a wonderful afternoon and I even had pizza delivered to the office for my whole team of twenty.

'To Australia's newest business tycoon,' Liza toasted me. 'You've only just begun.' And it felt like I had, like anything was possible.

Two short years later and my life was in chaos.

They did not take a new photograph for the article about my downfall, even though they could have gotten one of me in court with my shoulders bowed and my hair stringy and littered with grey. Instead, they used the old photograph so I looked like I didn't care, like I had nothing in the world to worry about, like I wasn't bothered by the crime I was supposed to have committed.

I shudder as I think about Ava reading the words in the article. She may have read them years ago and just dismissed them as she moved on to the next news story.

She will fire me when she finds out. I will be thwarted,

brought down, made to suffer by a young woman in her twenties.

Once in the apartment, I pace back and forth, too angry to make myself a cup of tea or to even sit down.

My whole life was brought down by a woman just like Melody once. I am not about to allow it to happen again.

Ideas churn through my head as I shower and get ready for bed. I had not anticipated this at all and I am angry with myself. I should have planned for what I would do if someone somehow recognised me and threatened to expose me.

I get into bed and try to sleep but eventually, just after 1 a.m., I give up and get out of bed, finding the bottle of vodka, opening it and inhaling the medicinal smell.

I close the lid and hold the bottle in my lap, turning it around and around, my fingers tracing the raised silver lettering on the label.

Words from the article circle in my head.

Grace Morton was the perfect example of an Aussie battler made good. Her parents threw her out of home when she was sixteen. 'I made a lot of bad decisions and put myself in an untenable position. It hurt at the time but I understand my parents felt they had no choice. They needed me to see the error of my ways,' Grace is quoted as saying in an article about her in Business Women Australia *magazine.*

I remember telling the eager young reporter that, and also that I had made peace with my parents. A lie, of course.

I tried to re-establish a connection with them. I went back again and again, despite vowing not to each time, because I wanted their approval, was desperate for their approval and their love.

Opening the article on my phone again, I stare down at the

words, reading what I have reread many times, giving the words the power to hurt me, to destroy me.

Grace Morton began her career as an assistant to a beautician, putting herself through TAFE and university to learn the tricks of the trade. At twenty-five she opened her own salon dedicated exclusively to waxing. Wax to the Max was the first of its kind in Australia, and Grace led the way in the opening of salons dedicated exclusively to one aspect of beauty.

By the time she was forty, her company comprised fifty salons across the country. She was living the high life with her greenspace architect husband Robert and daughter Cordelia.

A mansion overlooking the harbour, a fleet of cars and designer clothes were all part of her world until a problem with alcohol led to erratic behaviour at work.

'She changed,' an employee who did not want to be named has said. 'She used to be an inspiration to everyone but she began turning up drunk and sleeping in the office. She didn't seem to want to deal with any of the problems in the business.'

'She stepped away from the day-to-day running, leaving everything to Liza, the general manager,' another employee said. 'It was too much work for one person and the company suffered.'

'She accused her assistant of cheating with her husband,' a third employee told this reporter. 'One day she turned up drunk at the office and stood in reception screaming at her former assistant, calling her a "whore who ruined my life". Liza had to come out and drag her away.'

Friends and colleagues have all stated that they encouraged Ms Morton to get help for her alcohol abuse but she claimed that she did not have a problem.

A final devastating blow came with the death of her husband, Robert, in a house fire.

Tamara Reed, former assistant to Grace Morton, testified at her trial that Ms Morton had made threats against her husband.

'She told me that she would never let him go. She said she would never give him a penny of her money and that she would rather burn her house down than sell it and give him half,' Ms Reed said in court.

I never said any of that. Not a single word of it. But I couldn't deny it because I wasn't entirely sure. I had been intoxicated a lot in the last few months before the fire. I confronted Tamara on reception one morning when I dragged myself into the office and she was standing there, a smug smile on her face. I remember calling her a 'whore', and I remember her bursting into tears as Liza dragged me into my office and everyone else rushed to comfort Tamara.

I understand now, with the benefit of hindsight, that my reaction to Robert's cheating was extreme. Another woman, perhaps a woman who wasn't so terrified of losing everything she had in her life, would have asked for an amicable divorce, would have accepted the loss of half her company. But I wasn't that woman. I know there were moments in the months leading up to the fire that I understood I needed help.

But I had started with nothing and it seemed to me that Robert was going to take everything I had worked for and I would be left with nothing. I would be sixteen again, walking the streets with one suitcase, seeking shelter as I mourned the loss of my first love. I was terrified of having to go through that again.

The more I let alcohol take over, the worse I got. I know that. I know what I did and I have paid for my mistakes. I've lost everything.

It feels like I'm in the same place right at this moment. I have just started over and I'm going to lose it all. I pick up my phone and find a photo of my daughter, a wide smile on her beautiful face. It was taken when she turned sixteen and had some friends over for dinner. She looks so happy.

I knew that it was possible that my marriage would not survive Robert's cheating, especially because he wouldn't admit to it. I knew it was possible I would lose him but I never thought I would lose Cordelia as well.

Everything that has been taken from me crowds into my head as the hour grows later, and I make a vow to myself: I will not lose one more thing. And I will make sure that Ava doesn't lose anything either – except maybe a useless husband.

Melody has no idea who she is dealing with, no idea at all. And finally, I am able to return the bottle of vodka to the freezer and drift off to sleep.

TWENTY-NINE

AVA

'I think I should just confront Melody,' Ava tells Grace when they are driving to work on Thursday morning.

'No,' says Grace, 'she'll just deny it and then you'll look paranoid. I'm sure she's deleted the text.'

'But you haven't,' says Ava.

'I did, I'm afraid. I was reading it over and over and then I just couldn't stand seeing it anymore so I deleted it. It was impulsive and silly, but it's a nasty message and I didn't want it on my phone.'

Ava frowns, unsure what to say to this. Not having the message as proof makes it impossible to confront Melody. The young woman will obviously deny it.

This morning, she was almost ashamed of how grateful she was when Grace appeared at the kitchen door, ready to lend a hand. Once again, Finn was nowhere to be seen. He seems to be getting worse, or perhaps he knows Ava can rely on Grace to be there in the morning for the next couple of days so he doesn't have to be.

The person Finn was pleading with last night on the phone is on her mind. Is he cheating on her or is it something else entirely? And how will she find a way to ask him what exactly is going on? And why was he pleading with them about something?

And how will she confront Collin today about speaking to Finn? The urge to turn the car around and drive to a beach somewhere, to simply take a day away from everything, is almost overwhelming but of course she won't do that. She would never do something like that.

'I think Melody obviously dislikes you,' says Grace. 'She seems to have a strange relationship with Collin and that's why she felt she could send that message to me. I know she hates me because I keep trying to get her to be a bit more professional.'

'It's not that I haven't noticed it,' says Ava. 'It's just that...' She considers saying something about Collin, asking Grace for her perspective, but immediately dismisses the idea. She needs to really think this through so it doesn't blow back on her.

'You have so much on your plate already,' Grace finishes for her, and Ava is grateful to the woman for filling in the gap.

'Yes,' agrees Ava as they enter the building parking lot. She parks and Grace goes up first as usual.

When Ava walks into the office, Melody is behind her desk and Ava nods at the receptionist without greeting her. Melody frowns but Ava doesn't care. The message to Grace last night was unnecessary and also worrying.

Grace is in her office, scrolling through her desktop computer.

'Oh,' says Ava, a little taken aback, 'did you need something?'

'No,' says Grace, standing up, her cheeks flushing slightly. 'I was just checking up on the feedback for the last seminar run by Julian – for some reason it hasn't come through to my computer.'

'Oh, right,' says Ava, dropping her bag on the sofa and then coming around her desk to stand next to Grace, where she can see her computer is open to the file she said she was looking for.

'He's doing very well considering he's only just begun working for you, isn't he?' says Grace.

'He is,' agrees Ava.

'Sorry, let me get you a coffee,' she says, and Ava nods as Grace leaves the room. She sits down in front of her computer and closes the file and then she checks her emails, making sure to note those that she needs to deal with today.

But then instead of starting work, she finds herself back on Anita's Instagram page. Today she has put up not one but two posts. One says, *Finding love after divorce is hard but not impossible,* and the second one says, *Sometimes you have to fight fire with fire.* Ava feels her heart sink and then she's just irritated at herself for trying to figure out what the woman is saying, what she means. Collin is who she should be thinking about.

'Ava,' she hears and she looks up. Grace is standing at the doorway with Finn.

'Finn,' she says, quickly shutting down Anita's Instagram page and standing up. 'What are you doing here?'

'I thought I would drop in, just say hello. I had a meeting with Hector. I wanted to show him pictures of my latest piece.'

'Oh,' says Ava, 'do you want to go get a coffee?' It's a casual question but she is feeling anything but casual. Finn has never randomly turned up at her office and she can't help the anxious flutter of her heart.

'Sounds good,' he says with a smile, and Ava grabs her bag.

'We won't be long,' she tells Grace, who nods.

Ava leaves the office with Finn. On the way out they pass reception, where Melody is dutifully sitting. 'Finn, hi,' she says, her voice slightly squeaky.

'Hello,' says Finn politely, his gaze on the grey blouse Melody is wearing where more cleavage than necessary is on display.

'Let's go to the coffee shop downstairs,' says Ava. 'Did Hector like the piece?'

'He did,' says Finn, but instead of sounding happy, he sounds upset.

'What's wrong?' she asks.

'Nothing,' says Finn distractedly as they step out of the elevator and the building. It's hot but there is a breeze with a cool touch to it.

'Autumn's coming,' says Ava.

'Yeah,' agrees Finn.

In the coffee shop, once they are both sitting with their coffees in front of them, Finn says, 'Ava, we need to talk about something.'

'What?' she asks, her stomach immediately twisting with apprehension.

'I think I've screwed up,' he says, dropping his gaze to the table.

'Okay,' she says, guarded as she tries to steel herself for what she's going to hear. The portrait of Anita looms large in her mind, the cryptic post on Instagram about finding love again. *Is this really happening?*

Finn looks up and away from her and just stares at the door. Ava follows his gaze and sees Melody standing at the counter, ordering coffee. Ava hopes the young woman will not see them but just as she finishes this thought, Melody turns her head and smiles.

'Fancy seeing you here,' she says, coming over to their table.

'Yes,' says Ava although it's hardly a coincidence. The whole staff like this coffee shop.

'How are things, Finn?' she asks and he nods.

'Really good,' he says and then his phone buzzes. He takes it out of his pocket and looks at the screen. 'It's Hector,' he says, 'he told me he would get back to me with some possible dates for a show.' He stands as he answers the phone. 'Hang on, mate,' he says and then he looks at Ava. 'Look, I should go. I'll see you at home.'

'But, Finn...' she starts to say, but he's already walking away.

'I'll walk with you back to the office,' says Melody and Ava sighs.

What did Finn want to say? How bad is it? What has he done? Is he going to confess to an affair – and why come to my office to do it? How will we stay together if he does? If he is going to confess, is it because the affair is over? Or is he going to tell me that he's in love with Anita and wants a divorce?

'Melody,' calls the barista and Melody moves away from the table to collect her coffee.

Finn is out the door and gone before Ava even picks up her bag. She goes to the counter, where Melody is adding sugar to her coffee. 'I'm nearly ready,' she says but Ava has no desire to ride up in the lift with her.

'I need to make a call,' says Ava and she darts out of the café, hoping to catch Finn, but he's gone. She calls him once, twice, three times but he doesn't answer his phone. The conversation will have to wait until tonight.

Dread settles over Ava. *Who will I be, after tonight? What will have happened to my marriage?*

As she walks back to the office, trying Finn again and again, she curses Melody for coming into the café at the wrong time.

What was Finn going to say? And do I really want to hear it?

THIRTY

Dear baby girl,

At sixteen, I was completely alone. I wonder now if I would have achieved everything I did if not for that terrible start to life. I don't think so. It turned me into a determined fighter, into someone who was willing to do whatever it took to get the money, the security, the love I needed.

I know that the first night I was completely homeless, I missed my grandmother with an ache that took over my whole body.

I imagined her in her kitchen, mixing up some cake batter, a smile on her face, and in my mind I asked her what to do.

'Get help, there must be help,' she said. 'People are mostly kind and you will find someone to help you.' That was the lens through which she saw life and people were mostly kind to her. But I never had that ability. I expected to be treated badly, to be shunned and disliked.

I had no idea where to find help, so I walked away from Luka's house until I came to a park. I was cold, tired, hungry and deeply in despair. I sat on a bench with my suitcase and waited for the sun to drop below the horizon. There was a children's playground and I could see that there was a little cubby house. Once it was dark, I thought I would go in there. At least I would be protected if it rained. There was nothing I could do but get through the night.

And that's what I did. I waited for it to get dark and then I crept into the cubby house, opened my suitcase and pulled on as many clothes as I could, and then I curled up into a ball. It was still early but I was exhausted and I fell asleep, even as I shivered.

I was woken by a hand on my shoulder, and I went from fast asleep to on my haunches with my back pushed against the wall of the cubby house, terror in my veins as I looked at someone who was shining a torch at me.

'You can't sleep here,' said a man's voice.

Every terrifying scenario I had ever read about, been told about, came to me in a moment and I was certain I would die.

'Okay, I'll go,' I said quickly, praying that he would turn and leave.

'Why are you here?' he asked, moving the beam to the side so I could see him. It was a policeman in uniform, a young man with ears that stuck out and a nearly shaved head. 'Someone from across the road saw you sitting here in the dark and called us. Why are you here?' he repeated.

'I have nowhere else to go,' I said, bursting into tears.

'Your parents?' he asked.

'Kicked me out. They don't want me back. I can't go back. They hate me,' I sobbed.

'How old are you?'

'Sixteen,' I answered him.

'Well, they can't kick you out. And if they do, they have to make sure that you have a place to stay and money for everything you need.'

'They hate me,' I said.

'Come on,' he sighed. 'I'll find you somewhere for tonight.'

I didn't know if I could trust him but I had no choice. I climbed out of the cubby house, dragging my suitcase with me.

He took me back to the police station, where he gave me a hot chocolate, thin and tasteless but warm at least. 'I'm Jim,' he told me. 'Are you sure you can't go back to your parents?'

I nodded. 'Please don't make me. They never want to see me again.'

An hour after we arrived at the police station, he told me he had found a spot for me for the night in a group home.

In my mind, group home meant 'prison'. I thought he would take me to a place with bars on the windows and overcrowded rooms filled with angry, violent teenagers. I was utterly terrified as he drove me over there but I had no choice.

The 'mostly kind' people that my grandmother had talked about were actually running the group home. It was a large, ramshackle house with creaky floorboards and chipped kitchen cabinets, but it was run by Delia and her partner, Beverly, and they were the sort of people you always hope to meet. They emanated kindness, immediately giving me a bowl of hot soup and a sandwich before showing me to a room where one other girl was sleeping. The single bed had a thin mattress that dipped in the middle but it was covered in soft old sheets and warm blankets. I was so grateful to be out of the cold, I couldn't help my tears. 'It will be fine,' said Delia, patting me on the back as I cried. She had long grey hair and was wearing Christmas-themed pyjamas despite it being the middle of the year.

At some point someone must have contacted my parents. I remember a number of conversations with a social worker and then I know that my parents agreed to pay for me to remain in the group home. They really, really did not want me back. I hated them for rejecting me so thoroughly but I wasn't the only one in *that position. All the girls at the home hated their parents for one reason or another. We bonded over our enmity.*

Once I started making real money, I supported Beverly and Delia with large donations to their house until they both retired and moved away to live in Queensland.

I spent two years with them, and even though it was hard with the constant movement of teenage girls in and out, some of them violent, I never forgot their acceptance and warmth.

I dropped out of school at the end of year ten, which was acceptable in those days. I had no idea what I wanted to do with my life but the need to work and earn money led to me getting a job as an assistant in a slightly grimy salon run by a woman named Maria, who favoured thick make-up and false eyelashes and called everyone 'darling'.

Once I had been working there for a few months, she suggested I take some courses at TAFE. 'You're clever, darling,' she told me. 'Maybe one day you could own your own salon.'

Such a thing seemed impossible to me but it was an idea that got me out of bed every day. It got me to university to study business as well. All I wanted was to own one salon, just one. I never expected to do what I managed to do.

I never expected the life I managed to build. And you need to understand, baby girl, that I never expected to hurt people the way I have hurt them. I never expected that.

THIRTY-ONE

GRACE

Ava returns from getting coffee with her husband looking flustered and anxious. She has only been gone ten minutes so I can tell it must not have gone very well.

I want to ask her what happened but there is no chance with the phone ringing constantly and Ava taking Zoom meetings all afternoon on her computer.

At the end of the day, I tell her that I am going to go for a walk and take the train home. I need to be alone. Melody and I have completely ignored each other. Something that suits me.

'I'll see you in the morning,' Ava says with a sharp nod of her head, and I get the feeling that she needs some time alone as well.

I don't wish to see Melody on my way out but as I'm gathering my things, I see her going into Collin's office and I move towards the elevator.

It's after hours so it doesn't matter if the reception desk is left unattended, but as I pass, a low vibration sound alerts me to Melody's phone on the desk. It's surprising she has left it since it's barely ever out of her hand. She obviously didn't mean to be away for more than a minute but I suppose it's the curse of her generation to be so easily distracted. Collin is nice-looking and charming. I wonder briefly what's really going on in his office as I stare down at her phone. Taking a chance, I swipe the screen and I'm shocked when it opens and I find myself looking at a picture of a taut male stomach, a small tattoo of an eagle on one side. I look away quickly, hurrying over to the elevator just as I hear Collin's office door open.

Once again, I traipse through the city until I am exhausted and then I grab a sandwich from a 7-Eleven, swallowing the slightly stale bread quickly as I chase it with a bottle of water.

Despite not wanting to, I can't help but return to the article, reading the last few paragraphs more than once, and remembering every detail.

> In a final fatal mistake, Ms Morton came home drunk one night and, according to her, 'lit some candles to soothe my soul'.
>
> She then fell asleep and only woke when the house was filled with smoke.
>
> Neighbours called the fire department after seeing flames take hold of the house and then finding Ms Morton, intoxicated and barefoot, watching the house burn from the garden. Her daughter, Cordelia, was fortunately staying with friends.

I knew she was staying with friends. I paid for a night in a hotel for her and three best friends to celebrate the end of their final year of school. The part about the candles was a lie as well.

The night, the terrible night I set fire to not just my house but my whole life, comes back to me as I make my way to the station, remembering the smell of smoke, seeing the bright yellow-orange of the flames as they leapt from the roof.

My heart flutters in my chest, the imagined sound of wood splintering and glass shattering assaulting me on the train ride home.

I feel like I will never get there, never be away from the

gazes of others, but finally I am locked in the small garage apartment at Ava's house, where I grab the bottle of vodka from the
freezer, the icy glass immediately sticking to my hand. I clutch it
tightly, feeling the raised lettering imprint itself on my palm.

Cordelia explained at my trial that the night in the hotel
had been planned for weeks as a gift for finishing exams. She
described me as a good mother despite my addiction, even
though I knew she was furious with me because she wouldn't
even look in my direction, so perhaps there is still a tiny shred of
love in her heart for me. It's why I keep trying, why I will never
give up on her.

She's in Melbourne with a man who is like her father. I
know he's like her father. Girls either gravitate to the opposite of
their fathers or to the replicas of their fathers. Robert was opposite to my father in every way. He loved food and drink and
laughing and loving. He was loud and charismatic and joyful.
He was a cheater and a liar and an adulterer and I know, even
just through some light stalking, that Cordelia is with the same
kind of man.

Perhaps I am just suspicious of all men but perhaps I simply
know what to look for.

I can see, when I watch Ava and her family, that what
happened to me could so easily happen to her. I know it's
happening, even if she only just suspects it.

Before I can talk myself out of it, I open my phone and send
a text.

You and I need to talk. I know what's going on.

I add a time and where I am, just in case there's any confusion, and then I grab my bottle of vodka, letting the glass chill
my hands as I sit down to wait.

When there is a soft knock at the door, I know I have done
the right thing. I take a deep breath and draw on my strength,

all the strength I had to find as an unloved child, as a business-woman with no training, as a woman who had to recover after a terrible accident. I gather it together so I can do what must be done.

In the morning after very little sleep, I forgo breakfast and hurry to the kitchen to help Ava.

She is pale and snappy, telling Hazel to 'hurry up' and Chloe to 'stop it'.

'Can I help?' I ask tentatively.

'Finn didn't come home,' she whispers to me.

'Oh,' I say. I have no idea how else to react, so I say, 'Let me finish up with the girls.'

She nods her head and leaves the kitchen, and I wonder if she is calling the police and I assume that she will not be going into work today.

But when she comes back, she is dressed for work, her laptop case in her hand. 'Ready to go?' she asks and I nod. I feel a strange sort of pride for her. She is not doing what I did. When my life seemed to be falling apart, I fell apart with it, but Ava is carrying on. The CEO job is on the line.

We get the girls into the car and dropped at school. As we pull away from Chloe's preschool, Ava calls her mother. 'I need you to pick up the girls after school,' she says, her tone flat.

'Oh, why, where's Finn? I would be happy to, of course, absolutely,' her mother says over the phone.

'Finn has to work,' she says. 'Just take them home, you know what to do. I won't be late but you can order pizza for them as a treat.'

'I'm happy to cook, sweetheart. Should I—' her mother replies, but Ava doesn't wait to hear the question, just ends the call. She is jittery and tense.

'What do you think has happened?' I ask her.

'Something bad,' says Ava, shaking her head. 'I think something bad has happened.'

THIRTY-TWO

AVA

Grace is quiet, waiting for Ava to speak to her as Ava questions whether or not she should say anything at all.

She had been grateful for the drive home alone last night because she had imagined that she would be able to speak to Finn after his strange behaviour at the coffee shop. Sometimes it was easier to talk on the phone.

But as she drove, she called his phone and it simply rang until it went to his voicemail.

'Call me, Finn,' she said the first time.

'We need to talk,' she said the second time.

'This is silly, just call me. You can't just turn up at my office and say something like that and then not answer my calls.'

When she got home, Finn was not there. Instead, his mother, Doreen, was there.

'Doreen?' Ava said, shocked to see her mother-in-law.

'Ava, how are you? The girls and I have had a lovely afternoon and I've given them my special chicken nuggets for dinner. I brought everything with me when Finn asked me to take over for a few hours.'

'Why?'

'What do you mean, why? He said something about meeting Hector. Surely, he told you? He's nearly ready for a show, a show that's very important to him. I know he needs your support, Ava.'

Ava did not want to let Doreen know that Finn was lying, that he was definitely not with Hector because she had already called Hector to check.

Instead, she just thanked her. 'Oh yes, of course. It slipped my mind,' she said. 'Thank you so much for coming. Finn and I both appreciate it.'

'Anytime. Come and kiss Grandma goodbye,' she called to the girls, collecting her things from the kitchen, including a mixing bowl, and Ava understood the silent reproach – the idea that Ava might not have a mixing bowl because she was a working mother.

Chloe and Hazel came in from the living room to dutifully kiss their grandmother and then Ava did bath and bed time, counting down the minutes until she could be alone so she could call Finn again. She convinced herself that perhaps he had been waiting until he knew the girls were asleep so they could have a proper conversation, but then why not just be at home?

Finally, the girls were asleep and Ava poured herself a large glass of wine and called Finn again. This time he answered and she felt relief flow through her body. At least he was okay but then she was angry at everything he had put her through with his strange confession followed by his silence.

'What is going on?' she demanded.

'Ava, look,' he said, 'I need... some time. I can't explain anything right now but I just need some time.'

And he hung up the phone.

Ava called back but he didn't answer. She called ten times before giving up. And then she went upstairs to his loft, to see if there was anything there that would give her a clue as to what was going on with her husband.

But there was nothing there, just the chemical smell of paint and the portrait of Anita drying on the easel.

'Maybe I can help,' says Grace, dragging Ava away from her thoughts.

'Finn came to the office yesterday, as you know. We went for a quick coffee and he told me that he'd screwed up, but before he could explain what he meant by that, Melody came into the coffee shop and came up to us and then he just left. Last night he told me he needed some time and I just... I have no idea what to think. No idea at all.' She shakes her head.

'Strange,' murmurs Grace.

'Yes, and it feels like everything is falling apart. Patricia is going to make her announcement for CEO at the end of next week and I should only be concentrating on that. It feels like my whole life is in chaos and I don't know what to do about it.' Ava is embarrassed to find her eyes hot with tears.

Grace reaches across and pats Ava on the arm, just a light comforting pat. 'Until you know what he's done, there is little you can do. The girls are safely at school and your mother will take care of them this afternoon. Finn loves you. He loves the girls. He will contact you when he can explain.'

'Do you think so?' asks Ava as she pulls into the parking garage. 'I mean, what could he have done? Do you think he's having an affair with Sami's mum? Is he cheating and now he's got to decide between the two of us? It's just too much to even contemplate.' The tears she has been trying to control start to fall.

'Ava, listen to me,' says Grace. 'If Finn is cheating, you will survive. It won't be easy but you will survive because you're a mother and you have to. If it's something else, you may be able to help him. The only thing I can say is that you cannot let your worries derail everything. Trust me when I tell you that you must hold on to control.' The words are said firmly and they have the effect of stopping Ava's tears as she thinks about her girls. Whatever has happened, she will need to be strong for them.

'You're right,' she says. 'I need to concentrate on my work. I need to get through today and maybe he'll be home tonight.' She nods as she speaks. 'This can all get sorted out.'

'I know it can,' says Grace, and Ava is grateful for the certainty of her tone.

Finn is just not willing to talk to her yet.

She waits in the car for five minutes while Grace goes up, taking deep breaths and calming her pounding heart. 'I can deal with this, I can deal with this,' she tells herself and then she gets out of the car and goes upstairs, ready to let work distract her until her husband decides to call.

She will be, as Grace said, able to deal with whatever happens. She's a mother and her first duty is to her daughters. At least she has Grace to help her through this. The woman is the one bright spark in this strange and awful day.

THIRTY-THREE

GRACE

I am not as sure of Ava's abilities to deal with whatever is coming as I have suggested to her. I certainly couldn't have done when I was married – didn't, in fact – but I cannot let what happened to me happen to her. I need to help her through this.

Melody is in the kitchen getting coffee or, rather, flirting with Collin, who is also getting coffee. She stares boldly at me when I walk in and I drop my gaze. Let her think she's won. I know better.

'Morning, Collin,' I say.

'Good morning, Grace.' He smiles. 'Did you have a good night?'

'I did, thank you,' I reply to the banal question. 'What about you?'

Melody snorts, holding in a laugh, and I choose to ignore her, getting the mugs and making coffee as fast as I can. I feel like every moment I spend in the same room as Melody is a moment closer to her sharing that article with everyone.

'You know,' says Collin, 'you have a really familiar face – are you really sure we haven't met before?' There is another snort-laugh from Melody.

'We haven't,' I say shortly and I leave the kitchen. The reception desk is unattended and I wonder how long Melody will leave it like that.

'You need to see this TikTok,' I hear Collin say to her.

I put the cups of coffee down on the counter and go behind the desk.

I hear Melody and Collin laughing in the kitchen and I feel myself heat up with a flush of humiliation. I'm sure they're laughing about the article. It won't be long now until Ava is told and she confronts me about my made-up résumé and different name.

My heart races but I take deep breaths in and out. It's surprising how quickly that calms the body.

I gaze down at Melody's computer, where she has many tabs open, one of them a shopping website.

'So unprofessional,' I mutter.

After a few minutes, I decide the reception desk is not my problem and I pick up my cups of coffee and go back to Ava's office.

'You were a while,' she says.

'Melody is in the kitchen with Collin. I wanted to avoid them but couldn't in the end. It seems like they both have better things to do than work.'

'I really think I should talk to her about that message,' says Ava.

'Don't worry,' I say. 'I'm sure she was just having a moment. I'm going to let it go and you should too. Shall we take a look at the agenda for the board meeting with Patricia next week?'

'Yes,' groans Ava. 'I have a feeling I'm not going to be happy at the end of that meeting.'

'Best to say everything you want to say then,' I tell her and she nods.

For the next half an hour we work on points Ava wants to

raise and progress that's been made so she can tell Patricia everything she's doing.

It turns out to be advantageous that we have covered this because an email comes in from Patricia, asking Ava to meet tomorrow afternoon, sooner than we had anticipated. *I have a flight to catch on Sunday – sorry about pulling you in on a weekend*, Patricia has written in her email

'You'll be fine,' I tell Ava and she nods but looks worried.

'I know, it's just—'

We are interrupted by Collin yelling. 'Melody, what the hell?'

Ava stands up. 'I've never heard him yell before,' she says.

'What do you think has happened?' I ask and she shrugs.

'Should we go and see?' she asks me as we hear Melody saying, 'I didn't mean to, I didn't mean to, I'm sorry.'

'I think we should,' I say and together we walk towards the front of the office where the reception desk is.

Collin is standing over Melody, jabbing his finger at her. 'Do you even understand what you have cost this company? How the hell am I supposed to fix this now?'

Melody is looking down at her lap, wringing her hands.

'Collin, stop shouting, what on earth do you think you're doing?' says Ava.

Collin stops and looks up at her. 'She sent an email meant for me to the school.'

'Okay,' says Ava, 'it can't be that big a deal. What was the email about?'

'I can't,' says Collin, turning away from Melody. 'I cannot deal with this shit today. You sort this out, Ava. I need to go and make some calls.'

Melody is now crying.

'What exactly happened?' Ava asks Melody, and the young woman looks up, her face streaked with running mascara.

'I sent an email to Collin as a joke – it was just funny and I don't know how it happened but I accidentally sent it to the school.'

'I don't understand,' says Ava, and Melody hiccups and points to her computer screen. Ava walks around to have a look and even though she hasn't asked me to, I follow her.

There's an email exchange with a very prestigious school in Melbourne. I know that there's been a problem with the school getting the necessary materials needed for the students to participate in the Barkley programme and it's something Collin was supposed to be looking after. He obviously asked Melody to get involved. It's not part of Melody's job but James has been away for two days visiting his sick mother so I presume Collin asked Melody for some help with things. He really should have asked me. I am so much more capable than she is. I also know that the school has already complained twice because the parents have had to pay extra for the course despite their exorbitant school fees.

It seems the school sent another complaining email this morning and Melody forwarded it to Collin with her own amused take on the situation, except she didn't just send it to Collin, she sent it to the school as well.

The initial email from the school is a polite but angry complaint.

To whom it may concern,

This is the third time we have had to contact you regarding materials for the programme. At this stage we are concerned that we will not have time to implement things with our year eleven group before other school activities take over. Given the expense, we feel it should be your top priority to sort this out.

Liam Smith, Principal

Melody has written:

The stuffed shirt from the too-rich-for-their-own-good school has complained again. I swear the guy doesn't understand English. He's been told we're trying to sort it out. How stupid must the prick be?

'I didn't mean for it to go to him, obviously. I didn't mean it,' wails Melody.

It's a struggle for me to keep the smile off my face. We all have our bad days. We all make decisions big and small that we may come to regret. Melody is no longer smug and in control. Instead, she is a mess.

'Perhaps you should go and wash your face,' I say quietly, and Melody hiccups a sob and then nods her head, standing up. She is grateful for the time away.

It's lucky she's gone to the bathroom because at that moment Collin comes out of his office. 'They want their money back, that's thousands of dollars, thousands,' he says, gesturing at Ava like it's her fault.

'It was a mistake, Collin,' says Ava. 'She shouldn't be writing emails like that to you anyway. How often does she do it?'

'She... Look, I like to get on with my staff in a friendly manner. I didn't think she was a complete idiot,' fumes Collin as Melody returns from the bathroom.

'I only sent it to you,' says Melody. 'Someone else must have done that... They must have... I don't know how it happened.'

'It's your computer, Melody. And I'm afraid we can't overlook such a mistake. You need to leave,' Collin says through clenched teeth.

'What do you mean?'

'I mean that your time with us is over, Melody. You no longer have a job here,' snaps Collin.

'What?' says Melody. 'You can't fire me over this. I'm telling you that I only sent it to you. The computer must have glitched or something.'

'That's ridiculous. Computers don't glitch and send emails. Now please don't make this difficult. Ava, I'm sure you agree with me that we can't let this stand. Liam will only think about keeping the programme if she is fired.' Collin looks more panicked than I have ever seen him and it's clear that what scares this man the most is the loss of revenue. He stares down at Melody, his lip curling slightly as though she disgusts him.

'I think perhaps everyone just needs to take a step back,' I say.

'God, what am I going to tell Patricia? She and Liam are friends. She'll be furious,' says Collin.

'I think it's best if you just leave for the day, Melody. I need to talk to Collin and Patricia,' says Ava firmly, and I would like to cheer for her. She is taking control of the situation rather than letting her own worries and fears take over.

Melody comes around the desk and grabs her bag, throwing some stuff into it. 'You'll be sorry. I don't deserve to be treated like this and you'll all be sorry,' she mutters, more tears appearing.

And then she makes for the stairs and is gone, leaving everyone in the office standing around in stunned silence.

'Perhaps we should all just go back to work,' I say. 'I can work from here so someone is on reception.'

'Yes,' says Collin, nodding his head, 'thank you, Grace,' and he returns to his office.

I turn to Ava. 'I can log into my email from the reception computer. I just thought it would be best for me to man things out here.'

'Okay, good, good,' says Ava and I can hear that there is a touch of relief in her voice. It's just a touch, but it's there. She doesn't need one other thing to go wrong right now. 'I'll give

Patricia a call and see what she thinks.' She walks away to her office.

I sit down at the computer and log in, allowing myself a small smile.

What a silly girl to laugh at me, to threaten me. She had no idea at all what she was up against. Now she is gone and Collin is scrabbling to make sure he doesn't lose a huge client. Patricia will be very unimpressed.

Melody should never have been sending emails like that to Collin. Especially not when she leaves her computer unattended for such long periods of time.

All sorts of things could happen.

THIRTY-FOUR

AVA

Driving home, she is exhausted by the drama of the day, by her worry over Finn, over where he is and the state of her marriage.

They will need to tread carefully with what happened at work. What did Melody mean when she said they would all be sorry? Was it just the throwaway line of an angry employee? She messed up and she knew that Ava, at least, was dissatisfied with her performance at work.

Ava and Collin had a conference call with Patricia, who said she would try and sort things out with Liam but that it was necessary to fire Melody. 'It's the look of the thing, obviously,' said Patricia. 'I just wish she'd had a warning before at least.'

Ava bit her lip, wondering if she should say something. 'I did send her something just asking her to stay off her phone,' she said.

'Great, search up that email if you can and forward it to me,' said Patricia. But when Ava went looking for the email, she couldn't find it. It had somehow been deleted from her sent folder.

'Don't worry, I'm on the case,' said Grace and Ava was happy to leave it with her.

Patricia was very angry with Collin for his overfamiliarity with a staff member, and a young female staff member at that. Ava would be lying if she didn't admit that she had really enjoyed his discomfort.

'I think I should give Melody a good reference,' Ava says to Grace, who has come home with her tonight.

'Yes,' says Grace, 'that might be a good idea. She may just find something else and want to move on from... everything that has happened. There's no need to give her any more ammunition to turn this into something it doesn't need to be.'

When she turns into her street, Ava is a little worried that she doesn't see her mother's car. It may be that she's parked around the corner. Before she can let her worries take hold of her, she reminds herself that if the girls had not been picked up from school, she would have immediately received a call.

Pulling into the garage, she is shocked to see Finn standing at the door that leads to the house.

She stops her car and gets out. 'Finn,' she says.

'I'm sorry, we have to talk right now—'

'Mum, Mum,' says Chloe, dashing into the garage and grabbing onto her legs.

'Hello, sweetheart,' says Ava, rubbing her daughter's fine blonde hair.

'Mum,' says Hazel, coming up behind her, 'Gammy picked us up from school and then we had home-made pizza and Gammy was going to give us an ice cream but then Daddy came home and said no and Gammy went home.'

Ava blinks as she processes all this information. 'Well...' she begins.

'And we both want ice cream,' says Hazel, holding Chloe's hand.

'Ice cream,' says Chloe.

'Why don't I take these two little girls to the park, give you some time to relax before dinner?' says Grace, and Ava turns to her, having forgotten she was there.

'Oh no, I couldn't ask you to do that,' says Ava.

'That sounds like a good idea,' says Finn, his eyes darting from Ava to Grace and back again.

'I'm happy to do it,' says Grace.

'Thank you, Grace,' says Finn, his tone hushed, making Ava worry even more.

'But ice cream,' protests Hazel.

'Well, I know there is ice cream at the park and I know the shop that sells it stays open late in summer so I bet if Mum says yes...' Grace doesn't finish her sentence

'Yes,' says Ava.

'I'll get them ready,' says Finn, his gaze settling on Grace for a moment. And then he turns away with both girls following him.

'Thank you,' says Ava.

Grace touches her gently on the arm. 'It will give you the time you need, and I enjoy spending time with them. You can sort this out, Ava. I know you can.'

'I'm really grateful,' says Ava and she is but her overriding emotion is fear. *What is Finn going to tell me?*

Once they are alone, Ava takes off her shoes while Finn pours them each a glass of wine.

'Okay,' says Ava when they are sitting down. 'Tell me.'

'Okay,' sighs Finn and he stretches his arms above his head as though he has a kink in his back. Ava watches his shirt ride up, exposing the small eagle tattoo on his side. He's in great shape, still in great shape, and she's overweight and angry and tired and always complaining. Can she blame him if he is cheating?

'It's about Melody,' he says.

'We fired her today,' says Ava.

'You what? Why?' asks Finn.

'She screwed up one too many times. Why are you so bothered by it?'

Finn gulps his wine, his face colouring as he pours himself another huge glass, and Ava's heart rate speeds up while she waits for him to speak.

'I never wanted to have to tell you this,' he mutters.

'Tell me what?' she asks, fear making her still, her hand wrapped tightly around her wine glass.

'Ava, you remember the last Christmas party?' His gaze roams around the room, as though he is taking it in for the first time.

'It was only a couple of months ago, Finn, so yes.'

'Melody was drunk and I volunteered to take her home.' He looks directly at her.

'I know. It made me angry because we had to get home for the babysitter.'

Finn nods his head. 'Yeah. But we each came in our own cars so I took her home and you went home.'

Ava struggles to remember that night. She never really enjoyed the Christmas parties. Making small talk with someone she had worked with all day wasn't fun, and she was always worried that Finn would say the wrong thing or that she would say the wrong thing. It was mostly a tiring experience.

The last Christmas party was no different and really the only person who seemed to be enjoying herself was Melody, who had ploughed her way through a whole bottle of champagne and then started on cocktails. Every Christmas party reminded Ava of the first one she'd attended for Barkley, when she'd made the terrible mistake of a tryst with Collin, so she was glad to see Collin's wife clinging on to him all night. There was more than one young female employee he always had a special smile for.

When Melody came to say goodbye, Ava and Finn were standing together.

'How are you getting home?' Ava asked her.

'Catching the tr... train,' giggled Melody as though that was funny.

'You shouldn't do that alone,' said Finn, 'you've had a lot to drink and people are weird this time of year.'

'Maybe I'll make a new friend,' slurred Melody.

'No, I have my car and I've only had a couple of drinks. I'll drive you home,' Finn insisted.

Ava pulled him to the side and told him to just let the young woman go home alone. They could call her a cab.

'And if something happens to her?' he asked, and she felt guilty and responsible for her employee.

Finn puts his wine glass on the coffee table.

'Yes, you drove her home, but why is that relevant?' she asks him as she stares at her husband, who is shifting on the sofa as though the cushions have suddenly become uncomfortable.

He looks at her and then his gaze darts away again. 'Well, she... she and I...' Finn can't say the words but Ava looks at his pale face as he bites his lip and she doesn't need to hear them.

'Oh God, Finn. Oh God, you have to be... How could you, how could you?' she says, shaking her head. She touches her chest where she can feel a pain. 'You slept with Melody... with Melody?' She cannot believe such a thing is possible. They barely know each other.

'I don't understand,' she says. He isn't denying it.

Finn leans forward, drops his head into his hands as though he cannot bear to look at her. 'It was just, like, a one-time thing and I don't even know... She came on to me and in the moment...'

'You just had sex? In the moment you just had sex with my receptionist? This is insane.'

'I know,' says Finn, looking up at her. 'I know, okay, I know and I've regretted it every day since then and I've wanted to tell you but she... she's not willing to just let it go. She keeps contacting me and that's why I changed the lock pattern on my phone. She wants to meet me again. She wants to keep seeing me and she keeps threatening to tell you.'

'And have you seen her again? Have you slept with her again?' Ava is squeezing her wine glass so tightly, she worries she might shatter it, so she puts it down carefully on the coffee table, sitting on her hands so Finn can't see they are shaking.

'No, no,' says Finn, shaking his head. 'I wouldn't do that to you.'

'*Again*, you wouldn't do that to me again,' spits Ava.

'Listen,' Finn says, raising his voice. 'I don't want to ever see her again. It was a mistake and I know you're going to have to find a way to forgive me. You have to, you have to, Ava. I can't live without you, without my girls. I've screwed up, like really screwed up, but I don't want my one terrible mistake to end our marriage. I love you and our family. I can't be without my girls. Without you.'

'Without my money, you mean,' hisses Ava and she is gratified when he flinches.

'You know that's not true.'

'Have you done this before? How many other women have you *mistakenly* slept with?' asks Ava.

'No one. I've never done it before and I will never do it again. You can't know how this has affected me. I haven't been able to—'

'Spare me how it's affected you, Finn,' says Ava, raising her hand. 'What about Sami's mum? What about beautiful Anita who you just *had* to paint?'

'Anita?' asks Finn, genuine confusion on his face. 'Anita is just a friend. She's dating some doctor and fighting with her ex over custody. She's just a friend. I would never do that with someone from Hazel's school. What kind of a person do you think I am?'

'Someone who slept with my receptionist,' says Ava tightly.

Finn sighs, long and loud. 'Ava, I am beyond sorry about what I did. But I think we need to concentrate on now. Melody has been sending me texts, asking to see me, and I have kept refusing. Now she's sent me this.' Finn unlocks his phone and gives it to Ava. 'I shouldn't have come to the office. I didn't think about what would happen if she actually saw me again. It must have made her angrier than ever and just... look.'

How dare you treat me like I'm nothing? I will not be ignored, Finn. Wait till you and that bitch of a wife see what's coming. You're both going to lose everything.

Fear ripples through Ava's body as she hands the phone back to Finn. Melody will be even angrier now and Ava wasn't even the one to fire her but she can see that now, because of Finn's stupidity, she will be the one to suffer for Melody losing her job.

'I wasn't going to tell you. I was just going to meet her and try to talk to her but then I...'

'Then you what?'

'Then I... thought about it and I knew it was the wrong thing to do. I need to protect my family.'

Ava stands and starts pacing the living room, a thousand scenarios running in her mind.

Finally, she stops. 'You need to send her a nice text, asking her to leave us alone. If anything weird happens, like if we have to get a restraining order, at least it will be on your phone.'

'What's a nice text, Ava?' asks Finn, leaning back against the sofa, his face pale. 'I've sent her a whole lot of them and she hasn't taken the hint, she hasn't stopped.'

'Give me the phone,' instructs Ava and Finn doesn't hesitate, handing it over.

Ava sits down in a grey fabric armchair, briefly remembering buying the chair with Finn one Sunday when she was pregnant with Hazel. They had found it at a charity store and both loved the woven grey fabric and the whitewashed timber arms.

She takes a deep breath and opens the messages between Finn and Melody, bile rising in her throat.

Scrolling all the way back to the beginning of the conversation, she starts with the first text Melody sent him, the day after the office Christmas party last year.

That was fun, Finn, we should do it again.

Looking at the dates of the texts, Ava can see that Finn took a couple of days to reply. And when she reads what he sent, she understands why.

Hi Melody. Look, what happened was a mistake. I love my wife and I have no idea how I let things go that far. You're a lovely young woman but I'm married and I will never do that again. I feel really bad but there's no way I can ever see you again.

In the next text Melody sent, Ava can feel her anger.

You don't get to just brush me off like that, Finn. You like me, I know you do. I want to see you again. You wife doesn't have to know. It can be our secret.

Ava reads on through the rest of the messages and she is

able to see her husband becoming increasingly more desperate and Melody increasingly more threatening.

I'm sorry but I can't see you ever again. It was a mistake.

You liked it, you know you did, and it wasn't a mistake. We have real chemistry. Let's just meet and we can talk about it.

I'm sorry, but the answer is no. Please stop contacting me.

Just a meeting, one meeting.

You need to meet me, Finn.

Why are you ignoring my texts?

Please stop contacting me. I have a wife and children. My little girls are very young. Please just let this go. I'm sorry it happened.

I'm not sorry and I want to see you again. Maybe it would be better if I just told Ava everything. Then we can see each other when we want to.

Please, I am begging you, don't do that. I don't want to see you or be with you. Please leave me alone. You need to stop this.

Or what?

Just stop, please.

Just meet me and we can talk. I just want to talk and then I'll go away I promise.

No, I'm sorry but no. Please stop contacting me.

I have pictures, you know, of the two of us.

What????

Meet me and I'll show you.

OK, where?

Ava stops scrolling and looks up from the phone. Finn is leaning forward, his hands on his knees as he chews on his lower lip.

'You said you never met her again,' she says.

'I didn't. I arranged a meeting as you can see but I didn't go. I knew she was bluffing. I was just trying to get her to back down. I thought if I didn't turn up, she would be... I don't know, embarrassed and just let it go or something.'

Is that the truth or another lie? How can I trust anything you say at all? How can I ever trust you again?

Ava shakes her head and then looks down at the phone again. Her head is pounding, her neck muscles tense ropes as she squeezes Finn's phone in her hand, hating that she is here, reading this.

There's a café near my building on Axel Street. Meet me there at 1pm on Tuesday.

OK

Hi Finn, I'm here.

Where are you? I've been waiting for ten minutes and I only have forty-five minutes for lunch.

Where are you?

Where are you?

You'd better answer my texts.

I have to go back to work. You're an arsehole, Finn. You'll be sorry.

Finn gets up and comes to stand behind her, reading over her shoulder. 'That was the last message she sent until yesterday.'

'So if she only texted you after she saw you, what did you come to talk to me about?'

'I wanted... I wanted to tell you everything about my conversation with Collin. Truthfully, I hoped that Melody would just go away. I thought she would just leave me alone and move on to some other guy. But I came to talk to you about Collin because I felt bad for not telling you everything he said.'

The word **BETRAYAL** appears in Ava's mind. She can see it written in huge black letters as though the universe is shouting it at her. So many lies, so many secrets from the man who is supposed to be her partner in life. This is not what a marriage should be. She closes her eyes briefly, wishing this day had never existed and, for a moment, wishing Finn didn't exist. She shakes her head. What is she supposed to say to this?

'I know you want the top job but he told me that he doesn't think you're capable and he asked me to convince you not to take it if Patricia offers it to you,' continues Finn quickly as though he can read her thoughts and needs to tell her everything he's been hiding before she has time to react. 'He told me to think about our family. It wasn't the first time he'd called me either. He called me a few weeks ago and told me that I should know how much travel was involved with the top job. I wanted to say something to you but he did make me think about it and I... I was mostly thinking about myself and what would happen if you got the job.'

Ava nods as he says this. This is a truth she has known for a long time, a truth she keeps trying to push away. Finn is always only thinking about himself.

'I know you think I always just think of myself but I don't,' he says, coming to crouch down in front of her. He looks up at her and she can see some fear there. He is afraid of what all these secrets coming out will mean for his life.

'But even if you do have to travel, even if I do have less time to work, I don't care anymore. I know it will make you happy and you deserve to be happy... so I came to tell you because I thought you should know what he said, and we never seem to be able to talk at home... with the girls and my work.'

He seems genuine. Is he? Is he just afraid of his whole life falling apart or has he actually had a change of heart, actually understood that he has been selfish?

'So you came to tell me all this and then you saw Melody in the coffee shop,' she says, the pieces falling into place.

'Yeah, and I panicked. I thought she was going to say something so I just... left. I just left and I started walking and then later I got her text and it's such a mess, it's all such a mess.'

'And where were you last night?' *With her? Were you with her? Is this all just an elaborate lie?*

'Just... walking, thinking,' he says, rubbing his arms as he stands and moves around the living room. 'I promise you that's the absolute truth.'

Ava leans forward and picks up her glass of wine, finishing

it in a large gulp and pouring herself another. She is surrounded by people who seem to want to hurt her and she has no idea why. Collin is a real problem and there's no way she's going to let him get away with talking to her husband, but he's a problem for tomorrow. Right now, Melody is the bigger issue. Melody, who spends a lot of time talking to Collin.

Ava can feel her career, her family, her whole life teetering on a knife edge.

'You deserve better from me,' says Finn as he sits down again and finishes his own wine.

Ava nods. She does deserve better. She has always deserved better, and instead of demanding it, she has felt guilty for being a working mother, guilty for needing a real partner. She hates Finn for making her feel that way but she can't hate him enough to tell him to leave, to just go. He made a terrible mistake with Melody but ten years ago, she made a terrible mistake with Collin. She wasn't married but Collin was and she knew he was.

She picks up Finn's phone again and rereads the message Melody sent yesterday.

How dare you treat me like I'm nothing? I will not be ignored, Finn. Wait till you and that bitch of a wife see what's coming. You're both going to lose everything.

She has a flash of sympathy for Finn. He screwed up, no doubt about that, but she can imagine the anxiety he must have been feeling as this all unfolded. When she heard him on the phone, he must have been pleading with Melody to leave him alone. He had sounded desperate and sad and maybe that's exactly how he felt and how he feels now.

Without saying anything else, Ava begins to type a reply.

I'm sorry, Melody. I just couldn't meet you. I don't really believe you have pictures. You need to leave me alone or I will have to report you for harassment. I've told Ava and it's over now.

Melody's reply is instant. It's an image of Finn's torso, his small eagle tattoo on display.

Come and see me if you don't want your whole family to suffer. Imagine what everyone at work would think. What everyone at your daughters' schools would think. You've told Ava but I'm going to tell everyone, even Patricia.

'Shit,' says Ava.

'God,' says Finn, walking away from her, running his fingers through his hair and pulling in frustration. 'What now? What do I do now?'

'Just give me a minute to think,' says Ava. She gets up, taking the phone with her to the kitchen, where she fills a glass with water. She is shocked to see that the sun is setting. It's nearly 8 p.m. She and Finn haven't eaten dinner, haven't done anything except slog through the mud of the mess he made.

It's getting late and the girls should be in bed.

But where are the girls? Where is Grace? Surely they should be back from the park by now?

'Finn,' she calls and he comes into the kitchen. 'They should be back,' she says.

'I know, I was just thinking that.' Panic ripples through Ava. Melody couldn't know where the girls are. It's not possible, and she would never hurt... Ava shakes her head. They're safe with Grace.

Are they?

'We need to go and find them,' she says. 'We need to go now.'

Finn grabs keys and they leave, shutting the door behind them.

Once they are out on the street, Finn grabs her hand and they both begin to run, panting with fear and worry.

We are in this together.

But where are our children?

THIRTY-FIVE

GRACE

As we round the corner, I am shocked to see Ava and Finn running towards us, naked fear on both their faces.

Instinctively, both girls clutch my hands.

'Oh,' says Ava, stopping when she gets to us. 'We thought...' she pants, 'we thought...' She stops speaking and crouches down, hugging each of the girls.

'No, Mum, you're sweaty,' says Hazel, pulling away.

'I'm so sorry,' I say. 'I thought you needed time and they were so happy and it's still light. I had my phone on in case you wanted us back earlier.' I show her my phone as though she needed proof.

'It's fine,' says Ava, shaking her head.

Finn swipes at his eyes, looking stricken. I know what has happened between them. I'm just not sure what is going to happen now.

'I'm tired, Daddy,' says Chloe, reaching her arms up to her father.

'Okay, baby,' he replies, leaning down and picking her up. 'Come on, Hazel. Let's get you two into a bath and off to bed.' He takes Hazel's hand and turns to walk back to the house.

'Thank you, I had so much fun,' says Hazel politely with a wave at me.

'I'll be there in a second,' says Ava and she takes a deep breath, covering her eyes with her hands for a moment.

'Ava, are you okay?' I ask as we stand on the street, where a cool breeze is dissipating the day's heat as the sun sets.

'No,' she says, shaking her head. 'I'm not and I don't...' She stops speaking and looks at me. 'I need to talk to someone, to tell someone because I think we might be in real trouble here. But, Grace, if I explain it, you have to... you have to keep it to yourself. You...'

My heart goes out to Ava. It's so hard to trust someone you don't know well, especially when she works for you. I know that I trusted Tamara, that I thought of her as almost part of my family, but her betrayal was terrible and huge and then she compounded it by lying. I trusted Liza but, in the end, she sided with all those who were against me, and even now, as the new owner of my company, she only begrudgingly gave a reference to help me get back on my feet. I am shocked to think that I have no one left to trust in the world. My daughter won't speak to me and I am estranged from my parents. I mentally brush these thoughts away. I can be here for another woman struggling as I once was. I can be here for Ava.

'You can trust me to be the soul of discretion, Ava. I promise,' I say.

Ava starts walking slowly back to the house and I fall into step with her.

'Finn and Melody slept together after last year's Christmas party,' she begins.

'Oh,' is all I can manage as I feel a hollow form in my stomach. Why does this happen to us? To women who are struggling to be everything to everyone? Why do we get punished like this? My own spiral into alcoholism hits me with full force, making me stop for a moment. No matter how many ways I explain it to myself, it is what happened. Am I still an alcoholic? Will I always be one or do I now have control over my drug of choice? I have no idea. But it's not about me now.

'I know it's awful,' says Ava. 'But it's not the whole story, not even close.'

I nod my head. 'You talk, I'll listen,' I tell her. 'And then we'll figure out what to do.'

We walk slowly, making our way back to the house and then past the house as Ava keeps talking and I listen to what has been going on. Finn made a mistake and he is suffering for it now, thanks to Melody. Nothing like Robert, who turned my assistant into his sunshine girl and then lied about it and threatened to take my whole life from me. As she finishes speaking, Ava takes a deep breath. 'And now I don't know what we do, what we say to her. If she decides to show the picture or pictures to everyone at work, at school. Or even if she just tells people. It could be a bluff but after today, she must be even more angry. She's lost her job and Finn won't talk to her. I just don't know what she's capable of.'

We stop by a bench on the sidewalk. 'Let's sit,' I tell her and she does. I close my eyes and I am ashamed to say that the first feeling I experience is one of jealousy. Why was I not good enough for Robert? Even if he had slept with Tamara once, why was I not good enough for him to understand it was a mistake and move on? I picture a broom in my head, sweeping the thought away. I can't go backwards and I don't want Ava to suffer for her husband's choices the way I had to suffer for my husband's choices.

Ava sits in silence, playing with her wedding ring, taking it off and putting it back on again.

'Okay,' I say after a few minutes. 'Here's what we're going to do.'

THIRTY-SIX

AVA

When she and Grace walk back into the house, Finn is coming downstairs. 'They're both asleep, exhausted. Thanks so much for taking them, Grace. Ava, we need to talk.'

'I've told Grace what's happening,' says Ava.

Finn simply nods as though he knew she would.

'Ava needed another opinion,' says Grace softly.

Ava is gratified to see Finn drop his gaze. His face colours and she knows exactly what he's feeling. Humiliation and shame. *Good. He should be feeling that.*

But she still feels another flash of sympathy for him. When she was sixteen years old and had her first serious boyfriend, she remembers being on the phone to one of her friends, telling them everything that she felt was wrong about him, and her mother overhearing her conversation.

'You're no longer interested in this relationship,' her mother told her.

'Yes, I am,' Ava protested.

'No, my darling. You're discussing his faults with everyone. It means that your relationship is no longer private, no longer just between the two of you, and that you're not as invested anymore.'

Ava had wanted to argue the point but she realised her mother was right. She broke up with the boy shortly after that.

And now she has discussed her marriage and everything that has happened with Grace, a woman she barely knows. But she is still invested in her marriage. She still loves Finn. And she needs some help, they both do. Grace is older, wiser, and Ava trusts her. And she's told her now. There's no going back. At least Grace knows the kind of person Melody is and she knows what's at stake for Ava, what it means for her to get the top job.

'Do you want something to drink, Grace?' asks Ava.

Grace hesitates for a moment before saying, 'A glass of wine perhaps.'

'Good idea,' says Ava. The wine in the living room is finished even though Ava doesn't remember finishing it. She goes into the pantry to find a bottle of wine she was given last year by Patricia as part of her Christmas gift. She takes it down and looks at the label, letting the expensive wine cause her some pain as she thinks about last Christmas. Did Finn seem weird even then? She has no idea. Christmas is a manic time for her as she struggles to organise presents and Christmas Day lunch for the extended family. She and Finn agreed to save the bottle for a special occasion like when he was ready for a show or when Ava got her promotion. 'Screw it,' she says, grabbing three fresh wine glasses from a cupboard in the kitchen.

In the living room Finn is seated on the armchair and Grace on the sofa. They are not speaking. Ava pours the wine, handing a glass each to Finn and Grace and taking a large sip herself. She hasn't eaten since lunch and she's already had two huge glasses. The wine immediately settles into her empty stomach, creating acid but also making her feel slightly woozy.

Grace takes a deep sip and sighs. 'That's nice wine,' she says.

'Patricia gave it to me,' says Ava.

Grace nods. 'Finn,' she says. 'I know this is very hard, but would I be able to see the messages?'

'Um... okay,' says Finn, his gaze resting on Grace for a moment. Grace nods at him, holding out her hand.

'She knows everything, Finn, and maybe she'll have a solution. Just show her,' Ava says with a sigh.

Finn hands the phone to Grace, who quickly reads through the text messages as Finn looks away.

'Okay,' says Grace as she reads, stopping every now and again to take another sip of her wine. Ava refills her glass and then she and Finn sit in silence.

'Right,' says Grace when she's done. 'She's angry, but I don't think she's going to do anything. I think it's just threats. Here's what I propose.'

She types a message into the phone and then hands it to Ava, who reads it and nods her head. 'Do you think this will work?' Ava hands the phone to Finn, who reads the message as well.

'It's worth a shot,' he says.

'Send it,' says Ava, and Finn takes a deep breath and hits send.

Hey Melody. I can't apologise enough for what happened after the Christmas party but I also can never see you again. I love my wife and my girls, and if you need to show people that picture and any others, there is nothing I can do. But I know you got fired today, and if you do agree to just let this go, I will make sure that Ava writes you a brilliant reference and that she helps you get another job. You're a beautiful woman, Melody. You deserve a husband and family of your own. You deserve to move on. We both do. Please let

this go now. It's not doing you any good. I am
sorry again.

Ava feels her heart in her throat as the three of them silently sip wine, waiting for Melody's reply. When it comes through, the ping is so startling that Ava nearly drops her glass.

Finn reads the message. 'Oh God,' he says, handing the phone to Ava.

Watch what happens now, Finn. I'm going to ruin all of your lives. Yours. Ava's. And that uppity assistant of hers. Just you wait.

'What do we do now? What do we do?' says Ava, her voice rising in panic.

'I think,' says Grace softly, 'that you need to stop replying. There is obviously something very wrong with her. In the morning, you should go to the police and file a restraining order. And Ava, I think that you need to tell Patricia as well when you have your meeting with her. This is not going away, but if you speak honestly about it, you can mitigate the harm.'

Ava wants to protest, wants to tell Grace that they should keep talking to Melody until they reach a solution, but it's after 9 p.m. and between not eating and the wine, she feels like she can't think straight. She needs to sleep. They all do.

'Okay,' she says, standing up, 'we'll do that in the morning. Thank you, Grace, for trying to help and...'

'I know, don't worry,' says Grace, standing as well. 'I will never tell anyone.'

Ava walks her to the door.

'I'm leaving tomorrow afternoon. My building is done,' Grace says at the door. 'Thank you so much for letting me stay. I wish things were different for you right now. I have so enjoyed getting to know you and the girls and I hope... I hope that this is just a blip, just something that disappears.'

'I don't think it will be,' says Ava, 'but thank you for all your help with the girls, with everything.'

Grace nods and she leaves. Ava watches her go up the stairs to the garage apartment.

Inside, she puts the glasses in the dishwasher and starts it.

'Ava, listen,' says Finn, coming into the kitchen.

'Finn,' she says, holding up her hand, 'I need to sleep. I can't go over this anymore. Let's just go to sleep and then in the morning, you go to the police. I need to go to work because I have a meeting with Patricia and Saturday afternoon is the only time she can see me.'

'I'm so sorry,' says Finn hoarsely.

'I know you are,' says Ava.

Finn reaches for her but Ava steps back and then she walks away, leaving him in the kitchen.

She is numb with it all. The betrayal, the lies, the fear. She is just numb and she needs to sleep.

Tomorrow she will be strong again, will be Ava the mum and Ava the general manager and Ava the supporter of everyone. But tonight, she's just done.

THIRTY-SEVEN

GRACE

As I ascend the stairs to the garage apartment, I know Ava is watching me. My heart breaks for her but also for myself anew. I remember what it was like when I first knew Robert had cheated, remember the swirling questions about my marriage, my life, myself.

Cordelia was older then. I cannot imagine what it would feel like to be facing this with two very young children. I know what I did but I don't wish that on Ava, don't want her to go through what I did. She could lose everything the same way I lost everything. A broken heart can drive a person crazy. It certainly did that to me. And now Melody means to expose me to the world.

I shouldn't have had any wine and now my head is buzzing with my first alcohol in years, but at the same time, my thoughts have an edge, a certainty.

There was no one to turn to and no one looking out for me when my life fell apart but I am Ava's assistant and my job is to make her life easier and I will do whatever I have to do to make it so.

That's what I tried to do last night when I realised that

Melody had a picture of Finn on her phone. I should have realised that she'd left her phone unattended hoping that Ava would see it. Instead, I am the one who recognised the tattoo after seeing it the Sunday night I joined them for dinner.

As soon as I saw it on Melody's phone, I knew I had to do something to help Ava. I texted Finn, knowing that if there was nothing to worry about at all, he wouldn't come. He would question if I knew who I was texting.

I held my phone in my hand after I sent the text, waiting, hoping that he would reply, that he would say, *Hey Grace, I think you may have sent this to the wrong number.*

But he didn't reply. He came to see me instead.

'Grace?' he said when I opened the door to his soft knock. It was very late but I could see he hadn't gone home. His hair was a mess, his shirt stained with sweat, and there was stubble on his face. He looked... haunted.

'I know about you and Melody,' I told him as I stepped back to let him inside, closing the door behind him. And even as I said the words, I hoped that he would deny it, that somehow I was wrong.

'What do you know?' he asked, narrowing his brown eyes, sceptical.

'She has a picture of you on her phone. I recognised your tattoo.'

His shoulders sagged, his whole being heavier with the knowledge that I knew everything.

'Oh... God, oh my God,' he said, pacing up and down the small living area. 'I don't know what to do, I don't... Have you told Ava? Are you going to tell her? Please, please, I'm begging you. I'm trying to... fix it but I just... I don't know... what to do. I called Ava and told her I needed time but I just... don't know what to do.'

He sat down on the small sofa and dropped his head, and then his shoulders began to heave. I couldn't believe he was crying. I don't know what I had expected. The same reaction I got from Robert perhaps but instead he was devastated, ashamed, filled with remorse.

And I understood that Finn is a very different man to Robert. Not a perfect man. He is selfish and immature and spoiled but he is not manipulative and vindictive. He doesn't want to take everything Ava has and destroy her.

As he sobbed the story to me, I understood that he had made a mistake, a mistake that he had almost instantly regretted. He loves Ava and his children and there was no need for him to pay for his mistake any more than he was already paying.

'Tomorrow, after work, you tell Ava everything,' I said.

'No, I need to tell her now. I'll go wake her.'

'No,' I snapped and he looked at me, his face pale in the yellow light of the living room. 'She needs her rest. This is an important time for her and you will derail everything. Let her have the day at work and tell her afterwards. I will be there. I will help.'

'I can't just go home and not say anything. I can't be with her without telling her,' he said.

'Stay away, Finn,' I instructed him. 'I don't care where you go, just stay away.'

I felt bad sending him out alone but he's the reason Ava is in this mess now.

In the morning, I texted him.

Be there when we get home from work. Don't tell her I know anything at all, nothing.

Okay. I think my whole life is over.

I told you I will help, Finn, and I will.

And then I went downstairs to help Ava.

He has done exactly what I told him to do. But Melody will not let go. There is an agenda behind her desire to be with Finn and I need to know what it is. And I need to stop her.

Tamara is living her life somewhere and I have been left with nothing.

I will not let that happen to Ava. She has her husband on her side but Melody can still destroy her career and her family.

But I'm not going to let her do that. Not a chance.

THIRTY-EIGHT

AVA

Ava sleeps, troubled by dreams of losing her children in a crowded marketplace.

'My children are gone. I need help,' she keeps shouting.

A policeman laughs at her and tells her she needs to sell her house. Finn lies still on the ground, refusing to get up.

Her eyes flick open and she stares at the red numbers on her alarm clock. It's after 1 a.m. She wants to call her mother but it's too late to do that, too late to wake her.

It may be too late for everything else as well.

'Ava, are you awake?' The words are whispered from her bedroom door, only the light of a phone screen visible in the dark.

'Not now, Finn,' she groans.

'I understand but I can't... we can't... I feel like when the sun rises our marriage will be over. I feel like I've broken us and I can't just let the sun rise without talking to you.'

Ava sighs. *Why can't he just leave me alone until tomorrow, just give me some time to digest all this?*

'Please, Ava,' he says and she opens her mouth to send him away but she also realises that he may be right. Divorce has been circling in her mind for months and this was the last straw, it will be the last straw. *But what can he say to change things? What can he possibly say?*

'Fine,' she says because they have two little girls who are peacefully asleep in their rooms, unaware that their lives may be about to be irrevocably changed. 'Don't switch on the light,' she says, knowing that whatever he has to say will be easier to hear if she is not looking at him, if she can't see him.

Finn comes into the room and she feels the bed dip as he sits down on the edge.

'I've been a shitty husband and a shitty father,' he says.

'Yes,' she agrees because she's done propping Finn up.

'I know that I don't do enough around here, that I don't help with the girls as much as I should and that I've just left it to you to support us, and all of that would have been enough for you to leave me – I get that – but then this... Melody.'

Ava bites down on her lip, letting her silence be her answer.

'I've had... I've been downstairs just thinking and then I started to write some stuff down and at first it was all about how I was hurt and why I did it and...'

Ava shifts in bed, suddenly hot. *Is he really sitting there and saying this?*

'But then,' he says quickly, 'I turned it around and tried to see it from your perspective and I've... I haven't been the man I should be. I haven't helped and supported and done any of the things a good husband and father should. I know that. It feels like...' He stops speaking and she glances over at him, sees his face in the dim light of the phone screen and she can see the sheen of tears. 'It feels like someone hit me over the head and woke me up, Ava. And I wanted to come and ask you – no... to beg you – to give me a chance to show you that I understand how wrong I've been, not just because of my betrayal but everything else as well. I just want another chance.'

Ava is wide awake now, her heart racing as she listens to

him. She thinks about divorce, about finding a lawyer and starting again, about what it would be like to tell the girls that they are no longer living together in this house, about Christmas in separate houses for them and weekends when she won't see them and nights without their father here to do story time. And then, for the first time in a long time, she thinks about herself, about what she wants from her life and for her future. A single mother struggling to work and care for devastated children? A married woman who has forgiven her husband? It's too hard to decide right now but she also knows that she cannot make this decision lightly.

'Things will have to change, Finn. I mean really change.'

'They will,' he says.

'And you have to commit to therapy with me.'

'Absolutely,' he says.

'And I'm not making any guarantees. I'm not saying yes, one way or the other, but I think... I think I'm willing to try.' Because she is, and being willing to try means that whatever decision she makes in the future, she will have explored every possibility. She needs to save herself from living with regret no matter what she eventually decides.

'Oh God,' he says, his voice catching, 'thank you, thank you.'

He stands and she knows he is going to come to her and that it would be so easy to just let him touch her and hold her because she melts under his hands, but she also knows she needs to stay strong.

'I need you to go back downstairs now,' she says. 'I need some time and I need to try and sleep a bit before the girls get up. We can talk more tomorrow.'

'Okay,' he says. He moves towards the bedroom door. 'I love you. You don't have to say anything, but just know I love you and the girls more than anything in the world, and whatever it takes to make this right, I'll do, I promise.'

Ava stays silent and then she hears the soft click of the

bedroom door closing. She is exhausted – physically, spiritually, emotionally – and all she wants right now is just to sink into nothingness for a while.

She closes her eyes, concentrates on her breathing and mentally sweeps away every single racing thought.

This will be easier in the morning. It has to be.

THIRTY-NINE

GRACE

Grabbing the bottle of vodka from the freezer and a few other things, I make my way to my car. I've only had a couple of glasses of wine but they are definitely having an effect on me.

If I can talk to Melody, I may be able to save this situation before it blows up everyone's lives.

I drive carefully as I make my way to her apartment. I know her address from the personnel files I had a quick look at one morning.

Perhaps if she and I can share a drink, she will let down her guard and be open to discussion. I have not treated her kindly so perhaps I need to try that. Perhaps that will defuse this situation before the whole thing blows up, hurting everyone involved.

That's what I'm hoping for anyway.

I concentrate hard as I drive, not wanting to be pulled over, not wanting to have an accident, and when I make it to her building without any mishap, I take it as a sign that I am doing the right thing, that this will end the right way for everyone.

It's just before 11 p.m. when I ring the buzzer on her building, pressing down hard on the number six.

'Yes, who is it?' Melody asks, and her sulky little voice immediately irritates me.

'Package for you,' I mumble into the speaker, deliberately making myself hard to understand. There is a buzz and the door is opened. I knew it would be that easy. Melody seems like the kind of woman who has little idea how many parcels she has ordered or received until her bank balance disappears. And packages are delivered around the clock these days. Not at this time usually but I took a chance that she wouldn't question me.

Her apartment is on the second floor and I take the stairs. No need to be seen in the lift, where there are usually cameras.

I knock and she immediately opens the door, anticipation on her face of the present she ordered for herself and then forgot about.

'You,' she says and she moves to slam the door.

'Melody, please. I just want to talk to you. I don't think you deserved to be fired and I think I can help you get your job back,' I say, speaking quickly before she closes the door in my face.

She is dressed for bed in a silly pink pyjama set with Mickey Mouse on the front. Why would a grown woman dress like that? But even dressed like this, Melody is beautiful. Everything is plump and curved and smooth. The gift of youth. That's what Tamara had as well.

'I know what it's like to lose everything,' I try, dropping my gaze and humbling myself. 'I don't want that to happen to you.'

'It wasn't supposed to happen,' she says, her eyes narrowing.

There is a lot more to this story than I know but I need her to trust me before she says anything.

'I brought some vodka so we could share a drink and just talk,' I say.

'But aren't you an alcoholic?' she says and I flush, remembering that she's read the article.

'I was never really addicted. I just used it at a bad time and I can have a drink now. I'll be fine.'

There is a slight smirk on her face as she steps back to let me in, as though she is going to enjoy watching me get drunk.

Her apartment is furnished with the same cheap furniture I bought to furnish mine. A mass-produced blue sofa is covered in purple scatter cushions that match the ugly purple rug on the floor. The apartment is a one-bedroom with a tiny kitchen where dishes are piled in the sink and the counter is covered in bits of food. She's still a child with a messy room. She has no idea what she's doing, who she's up against.

'Did Ava send you?' she asks, folding her arms.

'Ava?' I ask. 'No, why?'

'Actually,' she says, 'I don't think this is a good idea. I want you to go.'

'Look, I just want to talk,' I say. 'We can have a drink and talk like mature adults. Maybe we can figure out a way to get you your job back.'

'I don't need your help but fine, whatever,' she says with a roll of her eyes and I restrain myself from smacking her silly face. She has no idea that I know everything, that I have seen the messages she sent to Finn and read her threats.

She turns and walks away and I follow her to her small kitchen, where she grabs two glasses and some cranberry juice.

'You sit down, I'll do this,' I say and she shrugs her shoulders. I don't like working in her kitchen with its sticky counter but I simply try not to touch anything.

Once I have poured us each a glass, I take hers over to her, where she is slouched in a purple velvet armchair.

'I'm sorry about today. I mean, you shouldn't have sent the email but they didn't even give you a chance to explain.'

Her face falls, and she takes a big gulp of her drink. 'I don't know how it happened. I would never do something so stupid and then Collin... he was supposed to always support me but today he just... didn't seem to care at all.' She takes another gulp of her drink. 'Anyway, I don't think I did send that email. I think someone set me up.' She looks straight at me, her chin jutting out with her accusation.

'Set you up?' I ask with a small smile. 'Barkley is just an education company, Melody, why would anyone do that? If you ask me, you're too good to just be a receptionist. I could see the work bored you. Maybe it's a good time to find something more stimulating?'

Melody nods her head vigorously. 'I have a business degree and Collin said...' She stops speaking, finishing her drink.

'Collin said...' I prompt and then I wait, letting the silence between us grow until she fills it.

'Collin was going to promote me when he was made CEO.'

I am not surprised by this. Melody is barely capable of running a reception desk but, like with a lot of people in her generation, she sees herself as a bright shining star. I blame Instagram and TikTok. If she had any intelligence, she wouldn't be allowing me to stroke her ego. 'You deserved a bigger job,' I say, 'not to be fired for a small mistake.'

'I did and I'll still get it,' she says darkly. 'No one will stop me.'

'Well, perhaps it would be a good idea to move on to something better, to go somewhere you're appreciated.'

'I'm not going anywhere, Grace. That's what you don't understand. You think you're so clever because you once ran a company, because you had money and nice clothes? You're not as smart as you think. It took me five minutes of googling to find you and your sad little life story and it's pathetic. You're nothing, Grace, nothing and no one. By Monday morning you will be the one without a job, you and Ava will both be unemployed, just like that,' she says, clicking her thumb and finger together, the snapping sound loud in her small apartment. 'I'll make sure of it.'

'How will you make that happen, Melody?' I ask, making sure not to raise my voice. I want to just seem curious but my mouth is dry as my heart rate speeds up.

She shakes her head. 'Just leave, Grace, just leave my apartment and the company. No one wants a sad old alcoholic hanging around. And if you just leave, I won't have to deal with you as well.'

I want to leap up and shake the little witch but I don't. I'm here for a reason. Melody must be hiding a lot more than just an encounter with Finn. Is there another reason she dislikes Ava so much? And why would Ava lose her job?

'I'm here to try and help you, Melody. You may not believe that but I am. I still have a lot of old contacts in the business world. I can help find you a new job, somewhere interesting and exciting. Wouldn't you like that?'

'I don't need your help. Everything is going to change at Barkley, trust me on that. Ava's going to find herself very unhappy.'

'Let me get you another,' I say, getting up and taking her glass from her as I hope she's had just enough to agree to one more drink. If she asks me to leave again, I will have to go, but she nods her head instead.

'You don't seem to be drinking much,' she says, and I pick up my glass and drink the whole thing down.

'I'm ready for another as well,' I say with a smile.

I hand her the new drink, made even stronger this time. Mine has a touch of vodka in it, just a touch, but I can taste the beautiful burn with every sip.

Her eyes are glazing over a little and I can feel she is close to letting the truth spill out of her. I think she wants to tell me why she seems to hate Ava. I know it can't just be the one email I sent on Ava's behalf. And I don't think she's actually in love with Finn after only one night together. Whatever secrets she has, it must be killing her to keep them. Her generation thrives on sharing everything.

Another small nudge, a bit more alcohol, and then I will know everything and hopefully I can convince her to leave Ava and Finn alone and move on with her life. I don't want her exposing me either. I can't let her do that. But my priority is to protect Ava.

I need to delete all the pictures she has of Finn, get rid of all the messages between them. That's why I'm really here. Without those, it's her word against his, and if my experience has taught me anything, it's that women are rarely believed.

'You have a secret, don't you, Melody?'

'What are you talking about?' She turns her head away from me and the smirk appears again. 'I don't know why you're here,' she says when she looks back at me, and I get a sense suddenly that Melody is not just a sweet young girl who got angry with me and threatened me, not just a young woman causing trouble because a man she shouldn't have slept with doesn't want to see her again. She is much more than that.

I decide to confront her.

'I know about you and Finn, Ava's husband.'

Melody shrugs and she finishes her drink in one quick gulp. I stand and hold out my hand for her glass, which she willingly gives me, and I'm quick with a refill.

'So what?' she says. 'What are you going to do about it?'

'I know that Finn doesn't want to see you.'

'How do you know that?'

'They have children, they're a family,' I say without answering her question.

'That didn't matter when he had sex with me. Then he seemed to forget he had kids at all. And now he wants me to stay away from him and his precious... precious family,' she says, gritting her teeth, and then she drinks again. 'And why do you care? What are you doing here? You said Ava didn't send you so why are you here? Just to tell me you know her husband screwed around?'

'Melody,' I say patiently, taking the empty glass out of her hand, 'I just want you to consider what's best for you as you move forward. I can get Ava to give you a great reference.' I refill her drink and hand it to her while she stares at me. 'I can help you look for a job where you're challenged and able to advance through the ranks. Ava's a nice woman and Finn is just a man and it's best if you don't make trouble.'

'Ava's a bitch,' she sneers, taking another sip of her drink, 'and Finn's an idiot. I don't care if he... doesn't want to... to see me.' She closes her eyes briefly. 'I don't care,' she says, leaning her head back against the chair. 'All he needed to do was meet me one more time, just one more time, and then Ava would have seen... seen us and it was all... arranged. She would have gone mad, like you did.' She giggles hysterically and the urge to hit her makes me press my nails into my palm. I take another sip of my drink instead.

'Just like you did,' she giggles again and hiccups.

She is getting way too drunk. I shouldn't have poured her such large amounts.

'If you think Finn is an idiot, why are you bothering him?' I ask, raising my voice a little to keep her here with me. The last thing I need is her passing out.

She lifts her head and drains her drink. 'You're so... stupid, you and your... boss don't know what I know. I want some more.' She holds the glass out to me and I get up and pour her yet another drink, adding extra juice and handing it to her.

'What do you know?' I ask quietly.

'Collin loves me. He loves me and he knows that Ava's job should be mine. We just needed her gone. Collin loves me and I'm going to have Ava's job and we're getting married.'

And there it is. Melody thinks she's going to get Ava's job. It's ridiculous but she seems to believe it's going to happen. She is enthralled by Collin and she probably believes everything he has told her.

I sit down on the sofa and drain my own drink.

Melody looks unsteadily around the room. 'I'm tired,' she says.

'And you should sleep,' I say. 'But first explain it to me, Melody. You love Collin?'

'I love Collin and he loves me,' she says, nodding her head, and I get a glimpse of sixteen-year-old Melody with a teenage crush. Except this is not a teenager.

'But Collin is married.'

'He hates her and he loves me,' she says, leaning forward, her glazed eyes brightening with her eagerness to share this particular secret with someone. 'He's going to leave her when he's CEO and we'll be together.'

'But Ava's not going anywhere. And what if Ava is made CEO?' I ask, a chill coming over me.

'No chance,' Melody giggles. 'I have video, I'm going to send her the video, I'm going to send Patricia the video. And just like that,' she rubs her hands together as though dusting off some dirt, 'no more Ava.'

I am starting to understand what's been going on. 'Did Collin tell you to seduce Finn?' I ask, too shocked to know how to feel.

'Ava needs to stay home with her kids. Patricia doesn't like scandal,' says Melody and then she leans her head back again and closes her eyes.

'Where is the video?' I ask, and she moves her head from side to side.

'I'm not stupid,' she sings.

'I don't believe you have a video,' I say.

In a burst of energy that only someone as young as Melody

would be capable of when drunk, she drops her glass on her coffee table and grabs her laptop from the small round matching side table. 'Look here,' she spits and opens her computer, clicking on a file.

An image appears, not grainy and dark like I had expected but shot in bright light. It is of Finn and Melody and I can see exactly what they're doing and it's disgusting. 'He wouldn't meet me... and he should have. He would have loved the video. But I'm sure Ava will love it and her kids will love it too.'

'But you wouldn't want anyone to see this,' I say, 'you're in it.'

'I think I look good,' she says, hauling herself off her chair and going to the kitchen, where she grabs the bottle of vodka, refilling her glass and spilling some.

'You need to sit down and you need some juice,' I say quickly as I leap up and grab her glass and take it back to the kitchen to add some juice. The image of her and Finn together is seared on my mind and I briefly wish I could drink myself into oblivion so I wouldn't have to see it.

I hand her the glass. She is slumped in the chair again, the laptop open, the video playing. I shut the laptop lid down, unable to bear looking at it.

'You need to delete that,' I say, slightly desperately. Ava would be devastated. This will ruin any chance she has of forgiving Finn. It's too brutally exposing; his enjoyment is too clear. Ava's family will fall apart. Ava will fall apart if the video is shared. I can almost feel her humiliation.

Melody sits up straight and I am suddenly aware that she's not as drunk as I thought she was. 'Make me,' she smirks. She lifts her glass to her lips and drinks it all.

'Please, Melody,' I say, hoping I can reason with her.

'No. You need to leave now.' She stands and picks up the laptop and I realise that she's been playing with me. The alcohol has barely affected her at all.

'Melody, you know that Collin was just using you, right? You know if you show this video to Patricia and Ava, you still won't get your job back. Collin doesn't love you. He just wanted to sabotage Ava.'

'He does… I wrote him an email and he'll take me back… He loves me and I'm getting Ava's job. You need to go,' she says, her tone low and menacing.

'I'm not going until you delete that video,' I say.

She sits down again and opens the laptop. 'I might just send it now. I have it ready to go to Ava and Patricia and Finn. And then I may just add it to my Instagram. There's no such thing as bad publicity, is there?' She arches an eyebrow and pouts.

'You can't do that,' I say weakly, watching her hand hover over her keyboard.

'Watch me, Grace, watch me,' she sneers.

Her fingers touch the keys and I jump up and grab the computer, pulling it away from her and throwing it onto a chair. 'No,' I yell, 'you won't do that.'

She stands and comes at me, her hands go around my neck, squeezing tightly. I am strong but so is she and she pushes me down onto the sofa. Flailing, I grab for something, anything, my hand touching a soft purple cushion, and I grab it and hit out at her. It can't hurt her but it makes her let go, and she steps back and tumbles onto the carpet, the alcohol now having some effect obviously.

'You bitch,' she roars. 'You made me fall over.'

'I'm so sorry,' I gasp, 'so sorry. Let me get you some juice. I think you need some juice.' I move to the kitchen quickly and pour her a glass of juice.

'I don't want to drink any more,' she says, sitting up on the carpet, but I hand her the juice anyway.

'You need some juice. You'll feel better, and if you drink it and if I can see that you're not too drunk, I'll just go,' I say, trying to sound motherly. She is the same age as Cordelia but so different from her that they may as well be decades apart. Cordelia would never behave like this. Cordelia would never want to hurt someone the way that Melody wants to hurt Finn and Ava. I don't understand this young woman at all.

She grabs the glass from me, spilling some, but then she drinks the rest down. 'There, now get out of my apartment before I call the police... you, you...' She lifts her hand to her head. 'I'm so tired.'

'Lie down and sleep,' I tell her, 'just lie down here.' I take the cushion and hand it to her and I can see that she is finally where I want her because she doesn't resist, just lies down on the floor, putting the cushion under her head and curling up on her side.

'Go away,' she slurs.

'I'm going,' I tell her and I stand and move towards the front door, where she can't see me from where she is lying on the floor behind the sofa. I act like I'm leaving, even opening and closing the front door, but I don't go anywhere. Instead, I stand by the door and wait until I hear her breathing change. It takes fifteen minutes and I feel every minute with my muscles tensed and my heart pounding. She doesn't speak again.

Finally, I think that she is really, properly asleep and I move over to her and touch her on the shoulder. She doesn't respond so I gently lift an arm and let it go; it flops to the floor. I lean down closer to her, listening for the deep breaths of sleep.

But she is not breathing and I realise that her body is still.

Very, very still.

'Oh,' I gasp. It was too much. I've given her too much.

'Melody,' I try, shaking her quite hard but she doesn't move. Her body is rag-doll loose.

'Melody,' I try again, slapping her lightly on the cheek but I get no response.

I move away from her, thinking about what I should do now.

I need to perform CPR and get an ambulance. I stand and go to my bag and get my phone but then I stop.

She wants to destroy Ava and me. And now it will all be much, much worse. There will be no clinic where I can recover from this mistake. If she wakes up, she will make sure I am sent to jail. I can't have that.

So instead, I sit very still on the sofa for another ten minutes.

'Melody,' I say but she doesn't respond. 'Melody,' I repeat a little louder but she doesn't move at all.

I stand up and grab her computer using the passcode I saw her enter. I find and delete the video, clear the search history and then delete the trash bin as well.

I don't delete the email I find in her drafts.

Collin,

I can't believe you did that. I didn't deserve to be fired. After everything I have done for you? How could you? I thought you loved me. You need to make this right. Call me. Please call me. I love you.

I don't delete it but I add some lines to the email. Necessary lines.

Please, Collin. I can't live without you. I can't exist without you. I can't.

I schedule the email to be sent an hour from now, to Collin and to Patricia.

And then I open another tab, finding job adverts for assistants, ones that are far beyond her capabilities.

I click on one and leave that open.

Are you looking for a new challenge? Do you thrive in a fast-paced environment? Then this might be the position for you. Our CEO is seeking a forward-thinking candidate with the ability to use initiative and adapt. Ideally, we are seeking a candidate who is able to be with the company long-term.

It must have made her very sad to realise that she wasn't even qualified to be an assistant. She thought she was going to be the general manager. I can imagine that losing her job and feeling like she'd lost Collin's love on the same day must have hurt her very much.

Her phone is on the coffee table, and I pick it up and use her thumb to open it. I search for the video for a few minutes, finding and deleting it from everywhere. And then I scroll through her whole gallery, making sure there is nothing else she could use to hurt Ava.

She has a copy of the article about me saved on her phone and I delete that as well along with all the text messages between Melody and Finn and Melody and myself. I delete Finn and I as contacts as well.

Melody sleeps on. *She's just asleep*, I keep telling myself. *Just asleep.*

I clean up after myself, wiping everything down, everywhere I touched, because I hate to leave a mess.

I place two boxes of Panadol, one empty and one half full on her coffee table. I place the empty blister pack of sleeping tablets on the table as well. I lie the empty bottle of vodka down next to her, briefly brushing my hand over the silver label before I wipe it down and then rest one of Melody's hands on it. I have had that bottle with me since I left the clinic but I don't need it anymore.

I don't know how she kept going with all the pills in her system. She was just supposed to fall asleep, that's all.

I take one last look around the apartment. Poor girl. She really thought he would give her Ava's job?

I open her front door, checking the landing and then quickly leaving. I drive slowly back to the apartment to pack.

It's over now. She can't hurt them anymore. She can't hurt anyone anymore.

FORTY

AVA

At 7 a.m., Ava's phone buzzes on her bedside table. She ignores it until it stops. The girls will be up soon enough, and after a troubled sleep she thinks if she can just get twenty good minutes before Hazel and Chloe come into the bedroom, she will be able to function and somehow manage to get through her meeting with Patricia this afternoon without bursting into tears in the boardroom.

A second later, the phone buzzes again and Ava grits her teeth as she hears Chloe shout her usual morning greeting to her sister: 'Hazel, I'm waked up, I'm waked up.'

The phone continues to buzz. Maybe she'll be okay if she can get a fifteen-minute nap at lunch if Finn takes the girls out. Maybe she'll be okay if she can just concentrate on talking to Patricia and forget all about her husband cheating with Melody and Melody's threats to expose him to the whole world. 'Yeah, right,' Ava says aloud as the phone stops and immediately starts buzzing again.

'Welcome to your life, Ava Green,' she sighs, picking it up and squinting at the screen.

It's Patricia. At just after 7 a.m. on a Saturday? The air

shimmers a little as Ava swipes her finger across the screen, her heart beating so fast she feels it may choke her. She knows her whole life is crumbling around her in this moment.

'Patricia?' says Ava, having no energy for a more polite greeting.

'We have a situation, can you talk?'

Hazel bursts into the bedroom, holding her sister's hand. 'It's pancake Saturday,' she yells.

'Pancake Saturday,' Chloe echoes.

'Just a minute,' says Ava.

She jumps out of bed, grabbing her light summer robe and pulling it on.

She takes the steps two at a time with the girls following her and finds Finn downstairs, sleeping on the sofa. She shakes him by the shoulder. 'Patricia is on the phone, you need to take the girls,' she snaps.

Finn sits straight up, panic on his face at what Ava's boss might know already. 'Okay,' he says and he stands as Hazel and Chloe get to the bottom of the stairs, repeating their chorus of 'pancake Saturday'.

'Come on,' says Finn, 'let's make chocolate chip pancakes.'

Ava darts back upstairs, picking up the phone. 'Patricia?' she says.

'Okay, Ava, I know it's early and a Saturday, but something has happened. I'm going to talk and you're going to listen and then you can ask questions.'

Ava has been working for Patricia for more than ten years. She is used to her slightly abrupt manner and she doesn't take it personally. But her body is flooded with fear. Has Melody sent the photo or photos? Is Patricia about to fire her? Is this how it ends? On a warm February morning with her husband making pancakes and her little girls joyous at the treat?

'Okay,' says Ava, clenching the fist of one hand, letting her nails press into her palm, reminding herself to keep calm and wait until she's heard everything.

'Right,' says Patricia. 'I've just had a call from the police. Melody is... Melody has taken her life. Apparently, she used a mixture of pills and alcohol. She had a friend arriving very early this morning to stay for a few days from Adelaide, and the young woman had a spare key to let herself in so she wouldn't wake Melody. She found her and called triple zero. The police called me this morning.'

'Oh,' gasps Ava, the idea too huge to take in.

'She didn't leave a note but her computer was open with a sent email to Collin. She sent it to me as well. I only just saw it. Apparently, they were having a thing, an affair. That's why I was called. It's not a suicide note but—'

'Collin and Melody?' asks Ava, unable to stop herself from interrupting.

'Yes, and now we have an issue. I called him before I called you and he's confessed that he was sleeping with her. Naturally his employment has been immediately terminated. This is serious shit, Ava, and I have no idea if her family is going to sue or what's going to happen but I do know that we need to keep things running as usual and you need to go in today and make sure that we're ahead of this mess. You need to take over all his clients and of course you'll be the new CEO. You have to hire a general manager.'

'Patricia, did they find anything else on her phone or computer, anything that may explain why she did it?' asks Ava, hot tears filling her eyes. Melody was only twenty-four – a baby. She did a terrible thing and she was not a good person but still, she was young enough to change her life, to learn from her mistakes.

'They found nothing – just work stuff and the email to Collin and me. There are a lot of calls on her phone to Collin, especially after he fired her.'

Ava feels her nails biting into her skin. She takes a deep breath. She can't believe any of this.

'I'll handle everything, Patricia,' she says firmly, 'don't worry.'

'Great, great. I knew I could count on you. To be honest with you, last year Collin overheard me talking to my husband on the phone about how I wanted you for CEO. I should have told you but he begged me to give him some time to change my mind. I felt I owed it to him since he's been with me from the beginning of the company but I didn't think I would actually change my mind and now I'm grateful I never did.'

'Me too. Thanks, Patricia. Don't worry, you do whatever you need to do. I can handle everything else.'

'Thanks, speak soon.' And her boss is gone.

Ava goes over to her cream bedroom curtains and pushes them open, staring out into the back garden and the street beyond as a pair of lorikeets fly past.

Collin was sleeping with Melody. Melody is dead. Collin knew last year that Ava was going to be the CEO? None of this makes sense. She can't make it make sense but she can get dressed and go into work despite it being a Saturday. She can do what she told Patricia she would do, and maybe after that, she and Finn can figure out a way to move forward in their marriage. They didn't find the messages to Finn? Why would Melody have deleted them?

She experiences a flash of angst for the young woman who was in so much pain, pain that she hid. Was she truly in love with Finn or with Collin? What was she trying to do with Finn? Ava shakes her head. She might never know the truth, but as long as her family is safe, she will have to accept that.

Without giving herself any more time to think, she jumps into the shower. Thank God she has Grace to rely on. Things are going to be tough for a while but she's confident she can keep everything on track.

When she's dressed and ready for work, she goes downstairs, where the girls are eating their pancakes as Finn nurses a cup of coffee. He looks up when he sees her, his face pale, already chewing on his bottom lip.

'Come into the living room,' she says and he follows her. She speaks quickly, explaining everything, touching his shoulder as an expression of horror appears at the news that Melody has taken her own life.

'Was it me?' he asks. 'Is it because of me?'

'No,' she says firmly. 'I don't think so.' And she believes that. Finn was just a pawn in whatever game Melody and Collin were playing. 'I think she and Collin... Look, there's more to explain, but right now I need to get Grace and go to work.'

'I'll sort the girls, don't worry.' He nods and she can see some colour returning to his face. 'It will all be... different now, I promise,' he says, repeating what he said only hours ago. He's relieved and so is she but mixed in with that relief are so many more emotions. Shock, despair, anger, concern.

Ava would like to take some time to think about this, to think about Melody and process what's happened, but Patricia is counting on her as are the people who work for Barkley. There is no one else here to run the company and by Monday, she needs to be in control. It is shocking to her that this is everything she has worked for but that it has come to her in such a terrible way. Collin must have been furious when Patricia told him he wouldn't be CEO. Would he really have set Finn and Ava up by having Melody sleep with Finn? Is such a thing possible?

She can't unpack this all now. She has to do what she told Patricia she would do because she needs her job, and because she has her own family to take care of.

She and Finn have a long way to go but right now she can see that he understands what needs to be done.

And so does she.

And she can't wait to tell Grace everything.

FORTY-ONE

GRACE

It is just after 4 a.m. when I close the door to the garage apartment. The keys are inside and my suitcase is in my hand. I have left the apartment the way I found it, clean and tidy. I glance over to the house, where all the lights are off. I hope Ava is getting some sleep. She will need her wits about her in the morning.

Whatever happens from here, I'm sure that Ava will be able to handle it. She's strong and clever and she deserves every good thing.

I make my way down the stairs and get into my car, hoping no one stops me. The car is a rental and I will drop it back off at the airport.

As I pull away from the house, I have a moment of grief for the Green family because I would have loved to know them better. I have a moment of grief for Melody, who got in the way and was used by Collin. And I have a moment of grief for the Grace I was and the Grace I will never be again, no matter how hard I try. I have to accept that but I know that there is a new Grace emerging and I know exactly what she's going to do now. She was forced out into the world by those who betrayed the old

Grace, those who tried to take her life from her. I suppose they succeeded but no one ever will again. New Grace cannot be touched.

The night of the terrible fire nudges at me.

I told the police, my lawyer, everyone, that I had come home and lit some candles and then had so much alcohol, I blacked out. But that wasn't what happened.

I came home late, sneaking into my own house. I knew Robert was home because his car was in the driveway.

I knew he would be asleep in the spare room, the door locked after I had tried once or twice to get in after a particularly intense drinking session, determined to confront him.

I had been out at a bar until the management suggested, gently and then more firmly, that I leave.

I had caught a cab to work and I had caught one home, struggling to get the key into the lock as I tried to be very quiet.

Inside I kicked off my shoes and sank onto the white sofa in the living room, meaning to drift off to sleep. I could already feel the delicious vodka buzz wearing off.

My phone pinged with a text.

I know you'll only see this in the morning, but thank you for this lovely night. We've had such fun. I hope things get better for you, Mum. I love you and I hope you can get better.

There was a picture of Cordelia with her three best friends in a hotel room, their faces covered in sheet masks, all of them wearing fluffy white bathrobes. I could see the remains of a room service feast but no alcohol. Cordelia didn't drink. I had booked the night away for her when she'd started her exams, showing her the wonderful reward that would be hers once she was done. She had been delighted and I think having a treat to look forward to helped her study and deal with all the stress that came from final exams.

I ran my finger over her beautiful face, knowing that she did love me and hated that I was drinking so much. She couldn't understand. Robert had discussed my paranoia with her, had told her that there was no way he was having an affair. She believed him. Everyone did.

Instead of going to sleep, I got off the sofa and made my way to Robert's office, hoping, once again, to find some proof of his affair. I didn't think I would. But I had to try. The need to try drove me forward, the alcohol veil receding from my brain as I searched through his desk drawers.

For some reason, and I will never know why, I pulled out the bottom desk drawer and then got down on my hands and knees, feeling my tight black skirt split along the seam as I did so, and rooted around in the space the drawer had left.

My hands touched a letter and I pulled it out.

Robert Morton, Greenway Architecture, it was labelled and then his business address.

I stared at it for a moment and almost dismissed it. It had been sent to his office and was obviously a business letter. Perhaps it had fallen down behind the drawer and been wedged in the space.

I sat back on the carpet, leaning against the matching bookcase that was filled with all of Robert's precious books on architecture.

And then I opened the letter, reading the words on the pink notepaper quickly and then more slowly and then even more slowly again.

Dear Rob,

This is such a weird way to communicate. I don't think I've written an actual letter since I last wrote a letter to Santa. But I feel like she's watching everything I do. I feel like she may have had that detective tap into my phone. I know I sound paranoid

– not as paranoid as her – but I can't get the idea out of my mind. I just needed to let you know I am thinking of you. I know we can't be together right now but I am holding on to the day in the future when we can be. She is more and more unhinged at work, and after she screamed at me last week, Liza told me that she doesn't think this can go on for much longer.

I think you can file for divorce now. She won't have the energy to fight you, not anymore. Half the house, half the company will be yours and it won't take us long to get rid of her.

I dream about that future as I lie alone in my bed. I know you said to be patient and I'm being patient. I love you so much, Rob. I love you my stars and moon. More than I ever thought possible.

Your sunshine girl,

Tamara

The vodka bubbled in my stomach and I covered my mouth with my hand, biting down on my lip, letting the pain concentrate my mind. I didn't want to throw up.

There it was, the proof. Undeniable proof. I was right. I had been right all along.

Even as I read the words again, I knew it wouldn't matter.

No proof would be good enough.

They were going to take everything from me. Even in my drunken state I could see that it had been planned all along. Robert wanted half my company, half my house and a new sunshine girl.

'No,' I whispered, looking at the words. 'No,' I repeated. I would not let that happen.

I struggled to my feet, hearing the skirt tear further, and looked at Robert's desk. In pride of place he had a gold lighter, given to his grandfather as a retirement present. They shared the same name so Robert had inherited it. *Presented to Robert Morton for fifty years of service. With thanks.*

I grabbed the lighter from his desk and made my way upstairs, the letter and the envelope in my hand. I stood outside the door to the spare room and leaned my head against the smooth cream timber, trying to feel my husband inside, trying to feel the love I used to have for him. But there was only a smouldering anger.

On each side of the door, I had hung beautiful hand-woven Persian rugs, bought on a trip Robert and I had taken to Turkey for a second honeymoon.

As my body swayed unsteadily, I opened the lighter and clicked it until I got a flame. I held it to the letter, watching the pink paper curl as it caught. Dropping the letter on the floor outside the door, I clicked the lighter again, holding it to the first rug and then the second.

They caught in a quick whoosh of blazing orange, a strange smell of burning carpet filling the air.

I moved quickly, making my way back downstairs to the living room, where I did use the lighter to light some candles.

Perhaps I imagined the carpets would burn themselves out and that would be it. But I do know that I was deeply thankful that Cordelia wasn't home. Everything would have been different if she had been. I was so deeply wounded by the truth in that letter, so angry. In sober hindsight, I should have kept the letter and used it to expose Robert, used it to show Cordelia and everyone else that I had been right all along but I was drunk and seething with the betrayal of it all. And I also suspected that it wouldn't be enough because nothing would be. My instinct wasn't enough, the pictures weren't enough and the letter would be denied or dismissed like everything else had been. I wasn't thinking straight and all I knew was that I couldn't let Robert and Tamara win.

Leaving the carpets burning I went downstairs and I lay on the sofa, woozy and dropping into an exhausted, alcohol-induced sleep. By the time I woke up, the whole house was ablaze.

I didn't even remember Robert in the guest room, just ran outside and stood there, watching until a neighbour came up to me, shouting at me, asking if I had called triple zero.

I hadn't. There was no emergency as far as I could see. My life had already burned down. All that was on fire was a ruin.

In the silent dark, I drive along the highway. Everything was taken from me anyway. And I even lost my daughter. I'm glad that will not happen to Ava.

The airport is quiet when I arrive and leave my keys in the special box outside the rental car company. I don't have a ticket so I sit down and use my new credit card to buy myself one.

The plane will leave in three hours.

I can wait.

I have the time.

FORTY-TWO

AVA

At 8 a.m., Ava races up the stairs to the garage apartment and knocks at the door, quietly first and then more loudly. 'Grace,' she calls once or twice, and then when she receives no answer, she tries the handle, expecting to find it locked, but it opens.

'Grace, sorry, it's me. I know it's early but I needed to...'

She looks around. Inside, the room looks exactly as it did before Grace moved in. Everything is neat and tidy. Ava moves across the living room into the bedroom, where the bed has been stripped and the sheets heaped in a neat pile to wash. She walks to the cupboard and opens it. It's empty but then she knew it would be. It's obvious that Grace is gone.

Shaking her head, she goes back to the kitchen, where she sees a white envelope on the benchtop. *Grace is gone? How can that be? Maybe she's just gone back to her apartment, although she said she was only leaving in the afternoon? But then a simple text could have explained that. Has Grace left because of everything she found out last night? Have I, through Finn, become the boss making ethically unsound decisions? Does Grace not want to associate with me anymore?*

Ava knows that if she asks Grace to come into work she will,

but before she texts her, she pulls a single sheet of thin paper
out of the envelope and reads the words written in Grace's
excessively neat handwriting.

Dear Ava,

*Thank you so much for the loan of this lovely little apartment. I
have left a list of suitable candidates to rent it for you to look at.*

*I am so sorry to do this to you at such a difficult time but
I'm afraid I had no choice.*

*The aunt in the UK that I told you about is very, very ill
now. I was called by her doctors to let me know that she will
not last longer than another day or two.*

*I have to get there. I have to see her and then I will be
responsible for winding up her affairs. I cannot apologise
enough for putting you in this situation but family is the most
important thing in the world. Remember that, Ava. You and
Finn have had a difficult time but your family, your beautiful
family, is the most important thing in the world.*

*I am so grateful I got to know you and work for you and I
know you will thrive in the top job. I just know you're going to
get it. Perhaps the garage apartment will be best suited to an au
pair so that both you and Finn can work and know the girls are
cared for.*

Thank you again for everything,

Grace Enright

Ava stands staring down at the letter, reading it again.

Is it just a coincidence? Is it the truth?

She can't lose Grace. How will she manage? How will she
run the company and hire someone to replace her at her own
job? How will she hold everything together? It feels impossible.

But it's not, Ava hears as though Grace were standing right next to her. *You're more than capable.*

'I'm more than capable,' Ava says aloud. She leaves the apartment, her phone at her ear as she calls Grace. She will wish her well and thank her.

'The number you have dialled is not in service. Please check the number before calling again.'

Ava looks down at her phone. It's definitely Grace's number, and even if she is already on a plane, the call should go to message bank.

She dials again but gets the same message. And she is just about to try again when her phone buzzes with a call.

'Oh God, Ava,' wails James, 'Patricia called me. What are we going to do?'

'I'm going in to the office, James, and I need you there as well. I know it's a Saturday but Grace can't be there and I need you. We're going to work together and sort it out,' says Ava firmly. 'I'm getting in my car now. I have a list to give you to get started with – are you ready?'

'I'm ready,' says James.

And Ava starts speaking.

EPILOGUE

I have bought myself a business-class ticket, despite Melbourne being just over an hour away. I hate flying, so if I do fly, I like to fly in comfort.

It's just after 7 a.m. Soon, Ava and Finn will know that Melody is gone, that she has taken her life. Poor girl. She was pushed into sleeping with Finn because of her love for Collin. Such a sad and silly thing to do. She should have known that Collin would quickly abandon her. It's a wonder Collin didn't think about the consequences when he fired her but then he is entitled, arrogant, self-centred. He was simply using Melody to get what he wanted.

Why are women still doing this? After everything we have learned and everything we know – why are we still letting men hurt us like this?

'Some juice?' a smiling flight attendant asks, offering me a tray, and I take a glass of orange juice.

'Thank you,' I say as she moves off.

As the safety announcements begin, I take the letters out of my bag.

I wrote them to my baby girl, wrote them to explain to her

and to myself, I guess. It was part of my therapy from Dr Gordon. He never asked to see the letters and so I confidently wrote the absolute truth.

'I believe that there is some trauma, some pain from your past that you have still not explored,' he told me. 'It's the secrets we keep from ourselves that cause the most damage. Write it down, Grace. Write it all down in a journal or as a letter but keep writing until you reveal what you're hiding, bring it out into the open and then you can face it.'

I may have scoffed at him when he told me to do this, but the moment I picked up a pen, the first words came: *Dear baby girl.*

I knew instantly who I was writing to.

I never mailed them and I never will, but I read over the last one I wrote on the day before I left the clinic. I had started making my plans by then and I knew what I would do.

Dear baby girl,

I couldn't have known the day I was kicked out of my house what would happen to me. Just like I couldn't have known I was pregnant.

When I found out, I made a decision not to tell Luka, not to share who the father was with anyone.

I knew I would have to give you up. I wasn't equipped to handle a baby but I loved you anyway.

Your birth was very different to the birth I had with your half-sister, Cordelia.

Giving birth to you was terrifying, painful and filled with sadness. One of the women who ran the group home, Beverly, was with me. She held my hand and told me to breathe, said all the things she could think of to keep me calm.

She had already organised an adoption. It was a couple who couldn't have children. I had never met and would never meet them but I hope they were good parents to you. I hope they loved you as I couldn't. I hope you are happy and have a family of your own.

I sigh, wiping a tear away. It felt so strange this morning to finally write her name on a letter, the name given to her by those who'd raised her. When I left her the note, I wanted to write *Dear baby girl* instead of *Dear Ava.*

Should I have told her? Would it have made any difference? I don't think so. I was never supposed to know who she was but I always wondered. And yet, I did nothing about it until I was in the clinic, in treatment for blowing up my whole life.

I had time to bring the trauma of her birth, of having to give her away, to the surface, to look at it, examine it and sit with the feelings.

And then I had time to do some research, time to track her down.

I don't think she knows she's adopted. Or perhaps she does and she never really thinks about it, but she's my daughter and if she's anything like her half-sister, she would want to know everything. I didn't want to hurt her or my beautiful grand-daughters by changing the way they viewed their whole lives. I just wanted to make sure she was happy, healthy, safe.

When I found out who she was, I started watching her and I knew she needed me.

A mother just knows.

I needed to make sure that my daughter got what she wanted, got to have the life she wanted. I had no idea just how badly she needed me. I had no idea how many people were plotting against her, trying to hurt her.

In just over an hour, I will land in Melbourne to see the daughter who won't speak to me but who also needs me very much. I will always hold love in my heart for Ava and her girls, and I will watch them forever, keep track of them as they grow up.

I am flying under the name Grace Morton but I will soon begin legal proceedings to change my name. I would rather be Grace Enright.

I like my hair the colour of copper.

I like Grace Enright.

She is a woman who gets things done, who does not let her heart lead her astray and who will always, always survive.

As the plane lifts into the air, I picture Cordelia's face.

I'm coming, my darling, I think. *I'm nearly there.*

A LETTER FROM NICOLE

Hello,

I would like to thank you for taking the time to read *The Assistant*. If you enjoyed this novel and want to keep up to date with all my latest releases, just sign up at the following link. Your email address will never be shared and you can unsubscribe at any time.

www.bookouture.com/nicole-trope

I know that many women will identify with Ava and her frustration as she juggles a family, a job and the mental load of being responsible for everything.

Her problems with Finn may not be over but I do feel that they are on a better path together now.

Perhaps not as many readers will identify with Grace, who had her own agenda, but I hope you can appreciate her anger after everything she went through to build a life for herself. Being gaslighted by someone who is supposed to love you is a difficult experience for anyone, and Grace could have handled it better. Even though you may question her choices, I hope you can understand some of her reasoning.

I'm looking forward to exploring what else Grace does as she moves forward with her life, and I hope she manages to reconnect with Cordelia. Spoiler alert: Grace will be back for a second book.

As always, I will be so grateful if you leave a review for the novel, especially if you loved the book – please just avoid those pesky spoilers.

I love hearing from my readers and you can get in touch on social media.

Every review is appreciated and I do read them all. I try to reply to each message I receive.

Thanks again for reading,

Nicole x

 facebook.com/NicoleTrope

 x.com/nicoletrope

 instagram.com/nicoletropeauthor

ACKNOWLEDGEMENTS

My first thank you goes to Ellen Gleeson, who has joined me in the pursuit of the perfect prologue. Thanks for all your insights along the way, and for your lovely comments to enjoy as I edit. Here's to the next book and more of Grace's adventures.

I would also like to thank Jess Readett for all the support and patience. And for helping me get my novels into the hands of many eager readers.

Thanks to DeAndra Lupu for the copy edit. It's so lovely to be working with you again. And to Liz Hatherell for the very thorough proofread.

Thanks to the whole team at Bookouture, including Jenny Geras, Peta Nightingale, Richard King, Alba Proko, Ruth Tross and everyone else involved in producing my audio books and selling rights.

Thanks to my mother, Hilary, who is an excellent beta reader.

Thanks also to David, Mikhayla, Isabella, Jacob and Jax.

And once again thank you to those who read, review and blog about my work and contact me on social media to let me know you loved the book. I love hearing your stories and reasons why you have connected with a novel.

PUBLISHING TEAM

Turning a manuscript into a book requires the efforts of many people. The publishing team at Bookouture would like to acknowledge everyone who contributed to this publication.

Audio
Alba Proko
Sinead O'Connor
Melissa Tran

Commercial
Lauren Morrissette
Hannah Richmond
Imogen Allport

Cover design
Mary Luna

Data and analysis
Mark Alder
Mohamed Bussuri

Editorial
Ellen Gleeson
Nadia Michael